Introduction

Christmas Confusion by Lena Nelson Dooley
Lori Compton, mayor of Mistletoe, Montana, needs ideas for ways to prop up the sagging economy. After having her heart broken by the former pastor, she doesn't want to spend time with the new pastor. Rev. Russell Brown has plenty of ideas, even one that includes his spending the rest of his life with the beautiful mayor. Will Lori be able to move beyond her hurts and recognize God's intentions for the future of the town—and for her own future?

Return to Mistletoe by Debby Mayne
Deanna Moss assumes Frank is the man she'll marry, until her old flame, Anthony Carson, arrives in town on business. Their attraction is as strong as ever, but she doesn't want her heart to be broken again. Anthony has a reputation for not staying in one place for long. Deanna loves Mistletoe and wants to protect not only her heart but the place she loves from people who only care about the bottom line. Will Anthony ever convince Deanna that he's serious about loving her and making Mistletoe his permanent home?

Under the Mistletoe by Lisa Harris
When Madison Graham leaves the quaint town of Mistletoe for New York City to buy products for her year-round Christmas store, Under the Mistletoe, she's positive she has met her man. Albert Tanner is everything she's ever dreamed of: successful, good-looking, and well off. But is worldly success really what she's looking for in a man, or have the bright lights of the city so blinded her that she's forgotten the real meaning of Christmas?

All I Want for Christmas Is. . .You by Kim Vogel Sawyer
When Kathy Morgan returns to her childhood home of Mistletoe for a stroll down memory lane before accepting the marriage proposal of her business-partner boyfriend, she doesn't expect to have her world turned upside down. But local postman Erik Hoffman ends up delivering more than mail—he delivers a disturbing message that Kathy needs to get her heart back in order with her Savior. Will Kathy heed Erik's advice before she makes a life-impacting mistake?

Montana
Mistletoe

Romance Has Perfect Timing
in Four Christmas Novellas

LENA NELSON DOOLEY · LISA HARRIS
DEBBY MAYNE · KIM VOGEL SAWYER

BARBOUR
PUBLISHING

Published by Barbour Publishing, Inc., P.O. Box 719, Uhrichsville, Ohio 44683, www.barbourbooks.com

Our mission is to publish and distribute inspirational products offering exceptional value and biblical encouragement to the masses.

ecpa Member of the
Evangelical Christian
Publishers Association

Printed in the United States of America.

Christmas Confusion

by Lena Nelson Dooley

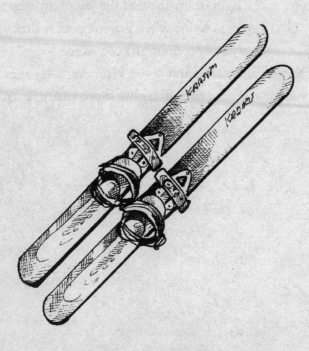

Dedication

Crystal, I welcome you into the family
by dedicating this book to you.
I received the contract soon after attending
your and Timothy's wedding.
I look forward to our days ahead
and the great-grandchildren you'll give me.

James Allen Dooley,
you are the light of my life and the joy of my heart.
God gave you to me when I didn't even realize
what a precious gift you were.
Now I understand and praise Him every day that
you have been a part of my life for so many years.

*In his heart a man plans his course,
but the LORD determines his steps.*
PROVERBS 16:9

Chapter 1

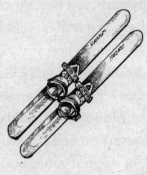

January

The doorbell chimed the first ten notes of "Have Yourself a Merry Little Christmas." Lori Compton dried her hands on a red and green kitchen towel, untied the cheery Christmas apron protecting her velour jogging suit, and gave the table a last once-over. Everything looked just the way she wanted it to.

She hurried to the door and pulled it open. "Welcome!"

Deanna and Madison, two of her best friends, stood on the small porch knocking slush from their boots.

"Come on in." Lori opened the door wider to give them plenty of room.

They complied with hugs all around, then removed their boots and left them on the rack in the foyer.

"Something smells good." A red-and-green-striped stocking cap hid most of Deanna's hair until she pulled it off using the snowball pompom on the very end. Static electricity gave her a strawberry-blond halo.

Madison headed toward the low round table in front of the stone fireplace. An abundance of goodies crowded the surface. "When you said high tea, you really meant it, didn't you?"

"Well, I wanted to start the new year right." Lori followed Deanna as she trailed behind their tall, willowy friend.

Lori's chalet perched high on the slopes of Sugar Mountain just north of Mistletoe, Montana. Her father had built it for her before he sold his construction firm and retired to Florida with her mother. A large, open great room boasted a wall of windows overlooking the town and surrounding areas. The view of the mountains was spectacular any time of year. A roaring fire added a warm glow to the expanse.

Deanna bypassed the table and went straight to the windows. She sighed before she turned around. "I just love it here. I don't believe there's a prettier spot in the whole world, Lori. You're so lucky."

"So you've often said." Lori joined her at the window. "I do feel blessed." Her gaze moved to the pristine white blanket covering the landscape; evergreens jutted through the snow in clusters. "I like it more than ever since I've been elected mayor. I sort of feel like I'm protecting Mistletoe." She gave an embarrassed laugh. "I guess that sounds ridiculous, doesn't it?"

"Not at all." Madison gave her a stern look. "I voted for you because you'll be good for this town. We need your creative thinking."

"I only hope I have enough."

This early in January, days were short in the Rocky Mountains. A weak winter sun sank slowly to touch the tips of the peaks across the valley.

Lori glanced at her watch. "Since it's past four o'clock, maybe we should start eating." The copper-bottomed teapot she'd put on the stove sounded a loud whistle as if on cue. "I'll set the tea to steep and bring it in."

While she fixed the beverage in the china teapot her grandmother had brought from England as a young bride, the murmur of lively conversation came from the great room. Lori set the teapot on a round silver tray and carried it through the swinging doors that separated the two rooms.

Madison and Deanna had already chosen to sit cross-legged on the thick carpet, and Madison held a half-eaten finger sandwich. "Is this cucumber and cream cheese?"

"Yes, Gram always made them for high tea." Lori set the tray in the vacant spot in the middle of the table.

"I'm going straight for the shortbread biscuits. Even though I know that's what the English call them, I have a hard time not saying 'cookies.'" Deanna reached for one and took a dainty bite. "Your grandmother's recipe produces the best I've ever eaten."

"And I made myself wait for you to get here before I had one of these raisin scones." Lori loaded a scone with strawberry jam and clotted cream before sinking her teeth into it.

By the time they finished eating, the fire needed tending. Lori placed a couple of large logs on the bed of glowing coals. "These should last us the rest of the evening."

Deanna rose from the floor and lounged on the leather sofa.

Lori smiled. She had saved a long time to afford the rounded couch that formed a conversation pit. Seeing her friend look so comfy made the cost worth it.

"So does anyone know what year this is?" A sneaky smile lit Deanna's face.

Madison raised her hand. "Two thousand—"

"I don't mean the date." Deanna huffed out a sigh. "This year is significant for us. . .and Kathy. I wish she were here."

Lori pictured their friend with the bright red curls and large, expressive eyes. "Yeah, I miss seeing her. Actually, I've missed hearing from her, too. How long has it been since any of us heard from her?"

"Well, we send cards for each other's birthdays, don't we?" Deanna placed a finger to her chin while she thought. "Who got the last one?"

As if she doesn't know. Madison and Deanna had been at the party Aunt Ethel and Uncle Hiram had thrown for her last night. Lori smiled. "I heard from her last, since my birthday is New Year's Eve. But this year her card didn't even include a note, just her signature. Maybe she's really busy."

Deanna cleared her throat. "Back to my original question. Why is this year significant?"

"We'll all be turning twenty-eight," Lori and Madison sang in unison.

"Yeah," Deanna agreed. "The year of the *marriage pact*." The emphasis she placed on the last two words indicated the weight of her pronouncement.

Silence descended on the room. Lori remembered the

agreement the four friends had made right before they left college—to be married by the time they were twenty-eight years old. Well, it hadn't happened yet. For any of them.

Lori started laughing, and the other two joined in.

"Do any of us even have a prospect?" She glanced from one friend to the other.

"Well, not exactly." Madison reached across the table and refilled her cup with tea. "This is empty. Do you want me to make more?"

"No, I'll do it." Lori jumped up and took the tray to the kitchen. Should she share the hopes she had hidden in her heart? She had one prospect, if she could call him that. His serious eyes and warm smile floated into her mind.

In a few minutes, she returned to her friends. "Well, I kind of have my eye on someone."

"And you haven't told us about him?" Deanna sat up and pulled one foot beneath her. "Is he someone we know?"

Madison gave a very unladylike snort. "How could he not be? Mistletoe isn't very large."

"Maybe," Lori said slowly. "But I'm not telling you who. He and I have known each other quite awhile, but the friendship seems to be moving toward a romance. I don't want to share until I know for sure."

No matter how many questions her friends asked, Lori didn't reveal any details. "What about you girls?"

"Well," Deanna began, stretching out the word. "You know Frank and I have been dating. I'm just not sure he's the one for me. I guess I want more zing or something."

"Zing?" Once again Lori and Madison spoke in unison. The two women thought remarkably alike—it was probably the reason they were the first to connect in college.

"Yeah, you know, a special tingle or something that sparks..." Deanna's words faded to nothing.

"When I was on a recent buying trip to New York..." Madison left a pregnant pause before dropping her bombshell. "I met someone."

"And you kept it a secret?" Lori leaned toward her. "Tell us more."

"There's not much to tell...yet." Lori sensed Madison's smile hid a world of meaning.

Deanna leaned back with a satisfied grin. "Well, we don't know about Kathy, but it looks as if there's a possibility that one or two of us will keep the pact."

Lori's friends left an hour later. She pondered what she'd told them about the silly pact they made in college. She hoped she hadn't said too much; she also hoped Matthew would make a move toward her soon.

Rev. Matthew Hogan, the handsome pastor of Living Word Chapel in Mistletoe's town square, was single. Lori had been active in the church for as long as she could remember. Since Matthew came to town, they had spent a lot of time working together on programs and activities. Of course, other people worked with them, but he did seem to pay a lot of attention to her. *Because you're often in charge of things*, she berated herself.

If she were honest, that was true. She'd always been a leader both at church and in other activities in town. After all, she never would have been elected mayor if she had been shy.

Lori took the leftovers to the kitchen and stored them. She'd have a ready-made lunch for the next couple of days. She brewed one more cup of tea before going back to stand by the fireplace and look out over her town. Darkness had stolen across the land, and Christmas lights defined various features of Mistletoe, especially the town square.

She loved this time of night because the area was full of activity. Even though the Christmas season was officially over, every day was Christmas in Mistletoe, Montana. The fact that every store displayed Christmas items year-round was a major tourist draw. But for the last two years, this type of traffic had gradually decreased, and the trend worried Lori. Her promise to make innovations to bring tourism back up to par had helped get her elected. Had she once again bitten off more than she could chew? She hoped not—for her own sake, as well as the town's.

Her attention settled on Living Word Chapel. Its steeple rose toward the indigo sky, now dotted with a multitude of twinkling stars. Evergreens in varying sizes and shapes formed a framework around the building, and light streamed through the stained-glass windows. From this distance, the colors ran together like those of a watercolor, adding to the charm of the quaint building. Looking at the picturesque church reminded her of one of the Christmas cards she'd received in December.

Could she and the good-looking man of God have a relationship? Would he be the answer to her longing for a husband and family?

Lori hung her hopes on that thought.

Chapter 2

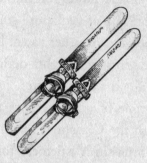

When Lori arrived at City Hall, which sat opposite Mistletoe Savings and Loan in the town square, jangling bells on the door announced her presence. Enticing fragrances of spices and evergreens wafted through the building. She inhaled, savoring the moment.

January second. Her first official day as mayor.

Lori glanced around the lobby, festooned with evergreen garlands and big red bows, seeing no one except the receptionist. "What's going on?" She unwound the long turquoise wool scarf from around her neck.

"We want to welcome you to your new job." Felicity Knowles rose from her chair behind her desk. "I'm supposed to escort you to the conference room."

Lori took off her coat, pulling one end of the scarf through the sleeve. "I guess the bells will let you know if someone comes in?"

"Yeah, they signal everyone's arrival."

"But what about answering the phone?" Lori hung her coat on the walnut hall tree beside the front door.

"There's one in the conference room. I'll stay close to it, just in case."

Lori returned Felicity's infectious smile before following her toward the hallway. When they arrived at the doorway to the conference room, the conversations coming from inside died down. Several people sat around the oblong table filled with enough goodies to feed the whole town of Mistletoe for a week. Lori could hardly believe her eyes.

Deanna and Madison sat on one side. Each held a half-eaten cookie. All of the members of the city staff crowded into the room, and several business owners were present, as well. Everyone stood when she entered.

"Welcome, Madam Mayor!" The large group must have practiced the enthusiastic greeting, because they were in perfect sync.

Lori smiled at them. "Thank you." She waved toward the table. "What's all this? Don't you know the holidays are over?"

"Not in Mistletoe." The city secretary perched on the edge of a nearby chair.

"Never in Mistletoe," the head of the parks department added.

Lori laughed. "You're right, but my holiday eating has to come to an end or I won't be able to climb the stairs to my office." *Or fit into any of my clothes.* However, she did pick up a sticky bun and place it on the small plate someone thrust toward her. She never could turn down one of Mrs. Flanagan's pastries. "Thank you for the welcome."

A staff member placed a steaming mug in her hand.

Lori took a quick sip. "This hot chocolate really hits the spot. I believe the temperature dropped even lower last night."

After the get-together, Lori climbed the stairs to her office on the second floor feeling thoroughly welcomed. The mayor's office faced the square, with a wall of windows across the front. She walked to them, stood with her hands behind her back, and let her gaze roam over the picturesque park. Each year, the town council chose the theme for the decorations. This year the trees wore mantles of white lights and gold ribbons. The bandstand took center stage. Weekly concerts brought people from near and far, but not as many as in previous years. That's why Lori was the youngest mayor ever elected in Mistletoe. The burden to help bring more people to their special town weighed heavily on her this first day in office.

Across the square, chimes from the clock tower on the Savings and Loan pealed forth the hour. Lori eyed her desk and decided to position it so she could see the square anytime she looked up.

A knock sounded at her open door. She turned to answer. "Deanna, Madison, I thought you had already left."

Her two friends hurried into the room, their excitement almost bouncing off the walls.

Madison reached up to flip her long hair behind her shoulder. "I can't believe this is now your office."

Deanna put her finger on her cheek and tilted her head. "It's pretty dismal. . .for the office of someone so important."

"So." Lori crossed her arms. "What brings the two of you to my office?"

"All this." Deanna's expansive gesture took in the whole room. "This room is so not you. We want to help you change it until it is."

How like the three of them to have similar ideas at the same time. Lori laughed. "I was thinking about moving the furniture first."

"We'll help." Madison studied the arrangement with a critical eye. "How about moving the desk so you're facing the windows?"

"Just what I wanted to do."

A half hour later, all of the furniture had been shifted, and the office felt more like home. "Thanks for your help." Lori hugged each friend.

Deanna studied the room one more time. "We'll be back with some other things to make this room feminine and perky."

"Just remember I'm the mayor, so this place still needs to look like a business office."

After her friends left, Lori went through the desk. She threw away anything that didn't look important and rearranged everything else to suit her. Then she attacked the file cabinets, trying to familiarize herself with all she needed to know.

Another knock sounded on her door, and she glanced up at the clock tower. How had the time gotten away from her? She'd missed lunch.

Lori turned toward the doorway. "Matthew, what can I do for you?"

Her pastor and friend entered the office and glanced around. "You've done a lot today. I like this arrangement better than the way Harvey had it."

She smiled. "I'm hoping the shake-up will help inspire me with ideas to bring more people into town."

Two steps brought Matthew close. "I really need to talk to you. How about I take you out for dinner? Are you free tonight? We'll celebrate your first day in the office of mayor and have time to chat."

In light of the conversation she shared with her friends yesterday, Lori saw Matthew in a different way now. Of course, he was tall, handsome, personable. What more could a woman want? *Love, maybe, but that will come, won't it?*

Matthew shoved his hands into his front pockets. "So how about tonight?" His tweed jacket opened, revealing a rust-colored turtleneck. He looked like a model in *GQ*.

"I'm free. Sounds like fun."

"I was thinking we might drive over to that new steakhouse on the way to Kalispell."

Lori tried to hide her surprise behind a professional smile. This was sounding better all the time. She took a deep breath.

"I'll pick you up when you get off at five. With all the snow, the drive could take awhile."

After Matthew left, Lori couldn't concentrate on work. What did he want to talk to her about? Maybe he was beginning to have feelings for her, too. This wouldn't be the first time they'd gone out together. On more than one occasion, they'd been in Kalispell for other reasons and ended up sharing a meal in a nice restaurant. At those times, she'd felt the dinner had just been convenient. But maybe not. He could've been working up to something else. After all, men don't express themselves as openly as women do. She smiled to herself. Perhaps it had just taken him longer to realize she would be a good catch.

Lori stepped out the door of City Hall just as the clock tower across the way chimed the last *bong* for five o'clock. She turned from locking the door to see Matthew Hogan pull up in his conservative charcoal gray sedan. Lori favored her red four-wheel-drive SUV.

Ever the gentleman, Matthew rushed around the front of his car to open the passenger door for her. "I thought I'd need to come up and get you. You must have finished delving into the files."

Not wanting to slip on a patch of black ice, she took a hesitant step off the curb on the way to the front seat. "I'm sure it will take awhile to get through all of them, but I stopped for the day."

Matthew drove slowly and carefully, expertly traversing the twisting mountain road. Soft instrumental gospel music surrounded them in a comfortably warm cocoon. Lori leaned her head back against the leather seat and relaxed for the first time since she arrived at the office that morning. The fragrance of Matthew's aftershave teased her nose. She glanced toward him, her eyes roving over his profile, silvered by the light of the moon, which hung low in the sky.

"Did you have a good day?" He smiled toward her for only an instant, then returned his eyes to the road.

"Yes. I got a lot done after Deanna and Madison left."

He chuckled. "Ah yes, the two best friends. Did they stay long?"

"They came to help me rearrange the office." Lori took off her gloves and stuck them into her coat pockets. "They knew I would want to make the space mine."

A comfortable silence reigned for a few moments.

"You know, actually, I had three best friends in college." Since the high tea yesterday, her thoughts kept returning to Kathy; she wondered what was going on with her.

Matthew's eyebrows quirked. "I don't remember you saying anything about another close friend. Does she live here?"

"No, we were inseparable all through college, but she moved to San Francisco and made a name for herself in advertising. We've kept in touch over the years. Deanna, Madison, and I talked about Kathy yesterday, so she's been on my mind."

"Sounds like you were close. I wish I could've gotten to know your other friend."

Matthew's comment took Lori's thoughts further into the discussion with her friends at high tea. Even though she carried on a conversation with him throughout the drive to the restaurant, her attention was divided. Visions of white satin and tulle danced in her head. Thoughts of ministering together with her husband and children did, too. Oh yes, this could be the night that changed the rest of her life.

Lori had never been to the upscale steakhouse. A string

trio on a raised stage in the center of the restaurant played a classical piece. The music enhanced the ambience of the room. Elegant burgundy drapes hung from the ceiling and puddled on the carpet beside expansive windows, forming a framework for the vista beyond. Scattered lights across the winter wonderland beckoned her gaze.

Matthew followed behind her with his hand at the small of her back as the maître d' led them to a secluded table. Flickering candles provided the only illumination. Candlelight and music. Just what a girl would want for romance.

The leather-encased menu placed in front of her didn't list any prices. She hoped that wasn't an indication they were sky high. But for a special night like this, perhaps the sky was the limit. Great. Now she was thinking in clichés. What next?

She enjoyed small talk all during the pleasant meal, which lasted a good hour. Lori relaxed and felt thoroughly cared for by the time they finished eating.

Matthew dabbed his mouth with the napkin and cleared his throat. He appeared a bit nervous. Was that a good sign?

"I wanted you to be the first to know." He leaned closer to the table and turned earnest eyes toward her. "We've worked so closely together that I've come to feel a special bond with you."

Holding her breath, Lori waited. *Here it comes.*

"I've been offered a wonderful opportunity."

For a moment the words didn't register. Then she let out her breath. This didn't sound as promising as she had hoped.

"You know I grew up outside of Boston."

Lori nodded, her throat too tight to answer.

"A rather large church in Boston has offered me the position of assistant pastor." Before she could let that sink in, he rushed on. "I know I'm the only pastor here, but this new position has much more responsibility than I would ever have in a small church like Living Word Chapel. Besides, I've really prayed before making this change." He stopped as if waiting for her to comment.

"That's good," she managed past the lump in her throat.

Matthew reached across the table and clasped her hand. "I knew you'd understand and be happy for me. I'll be very close to where my parents and grandparents live, too."

He released her hand and took a swallow of coffee.

Lori didn't know where to look. She didn't want him to read the disappointment in her eyes. She'd pinned all of her hopes on him. Now there wasn't a snowball's chance in... There she went again. Clichés.

Not a single other coherent thought took up residence. The rest of the evening passed in a blur. Soon after Matthew's announcement, they left for home. While he talked about his good fortune, she could only think about her lack of it. He let her out at City Hall so she could get her SUV, saying he'd follow her home to make sure she arrived safely. As if she didn't drive that road every day. The man's good manners stretched too far. Far enough for her to imagine he cared for her.

After she closed her door, she leaned against it and finally gave in to her swelling emotions. Tears streamed down her face. Then she remembered his comment about Kathy. *I wish I could have gotten to know your other friend.* As if that could ever happen now. Why hadn't she picked up on that clue?

How could she have been so foolish? Marriage pact or no marriage pact, she would not be married by the time she turned twenty-eight on the last day of the year.

Chapter 3

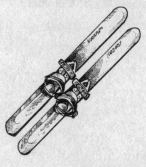

Lori spent a restless night thinking about the new turn of events. Hadn't she walked with the Lord long enough to understand He was in charge of her life? Why had she latched onto the idea of a relationship with Matthew without praying about it? She'd learned better. Finding out that nothing would come of it had hurt.

Morning came quickly. Her joy at the sight of bright sunlight streaming through her blinds told her the pain of losing Matthew was not heart-deep. She liked Matthew as a person, respected him as a man of God. But her emotions hadn't really been engaged. If it hadn't been for that silly pact she and her friends had made, she might've never looked at him as marriage material. He'd make someone a good husband, but he was actually more staid and stodgy than the man she'd want her husband to be.

She went to the kitchen and poured a cup of coffee from the pot she had preset to brew before her alarm awakened her.

She'd need a lot of caffeine today. Wondering how she would tell her friends what had happened, Lori decided they didn't need to know how silly she'd been. At least she hadn't blurted out his name. They could just go on wondering about the man she might be interested in. Maybe sometime down the road she'd be able to laugh about it with them, but not today. And probably not for a long time.

Russell Brown steered his heavy-duty truck up the winding road leading to Mistletoe, Montana. His college roommate had contacted him last week about the pastorate coming open soon. He'd even recommended Russell for the job and scheduled this interview. Russell had heard a lot about this unique town near Flathead Lake. Somehow he couldn't picture a town that had Christmas year-round. That might have been an exaggeration anyhow. He fully expected to see a quiet mountain town in the throes of winter. Even though he hadn't used four-wheel drive much in Texas, his vehicle had come equipped with it. If Montana winters were as bad as he'd been told, he'd have plenty of chances to test it out.

The farther north Russell traveled, the deeper the snow and colder the wind when he made a pit stop. He'd taken the time in Denver to buy a fleece-lined suede coat, which he huddled in now as he refilled the gas tank.

From afar, the first glimpse of the town confirmed that even though it was the middle of January, Christmas lights still outlined the buildings. They served as a beacon in the darkening evening. Reaching the cluster of lights clinging to the mountainside and sweeping across a high valley had taken longer than he'd thought it would. Evidently, light carried quite a distance in the crisp, cold evening air.

Russell pulled into an empty parking space in front of a building sporting a clock tower. MISTLETOE SAVINGS & LOAN was emblazoned across the front. He parked the truck and got out to stretch his legs after the long drive. He'd stopped somewhere in north Wyoming the night before at a motel by the interstate, but he'd pushed hard to reach the town today. Making his way across the slushy street took some doing. Maybe he shouldn't be wearing cowboy boots with leather soles. His feet slid across patches of ice a couple of times, but he remained upright.

Several people were out and about, even though suppertime had arrived. At least his stomach felt as if it had.

He turned up his collar, stuffed his hands deep into the warm pockets of the coat, and walked along the sidewalks in the park, admiring the decorated Christmas trees. Here, someone had cleared the walkways, and he wasn't in danger of making an undignified landing in the surrounding snow.

Russell studied each tree as he moved through the park. Christmas carols danced through the air, reminding him of the big gathering three weeks ago on the family ranch near San Antonio. The gaiety and glitter had been there, minus the snow and bitter wind.

Just as he reached the opposite side of the park, a woman opened the door of the City Hall building across the street. She glanced toward him, and their gazes locked. Even though she was bundled up against the below-freezing weather, warmth filled her expression.

"Are you looking for someone?" Her melodious voice floated on the frigid air, and a smile lit her eyes. "Maybe I can help you." She stepped out into the street and made a beeline toward him.

He watched her approach. "How'd you know I'm not from here?"

She laughed. "If I hadn't known before, your accent would've tipped me off." She stopped in front of him, pulled off one glove, and thrust her hand toward him. "I'm Lori Compton, mayor of Mistletoe, and I know everyone who lives here."

Her green eyes held a sparkle that left Russell at a loss for words. Curls the shade of rich coffee framed her face. Still clasping her delicate hand, he said, "Russell Brown." It was all he could stammer. Who was this woman, and why did he feel such a strong connection to her?

Lori withdrew her hand and started pulling the glove back on. Her demeanor gave no indication that she'd felt any of the sizzle.

"Can I help you find anything?"

At her words, he refocused. "You could point me toward Mrs. Flanagan's Bed-and-Breakfast. That's where I'm staying tonight."

Lori wasn't short, but Russell felt as if he towered over her.

She glanced across the park. "It's at the corner of Maple and Second, just two blocks off Main."

She paused and took a deep breath. How could she allow so much of the icy air into her lungs? Evidently, she had lived here long enough to be used to the freezing temperatures.

"You'll be glad you're staying there. She bakes the best pastries in town. But she doesn't serve dinner to her guests. Have you eaten yet?"

"I just arrived in town." Russell gestured toward where his dark blue truck sat across the way. "I parked and came over to see the decorations. Kind of late for Christmas, isn't it?"

Her musical laugh pealed into the cold night air. "Don't tell me you haven't heard about Mistletoe?"

Russell stuffed his hands into his front jeans pockets. "Only recently."

"Then you don't know that we're the year-round Christmas town." Lori hitched the handle of her handbag higher on her shoulder and headed toward a red SUV. "Come with me to Flossie's Café, and I'll tell you about it over a hot meal."

Sounded good to him. He wanted to find out all he could about the town before he made his final decision.

Lori turned back toward him. "Are you on your way somewhere else, or are you staying in Mistletoe for a while?" She sounded genuinely interested.

"I'm considering a move. Maybe it'll be to Mistletoe, so I wanted to check the place out." He whistled a happy tune as he crossed to his pickup.

Before he unlocked the door, he glanced back at her. She waited by her vehicle, probably for him to come around the block so she could lead him to the café. Sharing a meal with this woman could prove interesting, but he'd have to be careful not to reveal too much. He wasn't sure how much Pastor Hogan had told his parishioners about his plans to leave Mistletoe.

When Lori got home, she could hardly believe how long she'd talked to Russell Brown. They'd stayed at Flossie's until closing time, and then he'd followed her to the B&B. She couldn't remember ever having so much fun talking to a man, and this one was a stranger. Well, not anymore. By the time they left, she felt as if they were old friends. She hadn't had any male friendships like this since she came home from college. What a nice change.

While she got ready for bed, flashes of the evening invaded her thoughts. Russell had a broad chest and narrow waist. He looked as though he worked out. With his every move, his muscles strained against the western shirt he wore. The man dressed like a cowboy, but he looked more like a coach or an athlete. What would he be doing in Mistletoe? The high school had a coach, and there wasn't a workout gym.

They'd talked for hours but had never gotten around to that question. He did say he grew up on a ranch in Texas, graduated from Texas A&M, then later went to graduate school. All of his brothers were married, and he was uncle to a tribe of nieces and nephews. He hoped to have a houseful of children himself someday. She knew about a lot of his favorite things, but he never mentioned what he was doing here or what kind of work he did. She'd have to remedy that if she saw him again.

When Russell drove up in front of Living Word Chapel the

next morning, he took a good, long look at the building. Yesterday when he arrived, he'd noticed the church but hadn't given it much thought. Morning sun bathed the building with a golden glow. It looked like one of those Thomas Kinkade paintings his mother collected. And it was bigger than he'd first thought. He wondered just how large the congregation was.

He tried the front door, and it opened easily, even though he was early for his appointment with Pastor Hogan. Russell entered the sanctuary and walked down the long, carpeted center aisle. Sunlight streamed through the numerous stained-glass windows, making him feel as if he were in the middle of one of the kaleidoscopes he enjoyed so much as a boy. *Pretty impressive place.*

After mounting the few steps to the platform, he stood behind the hand-carved pulpit that matched the color of the wooden beams. He looked out over the pews, imagining them filled with people. If this room was full, it would hold several hundred parishioners. He leaned his hands on the ledge around the pulpit and bowed his head. *Father, please let me know if this is the place for me.*

"Getting the feel of it already, are you?"

The words, coming so quickly at the end of his silent prayer, startled him. Russell opened his eyes and looked around until he spied the man who had spoken.

"I guess I was." He smiled.

The other man, wearing a tweed sport coat complete with white shirt and tie under what looked like a cashmere sweater, joined him on the platform. "I'm Matthew Hogan, and you must be Russell Brown." He held out a hand.

Russell liked the man's firm grip. "Yes."

"Let's go to my office where we can talk." Pastor Hogan led the way through the door at the side of the platform.

The morning's discussion went well. By the time they were through, Russell knew he wanted to take this offer. He would like pastoring this church in the picturesque town. And he was told that Lori Compton was one of the most active members. A special bonus. He looked forward to spending more time with her. At that thought, his day brightened even more.

Lori had spent two weeks reading through documents, with several more file drawers to go. Nothing she'd found gave any indication that the last mayor had worked actively to help bring more people to town—hence the drop in tourist traffic. That couldn't continue. Right now her brain was too tired to come up with anything creative, but once she sifted through the paperwork, her brain would kick into high gear.

She took the last three files on her desk to the cabinet and placed them in the right drawer before removing the next three. She'd just sat down and opened the top one when her phone rang.

"Lori Compton here."

"Pastor Hogan and another man are here asking if they can see you." Felicity's dulcet tone brought a smile to Lori's face.

"Tell them to come on up." She closed the file and moved all three of them to her in-tray.

Footsteps tapped on the tile stairs. How like men to forgo

the elevator in favor of the stairs. Maybe she should do that more often. Sitting at her desk so many hours each day was a killer on her back—and her waistline.

Matthew ushered the Texas cowboy into the office before him. *Wonder why the two of them are together?*

Lori walked around her desk, and Matthew introduced the man to her. She thrust out her hand and shook Russell Brown's. "We met yesterday." She turned her warmest smile on the newcomer as she directed the two men to sit in the overstuffed chairs in front of the desk. Then she leaned against the corner of it.

Matthew glanced at Russell. "Why didn't you tell me you'd met our mayor?"

Russell dropped into the chair and hung his cowboy hat on his knee. "It never came up." He punctuated the statement with a shrug.

Instead of sitting down, the pastor stood between her and the newcomer. "I wanted to introduce you to my replacement, but now I can't do that."

"Replacement?" The question burst from her lips. "As in *new pastor*?" The warm smile slid from her face and changed into a polite but colder expression.

Russell didn't know what reaction he'd expected from her— but this wasn't it. Last night, Lori had been very friendly. He'd felt they'd bonded in a special way. Now she looked at him as if he were a stranger, maybe even one with two heads.

"Well." She moistened her lips. "That's interesting. . . . I had no idea."

He snagged his hat, then stood. "We never got around to discussing why I came here, did we?" Russell hoped his smile would coax one from her. It didn't.

Lori crossed her arms tightly across her midsection. "So when will the transition take place?"

Pastor Hogan stepped into the fray. The look on his face indicated he was as surprised as Russell by her iciness. "Since he's agreed to take the assignment, I'll be gone by the first of February. That'll give me time to pack."

He glanced at Russell. "The furniture and kitchen items in the parsonage stay, so all I have to deal with are personal things. When do you think you'll move in?"

"I'm not sure. Maybe we should go by and let me see the parsonage." Russell never took his attention from Lori, but her expression as a disinterested bystander remained. "Then I'll know what I'll need to bring with me."

"Actually, if you want to be here for the last Sunday in January, it would be fine with me." Matthew Hogan turned toward the mayor. "We're sorry we took you away from your work." With that, he led the way out the door.

For the rest of the day, Russell's thoughts were distracted. What had happened to the warm woman he'd spent the evening with? What had made her become the Ice Queen? Finding out would be one of his most important tasks when he moved here.

Chapter 4

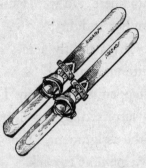

The last Sunday in January, Russell Brown stood behind the pulpit of Living Word Chapel in Mistletoe, Montana. Looking out over the congregation, he didn't see many empty seats. He wondered if the room was so full because everyone wanted to get a good look at the new pastor. He hoped that wasn't the case and that most were regulars at the services.

"Let's lift our praises to the Lord." Russell bowed his head for the opening prayer, filled with thanks to God for bringing him to this place.

The enthusiastic worship leader took over when Russell sat down. Although he tried to keep his mind on worshiping along with the music, Russell's gaze roved over each face, trying to locate one in particular. He'd expected to see the lovely mayor, but judging by the reception he'd received when the pastor told her that Russell would be taking over, why would he expect to see her here?

Still, Russell glanced over the congregation hopefully. One

of the taller men near the back shifted, and there she was. Lori. Standing behind him with her eyes closed and a smile on her face. The serenity in her expression lifted his spirits. This was the Lori he'd met that first evening.

Later, while the head of the church board pronounced the benediction, Russell quietly made his way down the side aisle toward the back. He wanted to greet each parishioner at the door. He knew it would probably take awhile, since this was the first time most of the people had met him.

Partway through the introductions, he noticed two other women join Lori—a dark blond and a strawberry blond. Their exuberant conversation would have been hard to miss.

"What are you doing way back here?" the strawberry blond chided Lori.

So Lori usually sits closer to the front.

"Yeah, we thought you weren't here today." The other woman pushed her long hair behind her ears. "We even saved you a seat."

Definitely near the front. He remembered the two women in the second row. *Now why would our esteemed mayor change her habits today?* He strained to hear Lori's response, but her reply came out muffled. Russell turned his attention back toward Mrs. Flanagan, who stopped to shake his hand and welcome him back to town.

"Since the party for you isn't until next week, I'd like to have you over to my B&B for lunch today. I've invited a few of my friends, too." The twinkle in the spry lady's eyes warmed his heart.

Church had been an ordeal for Lori. That new minister was too much of a distraction. She had been able to lose herself in the worship time because Hank Cowley stood in front of her. Hank had to be six foot five or taller, and the man really liked to eat. With Hank shielding her from other people, she'd felt as if Jesus was alone with her. A time of sweet refreshment in her spirit.

However, when the congregation sat down, Russell—Pastor Brown—was in her direct line of sight. Perhaps thinking of him by his title would help her forget the wonderful time they'd had together before she knew who he really was.

Lori had planned to delve deeper into the man she'd spent time with that night, but after learning he was a pastor, she stepped back instead. Hadn't she almost made a big mistake before the new minister came to town? She loved the Lord and His work so much that she had looked at Matthew as more than a pastor. All of the time they'd spent together, even when they were working on projects, had fueled her fantasy of being the wife of a minister. She'd flirted with that notion for a short while, but she refused to go down that road again. If God wanted her to be married before she turned twenty-eight, He'd have to drop a man in her lap. The picture that flitted into her mind brought a chuckle.

Lori slowed down in front of Mrs. Flanagan's Bed-and-Breakfast. Cooking for one bored her, so she had eagerly welcomed the invitation to eat with her old friend. Evidently, she wasn't the only person the elderly woman had invited, because Lori had to park down the block. She never took any of the spaces behind the Queen Anne house; those were used by the guests. As she walked back toward the inviting front porch, Lori decided she probably should have parked there anyway. The empty lot told a sad story. The inn appeared to have zero guests. How long could the town survive with the declining tourist trade?

Deanna opened the door to Lori's knock. "Come on in. Mrs. Flanagan's busy getting the food on the table. Madison's helping her, and I've been assigned as the welcoming committee."

She leaned closer to whisper, "Guess who else is here."

The parlor looked surprisingly full. "Quite a few people, I'd say."

"I mean what special person?" A conspiratorial gleam lit Deanna's eyes.

"Aren't we all special to Mrs. Flanagan?" Lori headed for the coat closet.

Deanna followed right on her heels. "I'm talking about the dishy new minister, Pastor Brown. Out of the pulpit he looks more like a pro athlete or coach." She sighed. "Maybe even a cowboy."

Don't I know it. Lori heaved a deep sigh. Now she would need to stay alert so no one would suspect how aware she was of everything about the man anytime he was near her.

Mrs. Flanagan had Lori sit beside her, and Pastor Brown was at the other end of the large rectangular table. With several people between them, Lori tried to keep her attention trained away from him, but her mind often drifted to the other end of the expanse. Until she could better control her emotions, she'd make sure she spent a minimum amount of time around the new parson. That might put a crimp in her work at the church, but she had a good excuse. As mayor, she had a lot of other commitments and responsibilities.

Russell's heart lifted when Lori Compton walked through the doorway of the B&B. Maybe he'd get a chance to talk to her. But it never happened. Somehow the woman was always on the other side of the room from him. When he ambled toward where she stood or sat, something caught her attention and she moved elsewhere. He'd almost think she was trying to avoid him, but why would she do that?

He did get acquainted with several people from the church, and he appreciated the effort Mrs. Flanagan took to make sure he did. She'd even offered to have him over for mealtimes until he settled in. He figured he just might take her up on breakfast, since she had to fix it for her guests. Come to think of it, he hadn't seen anyone who looked like B&B guests at the house, only church members. What was going on here? Maybe January was just an off month for tourists.

After the other dinner guests left, he lingered. "Mrs. F., I'm going to help you wash these dishes."

"You don't have to do that, young man." A blush spread across her wrinkled cheeks. "I can do them after everyone's gone."

"They all are, except me." Russell started toward the kitchen. "So don't try to talk me out of it." He noticed a ruffled apron hanging on a hook beside the refrigerator. He grabbed the garment and pulled it around his waist, but the ties barely reached. "I'm thinking about taking you up on cooking me breakfast, but I won't unless you let me help."

She took another apron from one of the drawers and donned it. "Okay, young man, you wash, and I'll dry. You don't know where anything goes. But first, I have to ask, have you ever washed dishes before?" A laugh accompanied the question.

He nodded. "I come from a big family. It's a rule that the men clean up after holiday meals. We even have a small TV in Mom's kitchen so we can keep up with the football games until we finish. I've washed a mountain of dishes in my time."

While they worked as a team, he asked probing questions. He hoped she'd just think he wanted to know about the church and its members. He enjoyed the lilting Irish brogue that colored the woman's words, though she'd been in the United States most of her life. Soon he ventured to queries about the town. Lori, he discovered, was the youngest mayor ever elected in Mistletoe. She ran on the platform that she would work hard to help bring tourism back to the town.

"Just how bad is the economy, Mrs. F.?" Russell glanced down at her face, trying to read in her expression if her own business was hurting.

She took her time answering. He could almost see the wheels turning under her cap of white curls. "I don't complain, but if things don't change, I might have to close the B&B and move in with my daughter."

"Where does she live?" By the worry lines that puckered between her eyes, Russell could tell this wouldn't be her choice. He dried his hands on the towel hanging on the handle of one of the drawers.

"Florida." She kept rubbing the plate she held, even though it was already dry. "I've never lived anywhere but in Mistletoe since I was a little girl, and my late husband, God rest his soul, built this house for me when we married." A sob slipped out, and she put one hand over her lips as if trying to hold back another. "I want to stay here until I go to be with him in glory."

Compassion overwhelmed Russell. He gingerly put his arms around the older woman. When she didn't seem to mind, he pulled her gently against his chest. She was so slight he was careful not to hurt her. "I don't think it'll come to that. We can all pray."

She sobbed until his shirt was drenched, but he didn't care.

Lord, show me what I can do to help. Is this one of the reasons You brought me to this town? There has to be some way to effect a change.

As small as she was, Mrs. Flanagan had a lot of strength. She stepped away and dried her eyes on the edge of the apron she wore. "I'm sorry, Pastor. I shouldn't have broken down like that. I don't usually." She stared at the front of his shirt. "I've really made a mess of your shirt, haven't I?"

He plunged his hands back into the sudsy water. "Nah. It's okay."

She put the plate in the cabinet and placed the damp towel

over another drawer handle. "But you can't go out in the freezing cold with a damp shirt, even under a warm coat." She tilted her head and looked him up and down as if taking his measure. "My dear Oscar was a big man like you. I still have some of his shirts. I know they'll be way out of style, but maybe you should wear one of them home."

The caring that poured from the tiny woman almost overwhelmed him. Russell's intention to help his new town grew stronger and more determined.

Lori hadn't slept well. The strain of staying out of Russell's way at Mrs. Flanagan's had worn her out. Her world felt topsy-turvy. She'd had a very satisfying life here in Mistletoe until that fateful New Year's Day. Why did Deanna have to bring up the marriage pact? Madison probably would've forgotten all about it. Since that night, Lori had felt pressured to be attached—or at least have a glimmer of hope that the Lord had an eligible bachelor for her in Mistletoe.

First, the disastrous evening with Matthew had shaken up her church life. She'd been sure all would settle down when the new pastor arrived, but he only brought more upheaval. Since she'd pulled back from taking on responsibilities at church this year, her life had a hole in it. Initially, Lori only wanted to see how much time her new job as mayor would require. Then Pastor Brown upset her equilibrium before she learned who he really was.

She missed sitting with her friends yesterday. Maybe she

could convince them to move farther back. Lori shook her head. Not likely.

Now here she was at the office having a hard time concentrating on the boring files. Maybe she should just throw them all out and start afresh. Wouldn't the city secretary have a fit if she did that?

Lori had closed one file and reached for the next one when her phone rang. "Lori Compton here."

"Mayor." How could Felicity always sound so cheerful? Maybe that's why she'd kept her job so long. "There's someone here to see you. Pastor Brown."

Not today. Lori thought fast. She didn't want to reveal her feelings to the receptionist. "Actually, I'm really deep into some important files right now. I can't see anyone. Hold my calls for the next couple of hours." When she hung up, her conscience pricked her.

Why did I do that? Because I'm a coward, that's why. She picked up the top paper and started to read every tedious word. Before she got halfway down the page, Lori glanced out the window toward the clock tower. Her attention was drawn to the tall man bundled up against the cold, making his way across the park. Every few feet, he stopped and studied one of the trees or bushes.

What makes you tick, preacher man?

What a silly thought. If she'd let herself really think about him, she'd remember the fantastic time they had the first evening he was here. She wasn't going to let her thoughts take her there, no matter how much a part of her wanted to.

Well, that didn't go very well. Russell glanced back toward City Hall before he reached the bandstand in the middle of the park. The building didn't look like a fortress, but it might as well be. He sure hadn't been able to get in to see the mayor. That first day he came for the interview, he had the impression the mayor had an open-door policy for the citizens of the town. Now he wasn't so sure. Or was he the only one denied admittance? Something decidedly strange was going on.

Russell unlocked the side door to the parsonage. Back home, no one ever used the front door, unless a stranger came to call. He'd continued the habit here. Besides, if he went out the side door, he was closer to the church building.

Monday was his day off, so he planned to spend it doing personal errands. Maybe if he came up with some ideas to help the town, the mayor would see him. He went into his office and started surfing the Internet, looking for activities in other cities, as well as schools and churches. Maybe something would click and turn on his creativity.

Several hours later, he sat at the large wooden desk in the office in the parsonage, a legal pad and a pen resting on the top. He bowed his head and spent time communing with the Lord, the Author of creativity. When he raised his head and opened his eyes, the room had darkened. He went around turning on lamps, then sank into the large leather recliner and set the pad on the ankle he rested on his other knee.

Visions shot through Russell's head—carnivals, festivals,

and myriad other possibilities he'd located online. How could any of these events help Mistletoe? Concrete thoughts took shape, and he began to write. Soon he had quite a list with subheads jotted underneath.

Now he had something to take to the mayor. He only wished she'd be the friendly mayor he'd first met, not the one he'd been seeing lately.

Would the man never give up? Lori looked at her calendar. Here it was near the end of the second week in February. Every business day since he'd arrived, the new pastor had called her. She was out of excuses. She hadn't even gone to church last Sunday because she was afraid of running into him. This would have to stop. She couldn't let Russell Brown affect her walk with the Lord. Of course, she did watch a church service on TV, but it wasn't the same as being in fellowship with other believers. *Lord, what am I going to do?*

"*See the man.*"

Lori wasn't sure whether she heard an audible voice or not, but the admonition reverberated through her mind and soul. *Okay, Lord, I'll talk to him if he calls again.*

The chirp of the telephone let her know the Lord was going to test her on this. "Lori Compton here."

"Mayor, Pastor Brown is here again. Is there any way you can see him today?" Felicity sounded more subdued than Lori had ever heard her.

"Send him up, Felicity." She hoped she wasn't making a

mistake, but hadn't the Lord just spoken to her?

Once again, the man came up the stairs with quick steps. Lori's heartbeat accelerated in anticipation as he neared.

He stopped in the open doorway. "Thank you for seeing me, Lori."

Somehow he didn't sound like the preacher when he said that. "Come in, Russell." She stood but kept the desk between them. "How can I help you?"

"Actually, I've come to help you." The smile that spread across his face took her breath away.

"And how do you propose to do that?" Silence hung in the air. *Why did I use the word "propose"?*

"May I sit down?" He quirked one eyebrow above his steel-gray eyes.

"Of course." She dropped back into her own chair and rotated it until she faced him squarely. "Tell me what's on your mind."

He scooted the chair close to the front of the desk and placed a folder on it. "I've been talking to a lot of people in town. I know what's been happening to the economy, and I think I have a few solutions."

Lori tented her fingers under her chin. This wasn't what she expected at all. "And what sort of solutions are we talking about?"

Russell told her about surfing the Internet for ideas, then he thrust a page toward her. He had done a lot of work on the presentation, and his ideas were good—initiatives that could potentially bring more people to Mistletoe. Lori read down the list as he explained each one.

He ended with a question. "What do you think?"

For the first time since the middle of January, Lori actually smiled at him. Russell felt as if the sun had just broken through storm clouds. Now if he could just keep her smiling. "I'd like to work with you on these."

Lori shook her head. "I don't think that's a good idea." And the smile disappeared.

He couldn't give up now. "I could be a lot of help. I have a cousin who's in PR, as well as other contacts. We could choose a project, get the whole town working on it, and I'll get the word out without it costing an arm and a leg."

A smile tugged at the corners of her mouth but didn't take hold. "Perhaps you're right. I just wouldn't want to keep you from your important work at the church."

He laughed, hoping to coax the smile back out. "I don't work every minute of the day, you know."

"All right." Lori clasped her hands on top of the paper on her desk. "How about if you help us with the first project, and then we'll decide about more later?"

"Okay." Russell didn't want to wear out his welcome, so he stood. "I'll be going, but call me when you have time to talk again."

He was going to make himself so useful that Lori would have no reason to keep him from helping her. As he walked across the park this time, he whistled a tune, and it wasn't a Christmas carol.

Chapter 5

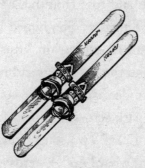

Lori took the list to the meeting of the town council that evening. They all affirmed her opinion: Russell's ideas were good. After much discussion and a vote, they chose to concentrate on two projects this year—a Christmas in July carnival and a Christmas harvest festival. When she arrived at work the next morning, for the first time since she took office, City Hall buzzed with excitement. For now she wouldn't even bother going over any more of the tedious files.

After she sat at her desk, Lori bowed her head. *Lord, I give this day to You. Help me make the most of it for the city's sake and for Your glory. Amen.* The ringing of her telephone punctuated her prayer.

"Lori Compton here." The excitement evident in her voice mirrored that in her heart.

"Pastor Brown wants to see you." Felicity's words held the same spark of life.

"Send him on up." Lori took a deep breath, then managed

a peek at the mirror in her top drawer before he reached her office.

Russell stood framed in the open doorway, and Lori took another deep breath and rose from her chair. *That man is just too good-looking to be a pastor.* She hoped he couldn't read her thoughts from her facial expression. "Russell, come in." This time, she went around the desk to greet him.

The megawatt smile that lit his face could have powered all of the lights in the park across the street for a month. "Thank you for seeing me, Lori." Two long strides bought him very close to her. "I meant what I said yesterday. I want to help with the projects."

With him standing so near, Lori felt the heat radiating from his body. She moved back behind the desk and took a surreptitious moment to calm herself, remembering why she had stayed away from him. When he wasn't at church, he didn't seem like a preacher. He was just Russell, the man she connected with in a special way the first time she met him.

"Have a seat." She slid into her chair as he dropped into one on the other side of the desk. "I have good news for you." Lori picked up a pen and started tapping it on the folder in front of her, a nervous habit she thought she'd broken years ago. Quickly, she laid the pen down. "The town council wants to go with two of the projects this year. Christmas in July and the harvest thing."

Russell leaned back and stretched his legs out in front of him. "Good. I thought those would be the best to implement first."

"So did they." Lori realized she was tapping her toe instead of the pen. Why was she so jittery around him? She willed her foot to be still. "Everyone in the office has a different perspective today."

When he stroked his jaw, her attention homed in on his chiseled features.

"Did they decide on a date for either one?"

Lori cleared her throat. "They want to make the whole month of July a festival month." She swung her chair to the side and rested one arm on the desk. "At first, I thought a week would be enough, but the consensus was that if July is in the name of the carnival, then we should have it the whole month. That will give people more time to come, instead of limiting it to a week and possibly cutting out those who already have plans. We're getting a late start for putting out publicity this year."

Russell rolled up out of his chair in one fluid motion. She watched him from under her lashes. For a big man, he was very graceful. *Be still, my heart.*

Standing, Russell seemed to take possession of the room. "That's a good idea, but won't it be a lot of work?"

Lori swiveled back around, then stood. "All of the preparation will be done before July, so it won't make any difference whether the carnival is a week or a month long. Remember this is the Christmas town, year around."

"How could I forget?" His hearty laugh echoed off the walls. "I'm here to help any way I can."

"Perhaps you should go see Deanna Moss. She's our director

of tourism. She'll know where your talents are most needed."

"Okay."

When Russell stuck out his hand, Lori shook it. His warm grip sent tingles surging up her arm. She hoped she didn't give him any indication of the way his touch affected her.

Russell left the mayor's office with a smile on his face and a lighter heart. Finally, the Lori he had met when he first arrived in Mistletoe had returned. The brief meeting in her office had brought all kinds of scenarios into his mind. Maybe God had brought him to Mistletoe to meet this woman. He'd never believed in love at first sight, but it hadn't taken him many encounters to realize he really wanted to get to know this woman with the intriguing green eyes—more than he'd ever wanted to know any other woman.

When she'd frozen up on him, he wondered what he'd done to push her away. Today in her office, he'd felt an awareness of her that went beyond anything he'd experienced before. And for some reason, he thought she felt the same thing. That could explain why she'd backed off from him when she did. Maybe the feelings were as foreign to her as they were to him.

He forgot to ask Lori where he could find Deanna's office. He'd have to ask Felicity.

Lori was blown away by how quickly everything happened after the meeting with Russell. Within little more than a week, a lovely brochure about the Christmas in July carnival was designed and printed. Russell, true to his word, sent them to numerous people all across the country. Soon inquiries flooded both Deanna's office and Lori's. There even were bus tours planning to come to Mistletoe.

Every day, Lori went to work with a lighter step, looking forward to whatever wonderful news the day would bring. She wasn't disappointed.

The whole town took on a different attitude. Where there had been a feeling of helplessness, now hope reigned. Shopkeepers got busy sprucing up their stores so they'd be ready for the influx of people.

By the middle of April, all of the inns were booked solid for the month of July, and the hotel out near the interstate reported an increase in bookings. Besides that, more people were coming to town even before the festivities. Lori had wondered when she ran for mayor if she really could help the town. Of course, not all of the changes were her doing, but she felt more confident in her job. She only had one problem—and he stood over six feet tall and talked with a Texas twang.

Rev. Russell Brown. For some reason, she had a hard time thinking about him as her pastor. Sure, he was a good preacher, and his sermons brought her closer to the Lord. But when the man was out from behind the pulpit, he became far too human in her thoughts.

Lori's phone chirped, startling her. Every time she started thinking about Russell, the phone rang. Was God trying to tell her something? If so, what was it?

"Lori Compton here." She swiveled the chair so she could look out over the park. A late snowfall still covered the ground, giving the outdoors a fresh look.

"Mayor, the Rev wants to see you."

When had Felicity become so flippant? Lori hadn't noticed, but she was sure she had heard Felicity call him "the Rev" before. "Tell him to come on up." She placed the phone in its cradle and took a deep, cleansing breath before turning back around in time to see him enter her office. At least the man was good for developing her lung capacity.

Russell came over and perched on a corner of her desk. "Do you have anything else you need me to do for the Christmas in July carnival?"

Lori shuffled through papers in front of her. "I don't think so. Looks like everything's running smoothly."

He thrust a folder toward her. "You might want to see these. I've just made the rounds of the shops, and the owners gave me their reports for you."

When she took them, he crossed his arms and waited. Lori scanned the bottom of the columns. "Every store is showing a substantial gain over last year's sales figures." She placed the folder on top of one of the stacks on her desk, then leaned back. "That's wonderful." Her gaze collided with his and lingered. The man's eyes mesmerized her.

The silver sheen of his gaze sparkled like the tinsel on the Christmas trees in the park. "I'm really happy for my new hometown."

Lori decided to give credit where it was due. "It wouldn't

have happened without your help."

The smile on his face could melt all of the snow under those trees in the park. "I didn't do it by myself. It took everyone pitching in—together."

"But the ideas were yours." Lori stood and moved around the other end of the desk to break the connection between them. Times like this made it hard to remember she didn't want a deeper relationship with a pastor, not after the fiasco with Matthew. She recognized that she couldn't trust her own feelings. Hadn't she read more into her former pastor's attention than he intended? She needed to remember the hurt she'd felt when, instead of declaring his undying love as she'd expected, he told her he was leaving.

Russell thought everything was going well until Lori moved away from him and her expression clouded over. He wasn't sure what caused the sudden change. He didn't think it was anything he said, so maybe whatever had caused her to avoid him before had come between them again. He'd hoped they were making some headway. After three months, he was ready to try to establish a different kind of relationship with Lori. If only he could find out what kept cooling her down in his presence.

He hadn't wanted anyone else in town to know of his feelings for Lori, but maybe it was time to talk to Deanna. Or Madison. One or the other could help him understand. He knew them well enough to trust they would keep the conversation confidential.

When he started toward Deanna's office, he saw her hurry to her car and take off. He turned the other direction and meandered toward Under the Mistletoe. Madison was clever to choose such a name for her business. No one would forget it. For a moment, he wished he could catch Lori under one of the bunches of mistletoe hanging in the store. *Whoa, don't go there!*

Jangling bells on the doorknob announced his arrival, and Madison quickly came to the front of the store. "How can I help you, Pastor Brown?"

"Madison, I'd really like you to call me Russell." He hoped she didn't think he was too informal. "I feel like we're friends now."

"Okay, Russell, how can I help you?"

He gave a quick perusal of the area. "Do you have any customers?"

She wiped her hands down the front of the decorated apron she always wore in the store. "Not right now."

"I'd really like to talk to you about something kind of personal." He shifted his weight from one foot to the other.

Madison replaced the OPEN sign hanging on the door with one that read BACK IN A JIFFY. "Follow me to the back. We can talk there."

Russell accompanied her quick footsteps to a back room. "Thanks for taking this time with me."

Madison headed toward a table and a couple of chairs off to one side. "I forgot to ask you if you wanted some spiced tea or cocoa."

"Cocoa would be nice."

While Madison went back into the store to get the drink,

he took the time to look around. The small space had been arranged efficiently to accommodate cabinets, a sink, a refrigerator, and storage shelves.

After handing him the cup, Madison leaned both arms on the table. "Tell me what I can do for you."

He swirled the drink around a few times, then took a quick sip. "I want to know what's going on with Lori Compton. You're one of her closest friends, aren't you?"

She nodded. "I thought everything was fine now that business is picking up for everyone."

"This isn't about the town." He cleared his throat and started again. "Sometimes she's really friendly to me, then she freezes up. Is there something I need to know about her?"

Russell could feel her intense gaze, and it made him uncomfortable, but he continued to stare into his cup, hoping she couldn't read his thoughts.

"I'm not sure I know what you're getting at."

He glanced up in time to catch a smile hovering on her face. *Might as well get it all out on the table.* "I'd like to pursue a relationship with her and see what develops."

Madison's smile widened. "That's what I hoped you meant." She leaned back in the chair and started rocking it gently. Then she proceeded to tell him about the marriage pact the four women had made before leaving college, ending with the fact that Lori would turn twenty-eight on the last day of the year. Amusement laced her words.

He mulled her words over before commenting. "Why would that make her act friendly sometimes but then cold?"

"I'm not sure, but when we talked about it on New Year's Day, she said she had someone in mind. She didn't say who, and Deanna and I have never seen her go out with any man since then. We don't know what's going on."

At least Madison was honest with him. "I'm not sure that helped me a lot, but it does give me something to think about."

Lori scanned the list of e-mails that Marsha Hawkins, the city secretary, had forwarded to her after Marsha had weeded through them. Lori wouldn't get much else done today if she responded to all of them. When the phone rang, she lifted the receiver without taking her eyes off the message she was reading.

"Lori Compton here."

"Mayor, do you know what time it is?" Sometimes Felicity's questions didn't make a lot of sense. The woman had a clock on her desk.

Lori glanced at the digital readout on the computer. "One o'clock." She sighed. "Okay, I get it, I missed lunch."

"Bingo. You're doing that a lot lately." Laughter provided a background to Felicity's comment, indicating that someone else was in the reception area with her. "But you won't go hungry today. Madison is here with lunch for the two of you."

At that pronouncement, Lori's stomach gave a loud rumble. She hoped the woman on the other end of the phone didn't hear it. "Send her up."

Now she was glad she and her friends had made a comfortable space for conversation on one side of the office. She and Madison could eat over there. Lori stood and stretched the kinks out of her back.

"You've been spending too much time in front of the computer, haven't you?" Carrying white paper sacks from Flossie's Café, Madison bustled through the door.

"Do I smell apple fritters?" At least the growl from her stomach wasn't as loud this time.

Madison set the bags on the low table in front of the couch. "Of course." She gave her friend a quick once-over. "You look like you're losing weight, not that you need to. According to Felicity, this isn't the first time you've worked through lunch."

Lori sat and pulled one of the sacks toward her. "She talks too much. What else is in here?"

Madison joined her on the overstuffed furniture. "A cheeseburger and fries. I want to put some meat on your bones."

Lori said a quick prayer over the meal, then sank her teeth into the juicy burger and smiled. This was better than the carton of yogurt waiting in the fridge in the break room.

Her hunger sated, she sat back and nibbled on an apple fritter. "I can't believe we ate without uttering one word." She grinned at Madison.

"You were as hungry as I was." Madison wadded up the burger wrapper and stuffed it into an empty sack. "Now we talk."

Lori laughed. "So this wasn't just a mercy mission to rescue your starving friend?"

"I thought it was time we discussed a certain matter." The smile that spread across Madison's face hinted at ideas Lori wasn't sure she wanted to hear.

"And exactly what is that?"

"Remember when we had the tea at your house on New Year's Day?"

"How could I forget?" Lori grimaced. "That discussion keeps popping into my mind at the oddest times."

"Deanna and I didn't want to push you on this. We thought you'd eventually tell us, but you haven't, so I'm just going to ask. Who were you talking about when you said you had your eye on someone?" Madison waited with an expectant expression on her face.

Might as well get this over with. Lori knew it would come up sooner or later. "I'm surprised you haven't asked before. Not that I really wanted to talk about it."

Madison huffed out a big sigh. "So tell me already."

Lori cleared her throat while trying to get her thoughts in order. "Matthew Hogan and I had been doing a lot of things together, so I kind of thought maybe something would develop there."

"Let me get this straight." Madison sat up and leaned toward Lori. "You were thinking you and Pastor Hogan would hook up?"

Lori didn't think Madison should have made it sound like such a bad idea. "Well, it wasn't impossible. We'd been to Kalispell together several times."

"Now I understand what's going on with you." A satisfied smile crept across Madison's face.

Lori stood and went to the windows to look out over the

park. "What do you mean, what's going on with me?" She didn't turn back toward her friend.

With quick steps, Madison strode toward her. "You know, sometimes you're friendly to the new pastor, and sometimes when you're around him, you're like the Ice Queen."

"The Ice Queen?" Lori whirled around. "Isn't that rather a junior high expression?"

"Did you think Deanna and I wouldn't notice?" Madison stood with fisted hands on her hips. "Well, we did. We've discussed it a time or two."

Leave it to her friends to get involved in every facet of her life, whether she wanted them to or not. "Okay. Here's what happened: Matthew took me out to a really nice restaurant. I assumed he wanted to start a more personal relationship with me. Instead, he told me he was moving. Those words completely destroyed my illusions. I've decided I can't trust myself to choose a mate, so now I'm waiting for the Lord to drop one in my lap." She tilted her chin. "There, are you satisfied?"

Lori didn't expect the laughter that filled the room. She scowled.

"Maybe—the Lord—has dropped one—in your lap," Madison choked out between snickers. The woman could be annoying to the extreme.

"And just who might that be?" Lori quirked an eyebrow at her smirking friend.

Madison took a moment to force her face into a serious expression. "Who is the best-looking guy to come to town this year?"

Heat climbed into Lori's cheeks. Oh, she knew the answer to that question, all right. She just didn't know if she wanted to verbalize it. A tall man with wavy, dark blond hair and steel-gray eyes popped into her mind, and he didn't have on the suit he wore on Sundays. Jeans on long, lean legs and a plaid Western shirt that rippled over his muscles, held together by a big engraved silver buckle, probably won at a rodeo. That's what she envisioned.

"You know who I'm talking about," Madison chirruped. "I can tell by your expression. The Reverend Russell Brown. But you don't want to think about him that way, do you? You're afraid you'll be hurt again." She draped an arm across Lori's shoulders. "Maybe you should ask the Lord what He thinks about a possible relationship between you and Russell."

Lori shook her head. "Russell probably isn't even interested in me."

"You should see the way he looks at you when you're busy with someone else. I'd say he's interested."

Lori's heart raced. Could Madison be right? Lori had a lot to think and pray about when she went home tonight.

Chapter 6

When Lori unlocked the door to her home, a feeling of sanctuary filled her heart. Within these walls, she could relax and be herself. After changing into her favorite velour jogging suit, she gathered up a load of laundry. While she prepared the washer, she replayed Madison's words in her mind. Did Russell really see her as anything special?

Pouring a capful of detergent into the machine, Lori remembered that Madison had a flair for the dramatic. Her heart sank. Russell was friendly to all—he was the town's pastor.

Lori continued her chores, but she was constantly distracted by the conversation she'd had with Madison. Finally, she gave up and plopped into the recliner that faced the window overlooking the town. Twilight quickly turned into the dark of evening, lit only by the Christmas lights in the square and from scattered windows casting a bright glow on the lingering snow.

Her Bible rested on the table beside her chair. She clicked on the table lamp and picked up the precious book. Letting the leather-bound Bible lay in her lap, she leaned her head back and closed her eyes. *Lord, was Madison telling me something You wanted me to hear? If so, show me.*

She held the unopened book close to her chest and waited quietly to see if God would make an impression on her soul. After a few moments, the phrase *Philippians 4:7* came to mind. She figured she might as well look it up and see if it applied to anything that was going on.

"And the peace of God, which transcends all understanding, will guard your hearts and your minds in Christ Jesus." After Lori read the words aloud, she mulled them over.

Maybe God did whisper the verse to her. Here she'd been trying all by herself to guard her heart from being hurt again, but this verse said the peace of God would guard hearts and minds. She hadn't even asked the Lord if He wanted her to pursue a relationship with Matthew Hogan. Maybe if she had, He would have given her a restlessness in her spirit about it.

Is it really that easy? Ask God what He thinks about something, then wait to see if His peace follows? Maybe she could try it.

Russell hoped Madison hadn't told Lori what he'd said, but the next few times he was near the mayor, he noticed a decided change in her attitude. Nothing spectacular, just more friendliness. He still felt wary, waiting for the freeze-out once again.

They worked together on many aspects of the Christmas in July carnival, which turned out to be a huge success. When publicity went out about the weeklong harvest festival in October, the inns booked up within two weeks. People who were too late asked for rooms either before or after the festival, thus helping the economy anyway.

Glowing reports from the merchants kept flooding in. The business climate of Mistletoe had definitely turned around. Russell reaped rewards from the increase in tourism, too. Most of the people who came on the weekends attended Living Word Chapel. If this continued, he might have to add another service on Sunday mornings. He'd never even considered that possibility when he accepted the position. What a difference a few months had made.

Christmas carols played softly in the sanctuary before the morning service, muffling the many conversations all over the room. Russell followed the choir through the doorway that led to the platform, taking his place behind the pulpit. As he looked out over his congregation, he saw many new faces scattered among the faithful parishioners. Unfortunately, Lori no longer sat in the second row with her friends. A month ago, she'd started singing in the choir. He'd missed sneaking glances at her while he preached. She always listened intently and even took notes. Not too many did that anymore.

When he and the choir were in place, silence swept across the room. He stretched his hands toward heaven and invoked the presence of the living God. "Thank You, Father, for being present with us today. Amen." His heart lifted with his words.

Lori hung back and let the other choir members crowd in to

hang up their red robes and golden stoles. She wasn't in a hurry, but many had families waiting for them. By the time she reached the front door of the chapel, only a couple of people waited to greet Pastor Brown. She stepped to the back of the short line.

Russell's hand engulfed hers, and he placed his other one on top of them. "Do you have plans for lunch, Lori?"

"No." She glanced up into his face, noticing the intensity of his steel-gray gaze. "The sermon really touched me today. God has been teaching me from that verse in Philippians 4. I'd never understood the full meaning until lately."

Russell continued to hold her hand, and she didn't want to pull away. He smiled. "I had a reason to ask you about lunch. There's a new chef at the hotel out on the interstate. I've been wanting to see how good he is, but I don't like to eat out alone. Would you rescue this poor preacher from loneliness?"

His question buried itself deep within her. How could he be lonely? Everyone in town loved him. Surely people often invited him to their homes for meals.

"And. . ."—his voice interrupted her thoughts—". . .we can discuss the insight the Lord has been giving you about this scripture."

"I'd like that."

They took Russell's truck to the restaurant. It was the first time Lori had ridden with him. She remembered thinking his presence filled her office when he stood. In the large pickup cab, his presence was even more overwhelming. Instead of being intimidated by it this time, Lori relaxed. Studying the depths of that verse had made an impact on her life.

She didn't know Russell had made reservations, but they were ushered to a table before those waiting in line. Had he assumed she would come with him? And why not? They'd been working together comfortably for months.

After they ordered, she started the conversation. "Have you heard the long-range forecast for next week?"

He undid the fancy folds in the napkin and carefully placed it in his lap. "I haven't paid attention to it."

"They're saying an arctic cold front is coming, and the west winds will bring moisture from the Pacific. We could have the first snowfall of the season during the festival."

"Would that be a bad thing?" He quirked one brow, as he often did when he questioned something.

"Actually, it might be good for adding to the feeling of Christmas."

"Great." He leaned his forearms on each side of the place setting. "Okay, tell me what you've been learning about the peace of God."

Russell's abrupt change of subject took her by surprise. She fiddled with the stem of her water goblet, trying to formulate an answer that didn't give away too much information. "I'd been struggling on my own with guarding my heart and mind. One night God led me to this verse. I'd read it before because I've read through the Bible more than once. But I'd never recognized that the presence or absence of the peace of the Lord should guide us in every situation." Lori shrugged. "In other words, I'd been trusting in myself instead of God."

He nodded, and his eyes held understanding. "That's a hard

lesson to learn. I've struggled with it over the years, too."

The waiter bringing their food interrupted the conversation. After he left, Russell reached for her hand across the table. "Let's return thanks for the food."

Lori welcomed his touch. Learning to have a comfortable, friendly relationship with Russell Brown had been a benefit of allowing God's peace to lead her. She no longer needed to put up a defensive wall to keep from being hurt.

In early October, Lori watched the Christmas harvest festival run without a hitch. People thronged the park in the square, enjoying the concerts in the bandstand and the decorations. They visited the area shops and eateries, as well. True to the forecast, snowflakes began to fall by midweek, but the conditions remained mild. Since many of the festival attendees came from southern and coastal states, they reveled in the increasing snowfall. The weather wasn't too much for the street department to keep up with, so it didn't slow the festivities. By the time the week was over, snow covered the yards and surrounding mountains, even though traffic moved along at a normal pace for winter.

The next week snow fell harder, leaving the mountains with enough of a base for skiing. Lori hoped she'd soon get a chance to try the slopes.

On Friday, she was going over reports that had sifted in from the festival. She was still smiling when the phone rang. "Lori Compton here."

"The Rev is on his way up to see you."

His entrance coincided with the end of Felicity's pronouncement.

Rubbing her neck, Lori stood. She'd been hunched over her desk too long again. "How can I help you, Russell?"

That wonderful smile spread slowly across his face, lighting up the office. "I want to go skiing."

"Skiing?" Lori blinked. "I've been thinking about that myself."

"Great minds, as they say." He chuckled. "So will you take me?"

"Have you ever been skiing?"

Russell jammed his hands into the front pockets of his jeans. "I know I came from Texas, but it's not *that* far from Colorado. I've gone a few times with friends or family."

"So what's your level of proficiency?"

He stared at the ceiling a moment. "Well, I don't use the bunny slope anymore. But I've never been on a black slope. Which resort do you usually use?"

Now it was Lori's turn to laugh.

"What's so funny?" A frown marred Russell's handsome features.

"You sound like a tourist." She tried for a solemn expression. "Natives don't often go to the resorts. We have favorite places to ski on private property."

"Okay. Where do you usually ski?"

"My family has owned most of Sugar Mountain for generations, and there's a wonderful place to ski on the other side of the mountain." She perched on the front edge of the desk.

"When do you want to go?"

Russell glanced toward the windows. "It's snowed several inches. Is there enough to ski on?"

She nodded. "There's plenty of base, and it's still snowing. Since tomorrow's Saturday, do you want to try out Sugar Mountain?"

His eager expression gave her the answer even before he spoke. "Of course."

Russell made a stop at Flossie's Café before heading to Lori's house. He loaded the backseat of his extended cab with thermoses filled with hot chocolate and several bags of food, including apple fritters. When he pulled into her driveway, Lori stood beside her SUV, which was parked outside her garage.

He exited his vehicle and walked toward her. A smile broke out on his face. Lori Compton was even more beautiful than the gorgeous backdrop. "I thought we'd take my pickup."

Lori shook her head. "I have four-wheel drive."

"So do I." Russell wasn't in the habit of riding with anyone else driving, especially a woman. If that made him a chauvinist, so be it.

With an exasperated sigh, Lori planted her fists on her hips. "But you've never driven on the other side of the mountain. There aren't as many roads, and I'm familiar with the terrain."

She had a point, even if he didn't want to agree. "Okay. I'll transfer some things from my truck to yours."

Russell carried the first load of goodies to Lori's truck,

went back to his vehicle, then filled his arms with a second load.

"How much stuff did you bring?"

He turned to find Lori on his heels. "Lots of food and drink. We might need it." He threw a grin back over his shoulder. "It never hurts to be prepared."

She picked up a couple of the containers and started toward the back of her vehicle. "It's just the two of us, not an army."

"I know, but. . ." With the blankets, emergency kit, and extra water in the back of her SUV, he had to cram to get all of his gear to fit. When he finished, he rubbed his gloved hands together. "We're ready to go."

"I'll say." Lori hopped into the driver's seat.

She looked adorable in her pink ski outfit. Russell walked around to the passenger door, his smile burying his doubts. Today it was just the two of them. They'd be alone in the SUV and on the mountain. It felt like a real date, but there was no telling whether Lori would revert to the woman who avoided him in church.

As she climbed behind the wheel, Lori couldn't help noticing how much this innocent ski trip felt like a real date—even if she was the one doing the driving. In the past, that would've bothered her, but no more. With a light heart, she turned onto the highway that led up, over, and around Sugar Mountain. Before they reached the ski slope, Russell would see some of the most beautiful scenery in Montana. Lori loved the ruggedness of the Rocky Mountains this close to the Continental Divide. Some of the peaks were so high that no vegetation grew on their rocky slopes, but down lower, the evergreens, hemlocks, and aspens were abundant.

"Fantastic," Russell said as the truck climbed higher into God's country. "Thanks for the invite, Lori."

"Oh, this is nothing yet. I hope we spot some antelopes or elk."

"No, this is enough beauty to last me a lifetime."

She shot a glance his way and stifled a nervous giggle. The way he was looking at her, he could've meant the beauty of the mountains or. . . Suddenly a lump formed in her throat. She wouldn't read more meaning into his words than he intended. Hadn't that gotten her into trouble before?

The drive on the wintry roads took almost an hour. When she turned off the pavement and drove up a snow-covered dirt track, she was sorry their time together in the SUV was almost at an end.

"Are you sure this road is safe?" Russell clenched his hands.

Lori restrained a laugh. "Like I told you, I know where I'm going." She smiled over at him, then quickly returned her attention to the road.

The lane led through a wooded area where the snow wasn't as deep under the trees that grew so close together. She slowed the truck and pulled up in front of the sturdy log cabin with a plume of smoke pouring from a pipe sticking out of the roof.

"Does someone live here?" Russell cleared the foggy window with his gloved hand.

"No, this is our family ski lodge. It's not as fancy as the ones at the resorts, but it comes in handy."

"Nice." He got out, went to the back of the vehicle, and started gathering up supplies. "Surely you didn't come out here earlier to start the fire."

"No." Lori picked up a few packages and led the way to the door. "I called my uncle, and he sent one of the men over to get the cabin ready for us."

While Russell continued to unload the vehicle, Lori unpacked the bags in the kitchen.

Russell brought in the last of their gear, then went over to the stove to warm his hands. "This really is nice."

"Thanks." Lori poured two mugs of hot chocolate and gave one to him before leaning against the bar that divided the kitchen from the rest of the room. "My great-grandfather was in Switzerland in World War II. He learned to ski there. When he came back, he didn't want to give it up, so he built this ski run on Sugar Mountain. It's been well cared for through the years, and three more generations have learned to ski on this slope."

Russell smiled at her over the rim of his cup. "That's some history. I knew that Keystone in Colorado was the first commercial ski run, and soldiers from that war opened it. I just never thought about anyone else doing the same thing. You said your uncle sent someone to start the fire. How come I haven't met your uncle?"

"You have." Lori laughed. "His name isn't Compton. He's my mother's brother. Uncle Hiram and Aunt Ethel go to Living Word Chapel."

"The Lanes. Of course I know them." Russell took another sip of cocoa. "I just never associated them with you. It takes awhile to put everyone together, even in a small town."

"They spend most of their time out on the ranch. You probably haven't seen us together." Lori switched her gaze from Russell's intense gray eyes to the bags on the counter. "So what's in these?"

He came over and lifted another of the sacks onto the bar beside her.

Lori's face heated. The hot chocolate had really warmed her up. At least she thought it was the cocoa.

"We can't go skiing without carbs for energy, so I brought some apple fritters. I'm afraid they're cold now." He stared down into her eyes until she became breathless.

Lori walked around the end of the bar. "Several years ago, Uncle Hiram had electricity run to the cabin, and we have a microwave." She opened the door of the appliance. "We can reheat them." She searched the cabinet and brought out two paper plates.

She needed to get a grip or Russell would see through her.

Russell loved the sparkle in Lori's eyes as they talked about their families and enjoyed the pastries. He could really get used to spending time with this woman. When he thought about that, he realized he felt God's peace in his heart. Once more, he visited the thought that this woman was one of the major reasons the Lord had brought him to Mistletoe, Montana.

When they finished eating and cleaning up, they gathered their ski equipment and went out the door. He looked around, and then it hit him: This wasn't a resort, and there wasn't a ski lift in sight. His gaze traveled the long way up the height of the ski slope before them. "Don't tell me we have to walk up there."

"Are you going to wimp out now?" Lori's eyes crinkled with her laughter. "Remember, no gain without pain, or something like that. We have to climb up before we can come down."

He took a deep breath. At this altitude, he needed it. "Lead on. I can go anywhere you can."

With her skis and one pole tied together over one shoulder and the other pole in her hand, Lori struck out. He started after her, surprised that the loose snow wasn't very deep. There truly was a strong base on which they could walk and later ski.

He soon moved up beside her, but their conversation was sparse because of the thin air. They needed all of their breath to climb. Before they reached the top, his legs let him know they weren't used to this type of exertion. He hoped he wouldn't make a fool of himself on his way down. What if his legs gave out under him?

Lori reached the top of the run before him. She went over to a wooden bench set to the side. After dusting the snow off, she sat down and started putting the skis on her boots. "We can take a breather up here before we start down if you want to."

Should he tell her the truth or just tough it out? Truth won. "That might be an excellent idea. I'm in good shape, but I'm not used to this kind of exercise."

Her chuckle warmed his heart. "Neither am I. Because of the pressures of my new job, I haven't been here since I took office. I'm glad you agreed to come with me. We can enjoy the view."

While they sat, Lori pointed out an elk and a small herd of pronghorns. It took him a few minutes to make them out against the woody backdrop some distance across the valley spread before them. He'd love to come back and investigate the animals further. Maybe she'd invite him again.

They didn't wait long enough to cool off before starting down the slope. Lori urged him to push off first, but he wanted them to go together, so he counted, "One, two, three, go!"

In tandem, they moved down the first third of the run. Then he made a mistake. He wanted to watch her for a moment. When he turned his attention to the side, disaster struck. Somehow, one ski slewed to the side and clipped her ski. When he tried to compensate, he did more harm than good. Everything escalated in a snarled blur from that point on.

They ended up with their skis entangled and went down, tumbling until they landed against a tree. While they caught their breath, he surveyed their situation. At least the tumble slowed them down. However, even though Lori's skis had released from her boots, one of his hadn't. His throbbing ankle was positioned at an awkward, unnatural angle.

Lori took stock of the situation, quickly releasing Russell's ski. "Does this ankle hurt?"

He closed his eyes before answering. "Yeah, it does."

"So don't try to be macho and not show it." She piled snow on the offending limb. "This should keep the swelling down. Do you hurt anywhere else?"

When he opened his eyes, he looked her over. "What about you? Are you hurt?"

"Maybe my dignity." She tried to laugh. "This is no position for the mayor to be in."

He tugged her gloved hand. "I mean it. Are you hurt?" His urgency touched her heart.

"I'm probably bruised some, but I don't think I'm injured. But your ankle could be broken. I hope it's only sprained, though."

"What do we do now?" Russell struggled to sit up with his back against the tree. He reached out and touched her cheek. "I'm so sorry. If I'd kept my attention where it should've been, I wouldn't have caused our collision."

Even though he was still wearing ski gloves, the imprint of his hand on her cheek warmed her face. "This isn't the first time, and it probably won't be the last time I've taken a tumble while skiing."

"Back to my question. What do we do now? If we were at a resort, the ski patrol would come see about us." He sounded worried.

"The ranch house is over there." Lori pointed across the valley. "Usually when someone is using the slope, one of the hands checks on it fairly often. We can wait."

He pulled her into a one-arm embrace. "We need to stay

close to share our warmth."

She didn't disagree. Being so near to Russell felt so right.

Sitting under the tall evergreen, they shared their hopes and dreams. Lori didn't realize how long they had been there until she began to shiver. "We can't stay any longer." She reluctantly pulled from his embrace and stood. "We'll end up with frostbite."

Russell watched her for a moment. "I'm sure you're right, but how do we get down there?"

"Can you stand on your other foot?" When he nodded, she helped him up. "You can use a pole on that side, and I can hold up this one."

Russell watched Lori stow their skis under some brush and make a slash on the tree in front of them. He knew it would be hard to get the rest of the way to the cabin. He didn't want to lean too heavily on Lori, but she insisted. Like a couple of cripples, they made their way down the slope a little at a time, taking frequent rest stops.

"So what has three legs, hops, and is icy cold?"

Lori's question surprised him. "What?"

"Two wrecked skiers." Her merry laugh bounced off the trees surrounding the ski run.

That set the tone for their trek down the slope. They laughed and joked almost the whole way. Finally, they stopped to rest at the last strong tree before making the final descent to the cabin. He leaned his back against the trunk and pulled her beside him. She looked up at him, and their gazes merged in a kind of strange, new event. Without thinking about the ramifications, he lowered his face toward hers, watching to see if she leaned away.

When her eyes slid shut instead, he touched his lips to hers. Even though they were both cold, heat quickly overtook the caress. What he intended to be just a gentle kind of thank-you took on a life of its own. And he wasn't the only willing participant. Her arms found their way across his shoulders, with her hands locking behind his neck. Savoring every nuance of the kiss, he cradled her closer to his chest. Never had Russell experienced anything like this. A fusing of two souls in a burst of love that took every other thought from his mind. He wanted *this* moment with *this* woman to go on forever.

"Lori!" A shout resounded from the bottom of the hill. "Are you still up on the slope?"

Russell reluctantly released her. At least they were on the uphill side of the wide tree where they couldn't be seen. The last thing he'd want to do is embarrass Lori. Later, they'd need time to explore what had happened. He smiled into her eyes, which held a dreamy expression, then touched his lips to hers for one last, brief kiss.

Lori stepped to the side, leaving him leaning against his support. "Uncle Hiram," she shouted and waved. "We're up here, and I think Pastor Brown's ankle is sprained."

"I'll send help." The sound of the motor of a snowmobile quickly followed.

Chapter 7

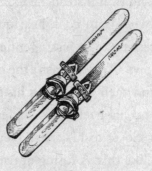

Lori stood beside her fireplace, staring out the windows but not really seeing the vista spread below. The fingertips of one hand lightly pressed against her lips while she relived every nanosecond of *the kiss*. One moment, she and Russell stopped to rest one last time before reaching the log cabin. The next, her world shifted on its axis and would never be the same again.

She had received brief kisses at the end of dates in college, but none of them had meant anything. Maybe that's why she had shied away from those kinds of meaningless associations the older she became.

What do I do now? She'd let down the defenses around her heart and made the choice to trust the Lord to guide her with His peace. Her heart was anything but peaceful right now. Alive was more like it. More alive than ever in her memory. All because of Russell Brown. The *Reverend* Russell Brown to be exact.

How could she face him in the pulpit? Thankfully, she

didn't have to watch him preach. She'd be behind him in the choir loft.

Was this love? This desire to run to him. . .be with him. . . hold him and never let him go?

Over the last few months, she'd come to really know the man. His integrity, his humor, his deep relationship with God. There was nothing about Russell she didn't admire. *Lord, where's Your peace in this?*

Tonight the choir would give a concert in the bandstand in the park. She imagined the carols wafting in the air with the bells in the tower of Living Word Chapel pealing forth as sweet as the bells she heard on the mountain when Russell's lips touched hers.

Into the silence, the still, small voice of God spoke to her heart. *"My peace is right here. Look at the man I've placed in your life."*

When the doorbell of the parsonage rang, Russell reached for his crutches. Mrs. Wendell, his housekeeper, hurried from the kitchen.

"I'll get it for you, Pastor Brown. You just sit there with your foot up like the doctor said."

After he settled back into the recliner, he lowered the sound on the TV, straining to hear who was at the front door. Although his housekeeper's words were strong, the visitor spoke too softly. Maybe it was another church member bringing food. If his freezer weren't so large, he'd need to start giving casseroles to neighbors.

"Hello, Russell."

His gaze shot to the doorway, and his heart skipped a beat. No matter what the doctor said, he wrestled with the crutches and stood. "Lori, come in."

She looked fantastic—vibrant and alive. The cold wind had brought bright color to her cheeks. He maneuvered toward her.

"Stay there." Her graceful movements brought her across the den.

When she stopped in front of him, he saw the peace in her gaze. Had something happened to her?

They both started to talk at once, but he stopped immediately. "You go ahead."

"I'm so sorry you're hurt."

"This isn't the first time I've been on crutches. Besides, it was my own fault." He wanted to brush the lock of hair from her cheek, but first they had to talk. "Lori, we have to discuss us."

Something flared in her eyes, and she glanced away. "What about us?"

He leaned on one crutch, touched her chin gently, and tilted her face toward his. "Our kiss changes things, don't you think?"

She nodded. "But do you want it to change things between us?"

"I decided a long time ago not to play the dating game, Lori. I asked God to bring me the woman I was supposed to spend the rest of my life with." His ankle began to throb, but what he had to say was too important to stop, and he didn't want to continue this conversation sitting down.

"I haven't dated in years, either." She smiled. "For much the same reason. But at the end of college, three friends and I made a silly pact. We'd be married by the time we were twenty-eight. That clouded my thinking earlier this year. I had confusing thoughts, but the Lord's peace has overcome my confusion."

"When will you be twenty-eight?" He didn't want to let on about his conversation with Madison.

"New Year's Eve of this year."

What an opening. "You can be married before then." He tried to convey with his eyes all of the love in his heart.

"This is no joking matter."

"I'm not joking, Lori. I'm asking you to marry me. . .soon."

Her startled expression worried him before she finally spoke. "I don't want to marry you because of some silly marriage pact. I want to marry you because we love each other."

Russell couldn't stand it any longer. He pulled her into a one-armed embrace, resting her head against his shoulder. "I do love you, Lori. I believe you're the woman God created for me. And I don't care when we get married, but the sooner the better. I'm not getting any younger."

Her laughter rumbled against his chest. When she looked up into his face, he did the only thing he could think of. This time when his lips touched hers, their kiss was no less potent than the first one. He was looking forward to a lifetime of sharing kisses, and much more, with this woman.

"So is that a yes?" he asked when the kiss ended.

"That's a yes." Lori stood on tiptoe and gave him another heart-stopping kiss.

Epilogue

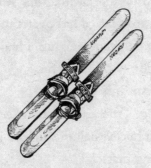

December

Christmas Eve morning, Lori arose early. She was too excited to sleep late on her wedding day. So much had happened in the last couple of months.

The first time Lori met Russell's mom, the delightful woman said, "So this is the woman who knocked my son off his feet."

During the visit, that comment had turned into a family joke. With four sons, Mrs. Brown's life had been boisterous, as she told Lori, but she loved every minute of it. The entire family had welcomed Lori with open arms. All of Russell's brothers were married and had children. Lori looked forward to more huge family gatherings.

Right now, all of the Browns were staying at Mrs. Flanagan's Bed-and-Breakfast. Her own parents would arrive today. They planned to take this opportunity to visit the rest of their family in Mistletoe for the holidays, in addition to attending her wedding.

Life couldn't get much better than this.

Deanna, Madison, and Kathy would come later this morning to help Lori dress for the noon wedding. The reception would be a sit-down meal, and everyone would have plenty of time afterward to get ready for the Christmas Eve candlelight service.

Russell didn't want to miss any of the holiday festivities this first year he was in Mistletoe for Christmas, so they would leave for their honeymoon cruise January second. Lori was glad he'd thought of that. Spending their first Christmas as husband and wife in this town that had brought them together would add a special significance to the season.

Russell stood at the altar beside his mentor at the seminary, Rev. James Dillon, who had been delighted to perform the ceremony. His brothers stood beside him, fidgeting in their rented tuxedos.

He watched as each of Lori's friends came down the aisle, wearing deep red dresses and crowns of holly and berries. They carried white poinsettias that matched those fastened on the end of each pew. Although the bridesmaids were pretty, he eagerly awaited his first glimpse of his bride.

Finally, the organ pealed forth the "Wedding March," and Mrs. Compton stood and turned toward the back. The rest of the congregation followed her example.

When the double doors opened, Russell couldn't take his eyes off the woman who walked through, accompanied by her proud father.

Lori had chosen not to cover her face with her veil. Her eyes met his, and her radiant smile seemed to be for him alone. Surrounded by clouds of white, she looked like an angel, but he knew she was human. A perfect helpmeet created specially for him, just as the Lord had promised.

LENA NELSON DOOLEY

Lena loves to write stories. She's blessed that this is her full-time job. Another of her favorite activities is mentoring other authors and helping them move toward publication. Because of this, she was awarded the American Christian Fiction Writers' Mentor of the Year award in 2006. Several times a year, Lena is a speaker at writers' and women's meetings across the country.

She holds a BA in Speech and Drama and completed many hours of post-graduate work. As well as serving as the Director of Drama at a large church, she has also written scripts and directed plays for community theater. She enjoys doing voiceover work for a local company that produces commercials, and she's been involved in a TV movie.

Lena has written nine books for Heartsong Presents and has stories in five Barbour novella collections. She has had books on one of the top ten favorite lists in the Heartsong Readers' Poll for four years. Last year, *Pirate's Prize* hit #1 on a Christian fiction bestseller list in the UK, and two others were in the top 25. Two of the novella collections spent time on the CBD bestseller list. In 2004, *His Brother's Castoff* was awarded second place in the Book of the Year contest at the American

Christian Romance Writers' national conference.

Married more than 42 years, Lena and her husband spend a lot of time with their children and grandchildren. They're active in church and love to travel. Some of the places they visit become settings in her novels.

She enjoys hearing from her readers. You can find out more about her on her Web site, www.LenaNelsonDooley.com, or on her blog at http://lenanelsondooley.blogspot.com.

Return to Mistletoe

by Debby Mayne

Dedication

This story is dedicated to the hardworking
emergency professionals who save lives every day.
A special thanks goes to the
Pinellas County Emergency operators,
the East Lake Fire and Rescue Department,
the Sunstar Ambulance Service,
and the cardiac unit staff at Mease Countryside Hospital.

I'd also like to dedicate this story to my husband, Wally,
my daughters, Lauren and Alison, and my son-in-law, Jason.
The Lord has blessed me with these amazing people.

This is the confidence we have in approaching God:
that if we ask anything according to his will, he hears us.
1 John 5:14

Chapter 1

June

Deanna's hands shook as she punched in the number of the mayor's office.

"Hey, girl, what's up?" Lori asked.

"Caller ID won't let me get away with a thing, will it?" Deanna grimaced. "And what are you doing answering your own phone?"

Lori chuckled. "The receptionist is out. But you sound strange. Are you okay?"

Deanna cleared her throat. "I'm as okay as I can be, considering I haven't been able to get Anthony out of my mind since I saw him last Christmas. To top it off, he just e-mailed and said he's coming back to town."

"Uh-oh. What about Frank?"

"Yeah, what about Frank? He's sweet and everything, but the relationship doesn't seem to be going anywhere."

"He seems to think everything's okay, though, right?"

Deanna sighed. "I haven't given him reason to think otherwise."

"And I'm sure you haven't told him how long it took you to get over Anthony. You didn't seem fazed the last time you saw him."

"Well, I—"

"Wait a minute. You did get over him years ago, right?"

"Of course I did." Deanna sniffled. "Well, I did—sort of."

"You need to pray about this, Deanna. Old feelings aren't something you can just ignore. Trust me. I've been there."

"Maybe we need to start a support group at church."

Lori chuckled. "We can call it the Get Over Being Abandoned by Mr. Wrong Club."

"I'll count on you to remind me he was Mr. Wrong." Deanna glanced at her watch. "I'd better run. I have a few things due to the committee before I can go home."

"Don't work too hard. You need your strength for whenever Anthony decides to grace us with his presence. Oh, by the way, Frank signed up for the covered dish dinner after church on Sunday. Maybe Frank will do something heroic to make you forget about Anthony."

"Maybe," Deanna replied, although deep down she doubted it. "Thanks, Lori. I knew I could count on you to give this situation some perspective."

"I didn't do anything you haven't done for me. Keep your chin up and keep praying. I'm sure the Lord will guide you if you pay attention."

After she hung up, Deanna took Lori's advice and said a

prayer for guidance and strength. Between her job as the director of tourism for the town of Mistletoe and the prospect of Anthony's return, she felt physically and emotionally worn out. But right now she had to get back to work.

Forcing her thoughts to the numbers she'd plugged into her budget spreadsheet, the shrill ring of the phone gave her a start. She grabbed the phone, which flashed the name of Madison Graham, another childhood friend.

"Hey, Madison, what's up?"

"Just checking up on you. I hear you had another blast from the past."

Lori sure didn't waste any time. "Yeah, but it really isn't anything worth worrying about."

"Are you sure about that?"

"What do you think?"

"Okay, I get the picture—you don't want to talk about it." After a dramatic pause, Madison continued, "Are you going to the covered dish dinner? Lori said Frank signed up. We think it would be good for you to go."

"I'll probably go if I can finish my proposal for the tour bus company."

"Look, I know it's none of my business, but you really do need to take a day off."

Deanna scanned the stacks of papers on her desk and decided Madison had a valid point. "Okay, I *will* go."

"Great. I'm sure Frank will be thrilled."

Deanna laughed. "I don't know about *thrilled*. He hasn't called me since last Sunday."

"C'mon, Deanna, you know how demanding his job is. Sometimes I get the feeling he's not happy at work."

"I get that feeling, too, which is why I told him he might want to start his own company. But he doesn't think there's enough business in Mistletoe for another accounting firm."

"He may be right." Madison sighed. "Look, I gotta run. I just wanted to make sure you were okay."

"Sure, I'm fine. See ya Sunday." Deanna hung up and clicked out of the spreadsheet. She'd have to finish first thing in the morning when she wasn't so rattled.

After clearing her desk and locking the door, she stepped outside and took a cleansing breath. It was almost dark. With her workload, leaving at dusk was getting to be the norm.

Even though it was June, the air was fresh and crisp. Evergreens and bows graced every door on the town square. Some houses still had a single light in the window, keeping the year-round Christmas theme alive. There never was a question of the Christmas mood lingering in Mistletoe. That was a given. But the sagging economy of the town from shops closing and people seeking their fortune elsewhere had the elders of Mistletoe worried. That was why she'd been hired: to help bring the special town of Mistletoe, Montana, back to life. The original year-round Christmas store was still open, but some of the smaller ones had closed their doors. Lori was doing an excellent job in her first term as mayor, and Deanna had managed to persuade one of the restaurant owners to remain open one more year, but the pressure was on her to do more. Not only did her job depend on an increase in tourism, but so did the livelihood of almost everyone in Mistletoe.

The next day was just as busy. Friday arrived before she had a chance to catch her breath, but she was relieved she hadn't been faced with seeing Anthony. . .yet. He'd told her he was coming but hadn't said when, which kept her constantly off-kilter and on alert. She'd barely settled into her office when the bell on the front door jangled. When she heard the familiar voice, her heart thumped out of control.

Anthony took a look around as he waited for the elderly receptionist to get Deanna. The last time he was in town, he didn't stick around long enough to allow these feelings to wash over him. The large picture window at the front of the small office building framed the town square; the view opened the floodgate to memories he'd long since shoved to the back of his mind. Mistletoe hadn't changed much since he'd lived here, but his feelings toward it had. His father had had a special secret government assignment in Montana, and his family had been able to choose anywhere in the state to live. His parents decided on Mistletoe because of its quaint ambience and small-town values. He'd thought it was boring—that is, until he met Deanna Moss, the prettiest and sweetest girl in the school. He fell for her head over heels the first time he laid eyes on her. It took him months to work up the courage to talk to her, but when he did, his opinion of Mistletoe made a complete turnaround.

"I didn't expect you so soon, Anthony."

He turned away from the window. Deanna stood in the doorway, looking even better than she had when he'd run into her last Christmas. His mouth grew dry, and his chest constricted.

Chapter 2

Anthony detected a note of annoyance in Deanna's tone, and he couldn't say he blamed her. After all, he hadn't called for an appointment or given her a concrete time. He'd thought about waiting until after the weekend to see her, but after communicating with her last Monday, he couldn't wait.

"Well?" She stood glaring at him, her arms folded, eyes narrowed, and lips pursed.

Her abruptness rendered him momentarily speechless. He cleared his throat and gathered his thoughts while she studied him. "I have business to discuss, but if you're busy right now, I can go to Mrs. Flanagan's and get settled." He paused for a moment. "Mrs. Flanagan is still there, isn't she?"

Deanna nodded, tossing her wavy, strawberry blond hair around her shoulders. "She's still there, but I'm not sure you can get a room. Her bed-and-breakfast has been packed lately. Ever since Lori became mayor, Mistletoe has been recovering."

Anthony's shoulders sagged. He'd been looking forward to the soft down bedding at Mrs. Flanagan's. He remembered staying there when he was a teen, while his family waited for the house they planned to rent to become vacant. He'd meant to call and reserve a room, but time had slipped away from him. He grimaced. "I guess I didn't realize how much things have changed. In the past, I would've been able to get a room at Mrs. Flanagan's on a moment's notice."

"Check there, but if she doesn't have a room, I'll see if I can find you something."

"But I had my heart set—"

"We don't always get what we want, do we?" Her annoyance came through loud and clear.

She was definitely mad about something. "I'll go check with Mrs. Flanagan. Do you work on Saturdays?"

The receptionist poked her head into the office. "See you in the morning, Deanna."

"Okay, Ginny. See you." After she left, Deanna turned back to face him. "You were saying?"

He smiled. "I'll be here in the morning, too."

A flash of pain flickered across her face. "I'm super busy, especially on Saturdays, so I'll only have a few minutes to spare." Her voice cracked.

Anthony said a few meaningless words before leaving. He knew deep down that something in his life was about to change. The Lord had led him here, and he wasn't one to stand in the way of divine direction, but he certainly had an unsettling feeling in his heart.

And there was that old flicker of love for Deanna he thought he'd gotten over.

The next morning, Deanna woke up before the alarm clock sounded. Her Bible rested on the nightstand where she'd left it after an hour of study before falling asleep. Having Anthony in town had disrupted her thoughts and sent her into sensory overdrive. The last time he was in town, they'd talked briefly, but she'd managed to keep the tone light to avoid the risk of losing her heart. But this time...

She noticed he hadn't lost the mischievous gleam in his eye. His hair was still the dark brown, almost black shade she remembered. Only now, it was cut shorter, and he dressed in a suit rather than a T-shirt and jeans. And he still had the ability to see right through her. From the moment they'd met in high school, she'd felt as though Anthony Carson was the one person who truly understood her. Then his father was transferred immediately after their senior year. Anthony had a full academic scholarship to a southeastern college, which was thousands of miles away, but she believed him when he said he'd be back to visit. One letter arrived, then weeks later a second one came. But he never mentioned returning. She saw him last Christmas, and he promised he'd be in touch. At first, she expected a call, but after a few weeks of nothing, she figured he'd simply disappeared from her life again. In fact, that was the last she'd heard from him until now.

And why now?

That question played over and over in her head as she got ready to go to work. When she rounded the corner to her office, she spotted Ginny's SUV and a rental car. It had to be Anthony's. Her heart picked up its pace as she parked, stepped out of her car, and walked inside.

"Your friend is waiting in your office," Ginny said, her face flushed with excitement. "He's very handsome, by the way."

Handsome had nothing to do with anything. Deanna had to find out what he wanted, then get rid of him before she imploded.

He stood to greet her when she walked in. As he took her hand in his, everything inside her shifted.

"I don't have much time." She quickly pulled her hand away and shoved it into the pocket of her slacks.

"Yes, I understand. I'll keep it brief."

She sat down behind her desk and motioned to the chair across from her. He remained standing.

"I'd like to discuss my tour bus stop in Mistletoe," he said.

"*Your* tour bus?" Confused, she tilted her head.

"Yes. You've been working with my representative for the past several months, and she says it's a done deal."

"Wait a minute," Deanna said. "Do you have something to do with Western Tours?"

He chuckled. "I suppose you could say that. I own the company."

Suddenly Deanna's head began to throb. She was totally unprepared for this revelation. "I had no idea."

97

"Obviously."

"Why didn't you say something before now?"

Anthony took a step back toward the door. "I suppose I should have, but I thought you knew. I'm sorry."

The project she'd been working on night and day was setting up the tour for Anthony Carson's company, and she was only now finding out. That was a fine how-do-you-do.

"I can see you have quite a bit of work to do, so I'll leave you alone. Here's my card." He came close enough to her desk to drop a business card on it, then turned toward the door. Before he walked out, he hesitated, turning back toward her as if he wanted to say something, but he just smiled, waved, and left.

Deanna was glued to her seat for a solid minute before she could move. By the time she got to the reception area, Anthony was long gone.

"What a nice young man," Ginny said. "I'm sure we'll enjoy doing business with him."

Right!

Deanna went back into her office, plopped down at her desk, and buried her face in her arms. *Please tell me it's a dream, Lord. Any minute now, I'll wake up and have a great laugh about this.*

"You shouldn't be sleeping on the job, girlfriend."

Deanna raised her head to see Lori and Madison, both smiling at her. She jumped up, came from behind her desk, and hugged each of them.

"We saw Anthony leave." Lori frowned. "What did he say to get you upset?"

"Upset?" Deanna jabbed her thumb to her shoulder. "Me?"

"Yeah," Madison replied. "I can tell when one of my best friends is hurting."

Deanna gestured toward the couch along the wall. "Have a seat. I might as well tell you the whole story about what's going on."

After Deanna wound down from her half-hour explanation, Lori shook her head. "It's just that spark from seeing an old flame. It'll fade away. You have Frank now, so there's no point in getting all worked up over someone like Anthony. . . who didn't have the decency to write or call."

"She's right," Madison agreed. "Remember our pact? You and Frank are well on your way to the altar, so forget about Anthony and focus on what's important."

"The pact," Deanna mumbled.

"You wouldn't let us forget, and now it's our turn to remind you."

Deanna shook her head. "Oh, I don't know what's going on. Frank and I aren't any closer than we were on New Year's."

"Look. Just don't worry about anything. The Lord's in control." Madison and Lori exchanged a quick glance before Lori continued. "Are you and Frank doing anything next weekend?"

"No. Frank is going to Colorado to hang out with some old college buddies."

"Good. We can talk about our strategy then."

Madison punched her finger in the air. "And we can call Kathy."

Lori chuckled. "Last time we called her, I thought she'd pass out from the shock of how the election turned out."

"I totally can't believe it, either," Madison teased. "Who'd have thought our very own Lori would wind up mayor of this town?"

Lori held up her hands. "Enough already. We have to concentrate on more important things. So don't forget. Saturday morning. My place."

As soon as her friends left, Deanna went right back to work to wrap things up before heading home. She'd just walked into her house when Frank called.

"You're going to the covered dish dinner at church tomorrow, aren't you?" he asked.

"Yes, of course."

"I guess I'll see you there."

She instantly thought about the difference between her fluttery feelings around Anthony and the total calm she felt with Frank. That had to be a good thing, didn't it?

"Deanna? Are you there?"

"Yes," she said with a sigh. "I'm still here. Why don't you stop by and pick me up on the way to church?"

"I wasn't sure if you wanted me to after you as much as told me to get lost last week."

"I didn't—," Deanna started before she remembered what she had actually done. But she'd only reacted that way because he'd ignored her to watch sports on TV. Still, she needed to apologize. "Sorry, Frank. It's just been so crazy busy at work lately. Nothing personal."

"That's fine. Don't worry about it. I'll be there at nine fifteen."

After she hung up, Deanna felt her shoulders sag. This had been one very emotionally exhausting week. She hoped her friends would help her sort through her feelings and her life would return to normal again.

Dream on, girl. Nothing will ever be the same.

The next morning, the knock came at Deanna's door at precisely nine fifteen. She grabbed the pan of brownies, along with her sweater and purse, and headed for the door.

Frank grinned as she handed him the pan. "I was hoping you'd bake."

"What did you bring?" She tried hard to lighten her mood and not compare her feelings toward Frank to the way she'd felt when she saw Anthony.

"I bet you can guess with one try." He flashed a quick grin.

"Chips and dip?"

"You got it." He shifted the pan of brownies to his left hand and put his right arm around her shoulders, giving her a quick squeeze. "You know me so well."

No, it was just that he was so predictable. The complete opposite of Anthony. It was impossible not to compare the two, no matter how hard she tried not to. *Especially* when she tried not to.

Chapter 3

After dropping off the food in the church fellowship hall, Frank guided Deanna to the sanctuary. She was about to slip into the fourth pew from the front when she glanced up and spotted Anthony—staring directly at her. He lifted his hand in a wave.

"You know him?" Frank asked. "I don't think I've ever seen him before."

"Yes, I know him." Deanna wasn't in the mood to share any of her past with Frank—particularly the heartache of losing the first love of her life.

Frank gave her a quizzical look, but the organist began playing and his attention turned to the music. She was thankful he didn't press.

Throughout the service, Deanna found herself focused more on Anthony than on the pastor's sermon. This was so not good. She decided to order a tape of the sermon after church and listen to it later.

When the last hymn was sung, Frank stood, stretched, and patted his stomach. "I don't know about you, but I'm starving."

"Yes, I'm hungry, too. . . ." The instant she spotted Anthony heading toward them, Deanna's appetite faded.

"The sermon was excellent, wasn't it?" Anthony said as his gaze met Deanna's, then held Frank's.

"It was excellent." Frank extended his hand. "I don't believe we've met. I'm Frank Bentley."

Deanna gulped. "Sorry about my manners. Frank, this is Anthony Carson. Anthony lived in Mistletoe several years ago. We went to high school together."

She glanced at Anthony and saw a pained look in his eyes. What was that about?

"So, Anthony, what brings you back to Mistletoe?" Frank asked.

Anthony held Deanna's gaze for several seconds—just long enough to make her squirm. Her face felt hot as she slowly looked away.

"Business," Anthony replied, his tone more clipped. "I own a tour bus company, and I thought this would be an excellent stop for some of our groups."

A frown line formed between Frank's eyebrows. "Oh yeah, I heard about that. We could use the business. Business was terrible the past couple of years. Sales were down in all of the shops—so much so that quite a few of them closed their doors. Lori has done a great job since she became mayor, but some people couldn't hold out any longer."

Anthony grinned. "Maybe this will be a mutually benefi-
cial business venture then. My representative has been the one
communicating with Deanna on my behalf, so I haven't been
involved in the nitty-gritty details."

As they chatted, several of the old-timers stopped by and
greeted Anthony. He recognized some of them, but others had
to be reintroduced.

"Hey," Frank said, "since this is a homecoming of sorts for
you, why don't you hang out with us in the fellowship hall?
We're having a covered dish dinner."

Anthony held his hands out palms up. "I didn't know, so I
didn't bring anything."

"That's okay," Frank said. "You can be our guest. We don't
expect visitors to bring anything."

Deanna wanted to crawl into a hole. She couldn't remember ever feeling so uncomfortable.

Throughout the meal, Deanna did everything in her power
to avoid contact with Anthony, but Frank was so friendly, the
task was impossible.

After they finished eating and said their good-byes, Deanna
nearly raced out of the church.

Frank followed on her heels. "Why didn't you tell me about
Anthony?" he asked. "You hung out in the same circles."

"I don't know," she snapped, instantly regretting her tone.
"I guess I didn't think it was important." She offered Frank a
look of contrition.

"Whoa, touchy subject, huh?" Frank frowned as he maneuvered the car out of the parking lot and onto the road toward her

house. Suddenly a look of awareness crossed his face. "Oh, now I get it. The two of you were an item back in high school, weren't you?" When Deanna didn't respond, he turned and patted her arm. "That's okay. You were kids back then. I understand."

No, he definitely didn't understand. "Let's just drop it, okay?"

He lifted one hand from the steering wheel, then slapped it back down. "Whatever you want. I didn't mean to hit a sore spot."

"You didn't." Deanna slinked farther down into the seat and folded her arms. She couldn't very well explain her mixed feelings about Anthony to Frank when she didn't understand them herself.

Frank took the hint this time and didn't say anything else until they reached her place. She opened the door and hopped out. "You don't have to walk me to the door."

"I don't mind." He opened his door.

She gave him her best smile. "No, really, I'll be okay."

"Fine, if that's what you want."

She quickly headed for the door, unlocked it, and waved to Frank to let him know she was safe. As soon as she got inside and locked the door behind her, she flopped onto the sofa. With a heavy heart, she prayed, *Lord, have mercy on me. I don't know what's come over me. It's been a long time since my relationship with Anthony ended, so why do I feel like he left just yesterday? Whatever the case, please help me get through this time. Frank is very sweet, and he doesn't deserve my bad mood.*

She was tempted to make a deal with the Lord—to tell

Him if only Anthony would leave and not come back, she'd be the best girlfriend ever to Frank. But she knew that wasn't right. The Lord was much bigger than that.

Deanna was glad when the end of the week arrived and Anthony was scheduled to leave Mistletoe. Her mom had invited her over for a cookout, and though she wasn't in the mood, at least she'd be able to avoid thinking about Anthony.

"Hey, Deanna," her mother's best friend said as soon as she walked into her parents' home, "I have a surprise for you." She took Deanna by the hand and led her to the kitchen, where Anthony stood over a pot of something on the stove, stirring.

When he glanced up and spotted her, his face lit up. "Hey! I'm making my mom's Italian sauce recipe—the one your mom always liked."

A lump formed in Deanna's throat. "That's nice." What else could she say?

He put down the spoon and moved toward her. "We have a lot of catching up to do. We've been talking business all week, and now it's time to relax. Let's go back to the sunroom so we can chat. I'm sure your folks will understand."

Deanna followed Anthony reluctantly. Once they were alone in the sunroom, Anthony turned to her. "So tell me about your life since we last saw each other."

"You mean since last year?" She shrugged. "I've just been working hard to bring more people to Mistletoe. There's only so much Lori can do with all of her mayoral duties."

He reached out and touched her cheek, making her pulse quicken. She tried hard not to react.

"I didn't get much of a chance to talk to you last year. I want to know about the past ten years."

As Deanna started talking, she noticed how he leaned toward her and seemed to hang on her every word. There was no doubt he was attentive. She felt her guard drop gradually. But when he jumped up to stir the sauce a couple of times, she reminded herself that he wasn't the type to settle down in one place.

"Hey, kids, we've been looking all over for you." Her mother stood in the doorway, grinning, almost as if she were in on some sort of secret. She turned to Anthony. "I can hardly wait to taste that spaghetti. I remember it from the church socials."

Everyone loved Anthony's sauce, including Deanna. And spending this time with him had confirmed her old feelings. She now realized that her puppy love for Anthony hadn't faded one iota. After dinner, he asked her if they could talk some more.

"I don't think that would be a very good idea," she said softly, in spite of her urge to talk to him forever.

"What's wrong, Deanna?" He reached out and touched her face.

She closed her eyes and took a step back. "Don't. We can't do this, Anthony."

He pulled back and studied her for a moment. "I see. You've moved on in your life."

She wagged her head. What was she doing? Of course she had moved on. She nodded, then turned away from him.

As soon as she could leave gracefully, Deanna approached her mother. "Mom, I'm really tired. It's been a crazy week. I hope you don't mind if I slip out now."

Her mother edged toward her and gave her a quick hug and a kiss on the cheek. "Of course I don't mind. This was a good party, wasn't it?"

"It was wonderful. Thanks, Mom." Deanna waved. "I'll call you later, okay?" She dodged out the door before her mother had a chance to urge her to stay and talk.

Early the next morning, Deanna grabbed the newspaper from the porch, padded into her kitchen, fixed some coffee, then sat at the table and perused the front page. Not much happened in Mistletoe, so most of the news was national. She skimmed the headlines and decided she needed something to cheer her up, not depress her. She grabbed a praise and worship CD and popped it into the player.

After listening for a while, sadness overcame her. Some of the older songs reminded her of Anthony. She pulled out the CD and opted for silence.

She took her time getting ready, arriving at Lori's place a few minutes late. They chattered about everything that had been going on.

Deanna brought up the marriage pact they had made in college, which started a whole new conversation that lasted almost an hour. She admitted that the chemistry still wasn't there between her and Frank.

Lori sighed. "Just remember, once the first flush of infatuation fades, you need confidence in the relationship."

Madison nodded. "How true."

"I know," Deanna replied. "That's why I'm not taking these

feelings for Anthony too seriously."

The conversation quickly turned to other matters. Deanna leaned back and enjoyed being with the people she cared about.

Afterward, she headed home to the small house she rented and settled down to her old routine. Once again exhausted, she fell asleep almost immediately.

Frank picked her up for church the next morning, but he didn't say much. She could tell something was bothering him, but she didn't feel like getting into a deep discussion, so she didn't ask any questions.

Anthony was at church on the front pew with some of his old friends. Their gazes met, and he waved before quickly turning back to his conversation. Deanna knew Frank noticed, but he didn't say anything until the service ended.

"How do you feel about us?" he blurted.

"Huh?"

Frank nodded toward Anthony. "You need to make a decision. It's either him or me."

A lump quickly formed in Deanna's throat. "Nothing is going on between Anthony and me, if that's what you're talking about."

Frank narrowed his eyes and nodded slowly as he put his arm around her and squeezed. "That's what I was hoping you'd say. Let's keep it that way, okay?"

Frank took her home, and she spent the remainder of the day reading while she finished her laundry.

Early the next morning, Deanna headed for work in a summer downpour. When she pulled into the parking lot, she was relieved to see that the only car in the lot was Ginny's. She got out and ran up the walk as the rain pelted her face. She took off her raincoat and had just changed into her dress shoes when the bell on the door jingled behind her. Even before she turned around, she knew who had come calling by the look on Ginny's face.

Chapter 4

I wanted to stop by and let you know I've called my office." Anthony smiled. "We're ready to roll with the new tours."

Good. He was keeping it all business. "Let me know what I can do on my end." She avoided holding his gaze.

He looked intently at her without saying a word. Deanna wished he wouldn't look at her that way—as though he was genuinely interested.

After an uncomfortable silence, he cleared his throat. "Some brochures touting the main tourist spots would be nice. We have the listing of sites you mailed. Just keep us up to date on what's still open so we don't get into any embarrassing situations."

His tone was different and much more businesslike, but he still had a questioning look. Deanna was unnerved by his presence, even if it only meant business.

"I'll fax everything to your assistant right away." Deanna's mouth felt dry, but she forced herself to look calm.

Finally, Anthony turned to Ginny and told her how much

he appreciated her patience. "And thanks for everything, Deanna," he said as he shoved the door open. He suddenly paused. "Oh, by the way, Frank seems like a nice guy, but don't you think he's a little too by-the-book for someone like you?"

Deanna was stunned, but she had to say something. "I don't have any idea what you're talking about, Anthony."

"I think you do. See ya later." He left the office as quickly as he'd come.

"Now that's the kind of man who knows what he wants and won't stop at anything to get it," Ginny said. "Too bad he can't stick around."

"Yes, too bad."

Deanna wandered back to her office, trying hard not to let her jitters show.

Anthony left town wondering at the wisdom of adding Mistletoe to the agenda for the tours. After all, he'd based a rather large business decision on his own nostalgia. He made a mental note to keep an eye on this venture. If it didn't work out, he'd have to pull it, no matter how much it hurt.

Mrs. Flanagan had to turn him down when he asked if she wanted to host a busload of eager travelers. She said her bed-and-breakfast wasn't large enough for some of the groups he anticipated bringing to Mistletoe. He understood, but he knew the hotel by the interstate wouldn't have the charm of her place. She did say she'd accommodate them for lunch if she had sufficient notice. And anytime he had a smaller group, she'd be glad to have them.

None of this was working out as he'd hoped. He'd envisioned his guests being mesmerized by the town that was all about Christmas. They'd spend time in the shops in the square before retiring for the evening at Mrs. Flanagan's Bed-and-Breakfast, a two-story Queen Anne house a couple of blocks from Main Street. They'd be able to worship at the Living Word Chapel and afterward head over to Flossie's Café for some of the fabulous apple fritters that made his mouth water at the mere thought of them.

His personal plans included accompanying them on occasion, just to get his fix of Mistletoe. Being honest with himself, he knew a big part of that plan included seeing Deanna.

Deanna. She hadn't changed much. She was still every bit the pretty, smart, spunky, interesting, dimpled, strawberry–blond-haired girl he'd known back in high school. Deanna had been the person who'd taken him to church, and through her, he developed a relationship with Jesus Christ. Within a year, his parents started attending church with him, and they became faithful Christians. He'd be forever grateful to Deanna for introducing his family to the most important aspect of their lives. Only now, she had her defenses up. He knew he was to blame for that, but he couldn't have changed anything if he'd wanted to.

After his family's move, he went off to college. His father retired from the air force and opened a paint store in a small town in northern Georgia. Halfway through his sophomore year of college, his father had fallen sick; his mother needed help at home, so he spent most of his weekends doing whatever work she needed done. He managed to finish college in three years by taking summer classes, then moved back home to get his family's business in order. During this time, his sister married a pastor and moved to the West Coast. When his father passed away, his mother moved to Atlanta to be closer to her sister, who'd also been widowed. That was when he decided to head west and start his own business.

Life had been hectic over the past several years, and there was nothing he could do about it but pray that he'd eventually find some direction for his own life. When he heard about the Boise-based tour bus company on the auction block, he jumped at the chance to buy it. After all, he loved travel, and this opportunity would give him a chance to see if he had the savvy to make it in the business world. The company had once thrived, but fewer people took bus tours these days. He immediately saw that he needed to change his clientele focus and began concentrating on senior citizens, who had more time and were less inclined to go long distances alone. During the first year of business, he'd recouped his investment. Now he was working in the plus column on the ledger sheet, so he knew he'd made the right decision.

For the time being, he lived in Boise, Idaho, but with the tour business, he could live anywhere he pleased. He'd chosen to rent an apartment until he could decide where to establish roots. After spending a little time back in Mistletoe, he felt a tug to head in that direction.

But then there was Deanna, the girl he hadn't been able to erase from his mind or his heart. Looking back, he knew he'd made a huge mistake by not returning sooner. Too bad she had a boyfriend. Frank seemed like a nice enough guy, though not a good match for Deanna. Frank was stiff, and Deanna was a strong woman who needed someone more spirited and fun-loving. Or was that just jealousy talking?

Anthony mentally shook himself. He didn't need to base long-term decisions on an old high school flame who wasn't willing to give him another chance. This had to be a business decision first and foremost. And he certainly didn't need a relationship while still growing his business.

The ten-hour drive home was exhausting, but he managed to make it in a day. Next time he'd fly. As he pulled into the parking lot of his apartment complex, he lacked the feeling of being home. It was definitely time to find a place to establish roots.

"Deanna, may I have a minute with you?"

Deanna glanced up and smiled at Ginny. "Sure, come on in." She gestured toward the chair across the desk. "Have a seat."

Ginny sat down and nervously looked around the room before settling her gaze on Deanna. "You have this place looking good. The last person here never bothered hanging any pictures. I particularly like the one with you and all your friends."

"Thanks. What can I do for you?" Deanna turned away from her computer to give her receptionist her full attention. She had a feeling Ginny was using stalling tactics.

"It's not really about me." Ginny fidgeted before looking

Deanna directly in the eye. "It's about that tour company you've been working with."

Deanna felt her forehead crinkle. "Is something wrong with the company?"

Ginny shook her head and steepled her hands before taking a deep breath and blowing it out. "No, it's just that. . ." She looked around the room again.

"What's wrong?" Deanna stood up, came around from behind her desk, and perched on the corner of it.

Ginny looked up at her with a sweet smile. "It's just that I think the owner might be sweet on you."

Deanna's jaw dropped. She was speechless.

"I know it's none of my business, but I couldn't sleep last night thinking about it. The way he looks at you gives me goose bumps." She rubbed her arms and giggled.

The last thing she needed was for Ginny to get involved in her relationship with Anthony—or lack of relationship. But she didn't want to hurt the feelings of this very sweet woman, who until now had never overstepped her position.

"Please don't lose any sleep over Anthony," Deanna said as nicely as she could. "We dated a little back in high school, but now all we have is a business relationship."

"When he looks at you—"

"He sees dollar signs," Deanna interrupted. "Mistletoe will be good for his company because they need destinations that bring back memories for his clients." Her voice was clipped, but she had to nip this conversation before it got out of hand.

The smile faded from Ginny's face as she stood. "Well,

I suppose you might be right, but I still think the two of you could rekindle what you once had if you'd give it half a chance."

After Ginny left her office, Deanna went back to her computer and stared at the screen, but none of the information registered in her head. All she could think about was the conversation with Ginny. She had to put a stop to any notions of getting back with Anthony, whether they were hers or Ginny's. And the only way she could think to do that was to nudge Frank into the next logical step of their relationship: engagement.

Yes, it was time to get him to pop the question. Maybe the spark wasn't there now, but so what? They were adults. They had mutual respect, they liked each other, they both had good jobs, and most important, they were equally yoked in faith. What more did they need? Maybe once they were engaged, she'd feel that same spark for Frank that she felt when Anthony was around.

Besides, she and her friends had a pact to find true love before they were twenty-eight. What better way to keep the pact than to get engaged to Frank? Sweet, unassuming Frank.

Deanna doodled on her memo pad beside the computer. *Deanna Moss Bentley. Mr. and Mrs. Frank Bentley. Deanna Bentley.* She resisted the urge to do the same with Anthony's name.

After several minutes of studying the names, she tore off the top sheet, wadded it up, and threw it into the wastebasket. She'd completed her work for the day. "Time to get out of here," Deanna muttered.

She'd just reached the door of her office when the phone jangled. Deanna hesitated before turning back. She grabbed the phone and sighed. "Deanna here."

"Deanna." The voice of Alan Reffler, the tourism committee chairman, was gruff as usual. "We've heard from Anthony Carson and decided it's time to pull out all the stops. Don't let this one get away. Do whatever you have to do to bring business back to Mistletoe."

Warning bells went off in the back of her mind, but she couldn't argue with her employer. "Yes, sir. I'll do whatever I can."

"That means spending most of your time with Mr. Carson when he comes to town."

Chapter 5

I t won't be so bad," Deanna mumbled to herself after hanging up with Alan. "All I have to do is treat him like any other business acquaintance."

Yeah, right. Anthony Carson was anything but just a business acquaintance. He was the first guy she ever had a crush on. He was the first guy to kiss her. He was the first guy to break her heart. And now he was back in her life, mixing her up and confusing her about her relationship with Frank.

Deanna squared her shoulders and walked over to the credenza, where pictures of her family and friends lined the surface. Her parents were on the very left, and her friends covered the middle section. Frank had his own special spot on the right-hand side. She picked up his framed headshot and studied it. Frank was a very good-looking man—much more traditionally handsome than Anthony. Both of them had dark brown eyes, but that was where the similarity ended. Anthony had darker hair, and Frank was a good three inches taller than Anthony.

She set down the photo and sighed. This wasn't about looks. This was about guarding her heart when Anthony was around and giving Frank half a chance.

That night, Deanna tried to refocus her thoughts. She wanted to push her old feelings for Anthony out of her heart and embrace the idea of a strictly business relationship with him. She fell asleep trying to imagine herself being married to Frank, but somehow the image never came into focus.

It was at least two weeks before she heard back from Anthony. His assistant sent her an e-mail announcing that he was coming to Mistletoe. Deanna shot back a response, stating that she looked forward to his arrival, then she picked up the phone and punched in Frank's work number to prevent further thoughts of Anthony from popping into her head.

"How about lunch?" she asked as soon as she had Frank on the line.

"Um, I'm pretty busy, but I guess it would be okay if I sneaked out for a few minutes. Where do you want to go? Flossie's?"

"Sounds good."

"Okay," he said. "Want to meet me there at eleven forty-five? That way we can beat the rush."

"Sure. I'll get there early and grab a table."

Today was the day she'd go all out and really let Frank know how special he was. With Anthony coming to town, she couldn't allow herself to harbor thoughts of anything with him but a mutually good business relationship that would benefit Mistletoe. And the only way to do that was to go after Frank with every ounce of love-seeking energy she could muster.

She quickly got back to her task at hand. Mistletoe was sponsoring an art exhibit in the newly refurbished town library conference room, and they expected more than a dozen out-of-towners to display their work. Lori was doing an excellent job on her end, but they needed to spread out more. Anthony's bus tours could be a huge boon and make a serious difference. She'd have to be very diplomatic around him.

Before she left for Flossie's, Deanna bowed her head and prayed for the right direction in matters of the heart. She prayed the Lord would work on her deep pain over the fact that Anthony hadn't bothered to contact her until now, when he wanted to do business—and he was acting as though he'd done nothing wrong. She prayed for something stronger to develop in her relationship with Frank. And she prayed for Mistletoe's future.

Flossie's was already starting to get crowded. Only a couple of tables were left. She grabbed one of them and sat down facing the door so she could spot Frank when he entered.

Several people asked her to join them, but she told them she was waiting for Frank. She sat there for a half hour before her cell phone rang. She pulled it out of her purse and glanced at the number. It was Frank.

"Sorry," he said, "I got busy and lost track of time. Can you give me another fifteen minutes?"

"Are you sure it'll only be fifteen minutes?"

After a pause, he sighed. "To be honest, I'm not sure if I can wrap things up in fifteen minutes. It might be a little longer." His voice sounded strained.

Deanna didn't feel like hanging out at Flossie's indefinitely by herself. "Why don't we take a rain check?" The instant the words left her mouth, she realized her tone was too harsh.

"You're mad, aren't you?"

No point in lying. "Not mad, just disappointed."

"I'll make it up to you," he said. "I promise. How about we go out for a special dinner Friday night?"

"Isn't that when your new clients are coming into town?"

"Oh, that's right. Maybe the weekend after, then. My buddies from college are stopping by Saturday, and I don't know what's on the agenda."

"Don't worry about it."

"Deanna—"

"Sorry," she said, "I gotta run. There's already a line forming at the door. I need to let them have our. . .my table."

"Don't be mad."

"I told you I'm not mad. Bye, Frank." She heard him trying to say something as she clicked off her phone. He called back, but she didn't bother to answer.

She stood and motioned for the waitress to take her carryout order. And rather than getting soup and salad as she'd originally planned, she ordered a hamburger, onion rings, and an order of apple fritters. At least that was something she could count on coming through for her. Flossie's mouthwatering apple fritters would make her feel better for at least a little while.

Deanna headed back to her office, frustrated. Frank had been attentive once, but he'd fallen into the trap of taking her for granted. It was time to either have a talk with him or move on. She sat down at her desk and quickly polished off the hamburger and onion rings. Then as she sat munching on an apple fritter, she heard the bell at the door. After a brief pause, she figured Ginny had the front under control, so she stuffed another bite of apple fritter into her mouth and turned back to the document on her computer.

"Ms. Moss?"

She glanced up, her mouth full of pastry, and spotted a flower deliveryman armed with a humongous bouquet of white roses and daisies. She hadn't finished chewing her food yet, and she couldn't speak.

"Where should I put these?" he asked, clearly unfazed by her lack of response.

Deanna pointed to the credenza before she realized there wasn't any room. She hopped up and carefully pushed all of the pictures to the side to make room in the center. At least Frank felt bad enough to send flowers. That was a good sign. Maybe she wouldn't have to let him have it after all.

She waited for the deliveryman to leave before taking a closer look at the flowers. The instant he was out the door, she reached toward the bouquet to see how Frank groveled. She chuckled as she lifted the tiny card from the prong.

Deanna, I want to let you know how much I look forward to doing business in Mistletoe. Call me if you need anything. And let me know what you think about my promotional package after it arrives in the mail.

Always, Anthony

Hmm. The flowers weren't from Frank. An odd tingling sensation washed over her as she took a step back. This wasn't the first time Anthony had sent her flowers. Back in high school he had daisies delivered on her birthday. He'd actually paid attention when she told him how much she loved daisies and white roses. In those days, he could only afford the daisies. Obviously, things had changed.

"That's a beautiful arrangement," Ginny said from the door. "Who are they from?"

"Anthony Carson."

Ginny smiled. "He's a very thoughtful young man. He cares enough to know what you like."

Deanna put the card back in its holder before going back to her desk. She had to change the subject. "Has the mail come yet today?"

Ginny frowned before shaking her head. "Not yet, but I expect it to be late with all this rain we're having. It's slow moving out there."

On a deep sigh, Deanna nodded. "Let me know when it arrives. I need to get back to this proposal."

After Ginny left, Deanna rested her head in her hands. She seriously needed to squelch this feeling that came over her anytime Anthony's name was mentioned. And he seriously needed to stop surprising her.

She pulled Anthony's business card from her file and picked up the phone to call him, then changed her mind and dropped it back into the cradle. An e-mail would be much easier.

After thanking him for the lovely flowers, Deanna let him

know that he didn't have to send gifts. She looked forward to doing business with him, as well. Then she read through the message and made a few changes before clicking the SEND button.

The rest of the day was filled with phone calls and work related to a new publicity campaign that wasn't due for another month. It kept her busy and her mind off Anthony, and that was important. The last thing she needed to think about was someone who flitted in and out of her life on a whim.

When she glanced up at the clock and saw that it was already almost four, she got up and headed to the reception area. Ginny was hunched over something at her desk.

"Hey, has the mail come yet?" Deanna asked.

"It just arrived. I'm sorting through it."

Deanna glanced at the large manila envelope teetering on the edge of the counter and reached for it. "What's this?"

"Oh, that's from Western Tours."

Deanna had to stifle the urge to dart back into her office and rip into the envelope. Instead, she forced herself to wait for the rest of the mail that Ginny was busy stacking in a neat pile.

"If you don't need me anymore," Ginny said, "I'd like to leave a little early today. Elmer and I are going to a movie tonight."

"That's fine," Deanna replied. "I won't be here much longer myself."

As soon as Ginny left, Deanna tossed the rest of the envelopes into her in-basket and tore open the envelope from Anthony. She carefully pulled a stack of brochures and advertising material from it.

She glanced at the press releases and documents related to his business expansion. Then she saw it—a four-color brochure of the highlights of his newest tour, with Mistletoe featured on the very front. Her heart flooded with emotion as she eyed the professional photograph of the town square during the peak of Mistletoe's best season.

She flipped through the pages to read about the other tour stops, and when she came to the blurb about Mistletoe, she had to sit down. After reading it a third time, she set aside the brochure and stared at the wall before picking it up and reading aloud.

"Mistletoe offers something for everyone—from nostalgic memories of Christmases past for the seasoned traveler, to early memory-makers for the very young. This tiny, romantic town is nestled in a valley known for its year-round Christmas spirit and friendly residents who always welcome their visitors with hot apple cider and delicious pastries from the bakery of Flossie's Café. Bring your loved ones for a taste of home-baked goodness, or go alone and find yourself falling in love."

Deanna's hands shook as she pondered a deeper meaning behind his words. A short note slipped out from the stack when she tried stuffing everything back into the envelope. *Call me. Love, Anthony.* She picked up her phone and punched in the number on the outside of the brochure but hung up when she got his voice mail.

She stayed in the office another hour, but after she tried calling Anthony again with the same results, she decided to head home. She'd already e-mailed him to thank him for the flowers. She figured she might as well give him a chance to respond.

Early the next morning, she checked her e-mail from home, but she still hadn't heard a word from Anthony. For the rest of the week, Deanna felt as though she was missing something, but she didn't know what. Later that week, Anthony replied to her e-mail, saying that sending flowers was the least he could do in exchange for her hospitality. His e-mail was brief, reminding her of the past. She couldn't expect much communication from him while he was away.

Frank called a couple of times to touch base, but he remained noncommittal about getting together. She remembered her plan to take action.

"Are you okay?" she asked.

"I'm fine. Just tired."

"Want to come over and let me fix dinner for you?"

"Maybe sometime next week. I just have so much going on, I don't think I'd be very good company."

She hung up, asking herself why she didn't feel all that disappointed. She tried to rationalize. What she'd had with Anthony was puppy love. It was easy to put someone on a pedestal when there were no adult obligations to deal with. Frank, on the other hand, had responsibilities and couldn't just drop what he was doing to cater to her whims. What she and Frank had was more real and made a whole lot more sense. After all, love wasn't just a giddy feeling in the heart. It went deeper than that.

Yes, she needed to keep trying to nurture her relationship with Frank and make an effort to stop thinking about Anthony outside the office. *Lord, the temptation to do something really stupid is always there. I pray You'll watch over me and keep me out of trouble.*

Deanna was definitely no stranger to trouble, and she needed all the help she could get to avoid it—especially if it meant falling in love with Anthony Carson.

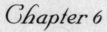

Chapter 6

On Friday, Deanna decided she would corner Frank after church on Sunday. She was tired of being alone, and she wanted to find out if their relationship had any hope of going anywhere. If not, they needed to break it off so she could move on.

Saturday dragged by slowly, but she managed to stay busy cleaning her house and running errands. She went to bed early so her mind would be fresh and clear when she talked to Frank.

He sat in their regular pew and was turned to the side watching the door when she walked into the sanctuary. He spotted her, smiled, and motioned for her to join him. She quickly made her way there and sat beside him.

"We need to talk," she said.

He offered a quizzical look but nodded. "Wanna go to Flossie's after church?"

"Sounds good." But no more apple fritters. Her skirt waistband was a little too snug as it was.

Deanna listened to the sermon as well as she could, but her mind kept leaping ahead to what she'd say to Frank.

Lord, forgive me for my restlessness.

As soon as the service was over, Frank turned to her. "Are you okay?"

She shrugged. "Like I said, we need to talk."

"Then let's go. I'm hungry. I'll bring you back to your car after we eat."

He took her hand and led her out the door. They walked to his car in silence, but once they were both inside, he looked at her, frowning. "Do you want to talk now or wait till we get to Flossie's?"

She sucked in a breath, closed her eyes for a second, then looked at him. "Frank, I need to know something."

"What?"

"How do you feel about me? About us?"

She watched his Adam's apple dip as he swallowed. "Um, exactly what do you mean by *us*?"

Deanna shrugged. "Do you consider us just friends or more than friends?"

He cleared his throat and looked around, tapping his fingers on the steering wheel. When he turned back to look at her, she tried to read his expression but couldn't. One thing she did know was that this conversation wasn't easy for him. Her heart filled with dread, but she needed to hear what he had to say.

"Deanna, I've never been good at expressing my feelings."

"Yes, I know. And that's fine. Just do the best you can."

"First of all, you know I care about you. It's just that. . ." He reached out and touched her face. "I've been so busy building my career. I guess I haven't been a very attentive boyfriend, have I?"

A nervous chuckle escaped Deanna's throat. "No, you haven't."

He cupped her chin in one hand and held her gaze. "I'll try to do better, okay?"

She nodded. This wasn't exactly what she'd hoped for, but it would have to do. For now, anyway. Getting a commitment from Frank was obviously going to take some work.

He leaned over and dropped a quick kiss on her lips. She closed her eyes, hoping for that heart-stopping feeling she longed for, but all she felt was the satisfaction that Frank was trying.

Frank quickly drew back. "Then let's go eat. I'm starving."

As soon as she smiled, he started the car and headed toward Flossie's. They had to wait a few minutes for a table. Frank held her hand and looked at her more often than usual. At least he was being more attentive than before. It was a start.

After lunch, he drove her to her car in the church parking lot. Trying again, she told him she wanted to do something fun, but he said he had things to do to get ready for work the next week.

"We can go out Friday night if you want," he said. "And maybe we can meet for lunch during the week if I can clear my schedule."

Deanna pasted on a smile as he walked her to her car. She drove home thinking about everything they'd discussed. She was disappointed, but not in what Frank said. Her disappointment came from the fact that she wasn't disappointed.

Then she remembered something her mother used to tell her: She would reap what she sowed in life. So if she wanted more out of her relationship, she needed to put more into it. Looking back, she realized she hadn't exactly put much energy into Frank, so why did she expect him to be such an attentive boyfriend?

When Monday came around, she called Frank, sent him an e-mail, and reminded him that they were going out Friday night. Friday morning, Frank called and canceled because one of his out-of-town clients had just contacted him and said he needed to do some last-minute work on a business that had just sold.

Okay, she told herself. *I shouldn't expect a complete turnaround overnight.*

Deanna went through an entire week without seeing Frank, but he promised that as soon as his schedule cleared, he'd take her anywhere she wanted to go. The most frustrating thing was that the situation was completely out of her control.

Lord, I know I shouldn't force a relationship, but how do I make this thing work? I want a man in my life. I don't want to be lonely. . . .

The phone rang, jolting her from her prayer.

"Hey, Deanna, Anthony here. What are you doing next week?"

"I. . .uh, um. . ."

He laughed. "Sorry if I interrupted something. Want me to call back later?"

132

"No, that's okay," she said, hoping her heart would stop hammering the way it did every time she talked to him. "What's up?"

"I'm coming back to town to nail down some plans for the tour, and I wondered if you could give me the dime version of what you show dignitaries when they come through."

"The dime version, huh?" Deanna chuckled.

"Yeah. An abbreviated tour. I don't want to take too much of your time."

"I, uh, I'm sure that can be arranged." Deanna wanted to kick herself for feeling like a lovesick teenager at the mere sound of his voice. "When exactly will you be here?"

"How about next week?" He paused, then added, "Unless that's too soon."

"No, that's fine." She could have taken him on a tour the very next day. Her schedule was clear for the next month.

"Can't wait to see you again." His voice had dropped to a very soft, personal tone.

She had to swallow hard to make her voice audible. "Drop me an e-mail with the exact day and time, and I'll clear off a couple of days for you."

"A couple of days?" he said. "I would have been happy with a couple of hours. Fantastic!"

After she hung up, Deanna's heart told her she was in deep water with a strong undercurrent. It was painfully clear that her old attraction to Anthony wouldn't go away just because she decided to amp up her relationship with Frank. This was so not good. Anthony was sweet, and she was almost certain he was a believer. However, there was the matter of his deeply ingrained wanderlust.

Frank, on the other hand, had always lived in one place until college. When he graduated, he met the partner of the accounting firm in Mistletoe during a campus recruiting interview. And he'd been in town ever since.

The biggest problem with Frank was that he didn't seem to understand the concept of a relationship, though he told her he cared about her and wanted to date her exclusively. He even said he eventually wanted to settle down and have a family once he reached his professional goals. His kisses were sweet but not earthmoving for her. Of course, that was probably her fault.

She picked up the phone to check on him and let him know she was thinking about him. His receptionist told her he was out on a business call. Oh well. What did she expect? Even if he'd been in, he might have had a client in his office.

The following Friday she was cleaning off her desk for the weekend when a shadow fell over the room. She glanced up to see Frank standing at the door, a bouquet of red roses in his fist and a sheepish grin on his face.

"Peace offering?" he said as he thrust it toward her and took a tentative step forward. "Sorry I've been so busy."

Deanna smiled and came around from behind her desk to take the flowers. "Thank you. You didn't have to bring flowers, Frank. I understand."

"I know." He shoved his hands in his pockets. "I've been thinking. Maybe you and I can go out tonight and grab a bite, then head over to your place and watch one of your old movies."

It was a start. At least he was trying. She nodded and managed a smile. "Sounds great, but I have a few things to do here before I go home. Why don't you pick me up in an hour or so?"

After Frank left, Deanna went back behind her desk and dropped into her chair. She scrolled through her e-mail and found a new message from Anthony marked "URGENT."

Chapter 7

Anthony had called Mrs. Flanagan and found out she was booked. So were all of the other inns within a hundred miles. She'd told him the mayor and the tourism director had been working hard to bring people back to Mistletoe, and obviously their work was paying off. He gave her his number and asked her to call if anything changed.

Disappointment overtook his enthusiasm, until fifteen minutes later when his phone rang. It was Mrs. Flanagan, calling to say she'd already had a cancellation. "Apparently, this was meant to be," she said.

"Obviously," he agreed.

They made arrangements for his stay. He hung up and thought about what to do next.

Anthony sat and stared at his computer, waiting—for what, he wasn't sure. It was past five o'clock. Deanna had probably gone home already, so he'd have to wait until morning to hear back from her.

He shoved away from the desk and stood, raking his fingers through his hair, trying to make some sense of it all. He thought he'd gotten Deanna out of his system, but now she was all he could think about. He had no doubt he was still in love with her. All it had taken was one look in those big brown eyes and seeing that she still had her same sweet nature to know she was the woman he wanted in his life. He was conflicted; he wanted more than anything for her to trust him, but he wasn't sure if he could be the kind of man she obviously hoped for.

His computer made the familiar *bing*, announcing an incoming e-mail. He froze before turning to see if it was a reply from Deanna.

It was!

As he sat and looked at the list of messages with Deanna's name, he felt a combination of dread and anticipation at what she'd say in response to his urgency to be in Mistletoe sooner than he'd planned.

His finger paused over the mouse, then he quickly clicked on the message. There it was, short and sweet. *That would be fine. Regards, Deanna.*

Yes! He punched his fist in the air.

Deanna felt sick to her stomach at the thought of seeing Anthony so soon. She'd mentally prepared herself to wait a week, but he was coming this weekend.

And it was Friday.

Emotionally numb, she grabbed her handbag and keys and

headed out the door. She still needed to freshen up for her date with Frank.

Frank arrived precisely when he said he would. He was the perfect gentleman, doing his best to be attentive, but she could tell his mind was elsewhere, which, for the first time, was fine with her. She wasn't mentally present, either.

He kissed her once, and she held her breath, hoping for a feeling other than friendship, but it didn't happen. When she opened her eyes, she saw that he'd already turned his attention back to the television.

At the end of the evening, when Frank left, she leaned against the door and blew out a sigh of relief. Now she was free to concentrate on a schedule for Anthony—one that would involve staying so busy showing off Mistletoe that she wouldn't have time to think about the way he made her melt inside.

She headed to her office early the next morning, hoping to get a few things accomplished before Anthony arrived. But when she turned the corner, she noticed an unfamiliar car parked alone in the lot. It had to be his. Ginny wasn't scheduled to work, and it was too early for most people to be out and about. She sucked in a deep breath and gathered her thoughts before she hopped out of the car and trudged toward the building.

"What are you doing here so early?" Deanna asked, trying her best to act annoyed to cover her excitement. . .and, yes, joy!

Anthony shrugged. "I flew in late last night, and I couldn't sleep. If you're not ready for me, I can leave and come back."

"No," she said as she stuck her key in the door. "We can get started. I'm sure you have a busy schedule, so maybe we can finish up today." She willed her heart to stop doing flips.

He frowned. "Is that possible?"

They were inside now, and she did everything she could to avoid looking him in the eye. "All depends on what you want to do. You said you wanted the *dime tour*."

She moved through the building, turning on lights, and he followed her into her office in the corner. She flipped the switch as he walked around looking at pictures and awards she'd won over the past year; then he turned around and grinned. "You're obviously quite good at your job."

She shrugged as she went behind her desk. "I just do what I've been hired to do. Now about your dime tour. . ."

"Maybe I should have said quarter tour. I need to run through all of the places we plan to take our clients."

Deanna couldn't keep from looking at him any longer. She turned and faced him head-on. He shoved one hand in his pocket and raked his hair with his other hand as he took a step back. Their gazes held.

She cleared her throat. "When do you need to be back to. . . wherever you plan to go from here?"

"No set time." His gaze remained on her.

"Okay, so we can go for a drive today and look around at some sites, but tomorrow's Sunday, and I don't plan to work."

"Same here." He picked up a picture of Frank and studied it before carefully placing it behind the flowers. "Where'd these come from?"

Deanna tilted her head, trying to decide if he deserved an

answer. She was about to speak when he interrupted.

"Okay, none of my business. Sorry about that."

"No, that's okay. Frank sent the flowers."

"I thought you liked daisies and white roses."

Deanna's jaw tightened. Of course, he was right, but she didn't want to let on that Frank didn't know what she liked. Frank actually knew very little about her—obviously less than Anthony—but she had to remain loyal to Frank.

She should be glad that Anthony and Frank were so different. She loved so many things about Frank, such as. . .his stability.

"Okay," Anthony said, "I'll drop it. Sorry if I overstepped."

"That's fine." She moved the mouse to wake the computer so she could pull up the itinerary. "Let me print this out, and we can get started." She found what she needed and printed it. On the way out, she flipped off the lights and grabbed her coat, which Anthony held open for her.

Anthony silently guided her to his rental car. They decided to start at the farthest point and work their way back. Within minutes, Anthony had her laughing.

He pulled into the parking lot of one of the small quilt shops on the edge of town, but he didn't make a move to get out. She put her hand on the door handle, but he reached for her other hand.

"Deanna," he whispered.

She pulled back from the door handle. The way she felt at the moment, even if she'd gotten out of the car, her knees would have buckled beneath her.

"We need to go in." She turned away to hide her jittery feelings.

He let go of her hand and huffed out a sigh. "Yeah, I guess we'd better. Stay right here. I'll come around and get you."

Even when he was a teen, Anthony had always been a gentleman, doing small things like opening doors and pulling out a chair for her at the table. Anthony quickly came around to her side of the car, opened the door, and reached for her hand again. The instant they made contact, her mouth grew dry, and her knees weakened. She stumbled as she stepped out of the car. He caught her and momentarily pulled her to his side. She swallowed deeply, offered a shaky smile, and cleared her throat.

"Thanks. I'm okay now." She carefully moved toward the door of the Quilt Cottage.

Deanna introduced Anthony to Angelina Smith, the shop owner, who gave him her card. Angelina said she'd be very glad to be one of the stops on his tour, and she even offered to set up some short classes if they had enough people. Deanna headed to the back to pick up a book for her mother, while Anthony chatted with the owner and nailed down a few details.

On their way back into town, Anthony stared straight ahead, while Deanna tried to keep her wits about her. Everything about Anthony pulled her to him—from his purposeful stride, to the way he looked at her with that mischievous gleam in his eye. She needed to focus on the work rather than the man.

She had to stop thinking so much and switch to business mode. "That was a successful stop," she said to break the silence.

"I think so." He turned toward the next destination—Mrs. Flanagan's Bed-and-Breakfast. "I figure the vacationers will be ready to relax for a little while after the long ride."

Deanna gathered her wits and nodded. "I'm sure you're right."

Simply being around Deanna made Anthony want to settle down, get married, buy a house with a white picket fence, and start a family. That wasn't what he needed at the moment—not while he built his business. Besides, Mistletoe wasn't exactly the center of commerce.

"I called Mrs. Flanagan while you were shopping," he said. "She's expecting us."

As soon as they arrived, Mrs. Flanagan greeted them both with a platter of pastries. "I made them just for the two of you. Have a seat and I'll go fetch some tea."

"Some things never change," Deanna said with a smile that brightened the room.

"That's what I'm counting on."

Deanna turned and shot him a look that turned him inside out. But there were a few big problems. She didn't appear to feel the same way toward him. She already had a man in her life. And he couldn't make promises.

What is the Christian thing to do?

Fortunately, Mrs. Flanagan saved the moment by inviting them into the dining room and seating them at a table. Within a couple of minutes, she had tea and a platter of food before them.

Mrs. Flanagan apologized for not being able to accommodate a busload of people overnight, but she reiterated how much she valued her favorite customers, like him. "I wouldn't want to turn away nice folk like you," she said in her hearty Irish accent.

"I understand," he said. "At least they'll get a taste of your wonderful cooking."

She shook a finger at him. "Just make sure you give me plenty of warnin', lad. I don't want last minute surprises."

Deanna's laughter filled the room—and his heart. Anthony turned and studied the girl he'd fallen in love with many years ago. At some point along the way, she'd become a full-fledged woman. And she continued to show her big heart, her gentle spirit, her ready laugh, and the outgoing personality that had reeled him in when he first met her.

Anthony kept looking at her in a way that made her squirm, almost as if he could read her mind. Deanna shifted, meeting Mrs. Flanagan's knowing gaze. Grinning, the woman looked at Anthony. "You two are lovely together."

Heat shot into Deanna's cheeks.

Anthony stood abruptly and dropped some cash on the table. "Thanks, Mrs. Flanagan."

Deanna's heart sank, but Anthony reached for her hand. "Why don't we head on over to Under the Mistletoe before we call it a day?" he said. "I'm really looking forward to seeing Madison and her shop."

"Okay," Deanna managed to squeak as she took his hand and followed him to the door.

"You kids have fun," Mrs. Flanagan called out. "I'll see you next time you're in town, Anthony."

He waved at the elderly woman, then stepped outside with Deanna. "Should we drive or walk?" he asked.

Deanna's smile made him want to kiss her on the spot. "Let's leave your car here and walk. It's just a few blocks away."

Anthony nodded. "Exercise will do us both good." He reminded himself to get back down to business.

Chapter 8

Deanna waved as she crossed the street to Under the Mistletoe.

Madison was standing in the doorway of her shop, and her face lit up with a grin. "Anthony! It's great to see you!"

Deanna took the opportunity to step back, observe, and regroup. She needed a little space to breathe.

"I heard all about your business," Madison gushed. "So you're here to help us save Mistletoe from extinction."

Anthony chuckled. "Not exactly. It's more of a scouting trip to discover which stops my clients won't want to miss."

Gesturing around the shop, Madison continued to beam. "You're at the right place. Take a look around and let me know if you have any questions."

Anthony meandered to a corner with a Christmas scene display. Deanna studied him as he paused, looked it over, and took a step back. He had an odd expression on his face—one she couldn't identify. He didn't appear distraught or sad, but he wasn't smiling, either. It was more a look of nostalgia.

He cleared his throat. "If you don't mind, Under the Mistletoe will definitely be on the tour agenda."

"Of course I don't mind! I could use the business."

"I guess we'd better go look at some other places." He lifted a hand to wave good-bye to Madison. "See you at church tomorrow?"

She nodded. "Yes, of course."

Deanna wanted to ask him what he was thinking, but she needed to maintain her business persona and deal with her feelings later.

"Madison hasn't changed," Anthony said as they walked toward his car.

"Yeah, she's always pulled together. And I'm glad you'll make Under the Mistletoe one of your stops."

They were a block from where he'd left his rental car when he stopped, turned, and looked down at her. "Deanna. . ." His voice was a hoarse whisper.

She swallowed hard and looked into his eyes, which were impossible to read. After several seconds of silence, she frowned. "What's wrong?"

Anthony licked his lips and shook his head. "Nothing. I was just thinking. . ." His voice trailed off as they continued to walk.

"About what?"

He shrugged. "I dunno. Mistletoe has a way of getting under my skin. Every time I come back here, I feel something."

"How many times have you been back?" Deanna asked.

"Several." He sighed.

So he had been back without letting her know. The only time she knew about was last year, and that was for such a short time it didn't matter anyway. She tried her best to focus on the moment rather than the fact that he hadn't been in contact with her.

"I'm sure it's nothing but some old childhood memories," he said.

"I can only imagine. I've never lived anywhere else, so I don't know the feeling, but memories are something that follow you everywhere."

"It's more than that," he said as he held the car door open for her. He quickly rounded the car and got into the driver's seat, continuing his conversation without missing a beat. "Mistletoe is unlike anywhere else I've ever been. It hasn't changed. Other places change."

"Oh, Mistletoe has changed, all right. With the interstate, we don't see as many tourists because everyone's in such a hurry to get to their final destinations."

Anthony nodded. "I see that. What I don't understand is why Mistletoe isn't the final destination for more people."

Deanna laughed out loud. "Good point. And it's my job to get that exact word out to the world."

He frowned. "I'm serious. I can take my clients through Montana and show them the clear lakes, the trees, and the wild animals. All that is fine and wonderful, but it won't give them the feeling they'll get when they have a taste of Mistletoe."

"The town that celebrates Christmas year-round," she added.

"Yes, there is that," he said slowly. "But there are other aspects I think they'll enjoy."

An odd sensation flooded Deanna—a blend of nostalgia, pride, and protectiveness toward the town she loved. She cleared her throat to break the silence and pointed to the ignition. "The car won't go unless you turn the key."

"Right." He started the car. "Oh, by the way, I'm thinking about buying that old hardware store right off the town square."

"For what?"

He shrugged. "An investment?"

She instantly felt her hackles rise. He wanted to be an absentee business owner? "Mistletoe isn't just some silly little town where you can drop a few bucks for an investment and take off, Anthony. In case you haven't noticed, there are some people who truly love it here, and I don't want the people in this town to get hurt."

"I wasn't. . ." He cast a glance her way, then sighed. "Oh, never mind."

The sudden tension in the car silenced them during the drive back to Deanna's office. When they arrived, she turned toward him. "I'll let myself out. See you tomorrow." She quickly hopped out of the car and slammed the door before he had a chance to respond. She was safely inside the building when she saw him pull away.

Conflicting emotions flooded Deanna's heart. Being in

such close proximity to Anthony wasn't good for her. Based on his history and some of the things he mentioned, she knew better than to let her guard down. And she certainly didn't need to get involved with a man who'd buy a business in Mistletoe and then ride off into the sunset.

She crossed the room to her desk, where she gathered her papers to file. The phone rang. Deanna dropped the stack of papers and picked it up.

"Hey, girl! This is Lori. I just got off the phone with Madison."

"So I guess she told you about Anthony."

"Yes," Lori said. "She told me he couldn't take his eyes off you. . .except when he was looking at her Mistletoe display in the corner."

Deanna needed to change the direction of this conversation quickly. "He's planning to make Mistletoe one of many stops on his Montana guided tours." She left out what he'd said about investing.

"That's more than the rest of the companies do," Lori said, "which is why I'm calling. Is there any way you can talk to him about coming for the next festival?"

"I can try, but I figured all of the hotels would be booked."

Lori chuckled. "Oh, I'm sure Mrs. Flanagan can find a spot for him. You know how she is with special friends. In fact, I think she has a room she holds back in case someone local needs it for a special guest."

They chatted for a few more minutes. After she hung up, Deanna finished her work and headed for the door. She needed to get out of here before another call came in.

For the remainder of the day, Deanna thought about her feelings toward Anthony and tried to figure out how to get through to Frank. She wanted Frank to be himself, but he obviously needed to learn more about how to nurture a relationship. With Frank, she felt safe, confident, and comfortable. With Anthony, she felt as if the earth were shifting constantly beneath her feet. As wonderful as that felt, in a way, it was like overloading on sugar: It couldn't be good for her.

As inattentive as Frank often seemed, she never doubted he'd be there if she really needed him. He was steadfast, although sometimes a little unbalanced between work and play. Maybe she was partially to blame because she'd often put work before time with him when they first started dating. Perhaps she needed to give more attention to Frank to set the pace. She couldn't forget about the pact.

Okay, so it was time to try once more to pull out all the stops with Frank.

As soon as she got home, Deanna sat down and mapped out a plan. She needed to be careful not to overwhelm Frank, but she'd give him all of her attention and be the best girlfriend she could possibly be. He'd either have to fall into her plan or tell her to get lost. Naturally, if her plan worked correctly, she'd reap the reward of each of them falling completely in love with the other.

She stuck her notes in her nightstand drawer, then called Frank's cell phone. He answered right away.

"Are we going to church together in the morning?" she asked.

"I guess." He sounded distracted. "What time do you want me to pick you up?"

"Nine fifteen?"

"Sure. See you then."

"Uh, Frank?" She took a deep breath, closed her eyes, and blurted, "Would you like to come over tonight and watch a movie?"

"Oh man, I can't. I brought home a stack of work I need to plow through. One of our prospective clients is dropping by the office first thing Monday, and I don't want to have to work on Sunday."

"Maybe we can do something tomorrow afternoon," she said, hoping for at least a crumb.

"Sounds good. See you tomorrow. Bye." *Click.*

Deanna held the phone out and stared at it. Frank needed some serious work. He hadn't been in many relationships in his life, so his boyfriend skills hadn't been developed. She needed to be subtle about the way she did this so he wouldn't think she was trying to change him—but forceful enough to get his attention.

The next morning, Frank was at her door precisely at nine fifteen. Deanna knew he hated waiting, so she was ready.

When they arrived at church, Deanna noticed a crowd standing off to the side in the narthex. It wasn't until she walked closer that she realized everyone was clustered around Anthony, asking one question after another. He spotted her immediately and motioned for Frank and her to join them.

Deanna felt awkward, but Frank sauntered over, smiling.

He even handed Anthony his business card and invited him to consider working with his accounting firm. Anthony turned to her and winked. Her cheeks flamed, and she quickly turned away.

After church, Frank invited Anthony to join them at Deanna's place to watch a movie. Deanna held her breath until Anthony said he'd take a rain check. Once they got in the car, she told Frank they needed to talk. He shoved the key into the ignition, then paused.

"What's up?" he asked.

"Why did you ask Anthony to come with us?"

He shrugged and looked out the window for a minute before turning back to face her. "I dunno. I guess it just seemed like the right thing to do. Are you mad?"

"No, not mad. Just a little annoyed."

"Look, Deanna, if you're still hung up on the guy, I understand. It's just that I thought you said it was over a long time ago. You were just kids."

She nodded. "Yes, you're right. It's just that. . ."

He grinned and placed his hand over hers. "You were putting yourself in my place, right?"

"Well, sort of. . .but not exactly."

"You already assured me you were over the guy. I care about you a lot, but I know you had a life before we met. And, hey, I want to be nice to a guy who can help bring more business into Mistletoe."

He was being entirely too understanding. She didn't have any grounds to stay annoyed with him. . .but she was.

"Is there something else?" he asked as he wrapped his hand around the keys to start the car.

She braced herself, then turned to him and nodded. "Yes. There's another thing."

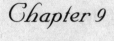

Chapter 9

Frank closed his eyes before turning to face her again. "What else did I do wrong?"

"You didn't do anything *wrong*. It's just that. . ." What could she say? That she was angry Frank trusted her enough to invite Anthony to watch a movie with them? She lifted her hands before letting them drop. "I don't know. Never mind."

He snickered. "Women. I'll never understand what goes on in that female brain of yours, so I might as well not even try to figure it out."

Irritation grew inside her, but Deanna kept it to herself. She needed to concentrate on more important things—such as falling in love with Frank and making him fall in love with her.

When they got to her place, she fixed a platter of sandwiches and handed him her case of DVDs so he could choose a movie. He picked an old Jimmy Stewart film, and she placed it in the DVR. From that point on, Frank was so engrossed in the movie that he basically ignored her. She decided that in the future she'd need to use a different tactic to take their relationship to the next level—one where they could communicate and honestly profess their undying love to each other. Watching old movies clearly wasn't the answer.

To her relief, the next morning, Anthony wasn't waiting for her at the office. She greeted Ginny on the way in.

"Good morning, Deanna. I need to leave early this afternoon if that's all right with you."

"Sure, that's fine," she replied as she headed straight to her desk. She sat down and read her new e-mail messages for about fifteen minutes before she heard Anthony come in the front door.

"I'll see if she's available," Ginny said.

Deanna took a deep breath, exhaled, and tried to remain as calm as possible, considering the turmoil inside her. When Ginny knocked on her open door, she glanced up and feigned surprise.

"Mr. Carson is here. May I send him in?"

"Sure." Deanna turned back to her computer monitor and remained fixated on the screen, even after Anthony entered her office.

"Hey, Deanna. Did you and Frank have a nice time yesterday afternoon?"

She glanced over at him and smiled as she folded her hands on her desk. Hiding her shakiness was difficult, but she was fairly certain she pulled it off. "A very nice time, thank you. Did you have a chance to visit with some of your old friends?"

He nodded. "I hung out with a couple of the guys, and then I went back to my room at Mrs. Flanagan's and charted a few places I want to take my clients."

"Good. So you won't need me today after all?"

"I do need you."

Silence and an electric charge filled the room as they stared at each other. When it became painfully obvious that Anthony wasn't going to say anything else, Deanna forced a smile. He grinned back at her without saying a word.

"Did you have a chance to talk to Lori at church yesterday?" she asked.

"Yes. In fact, she said she wanted me to return for the next town festival."

Deanna felt a thudding in her chest, and she worried he could hear it. She cleared her throat. "There might be a problem booking a room," she said.

"I've already talked to Mrs. Flanagan about that, and she said there was a cancellation for the event. I'm covered."

Deanna clicked out of her e-mail and stood. "Well, in that case, I suppose everything is in order for you to put the finishing touches on your tour plans."

He hooked his thumbs in his belt loops and nodded, his gaze resting on her. "Looks that way."

"Then let's go check out the rest of Mistletoe. I have other work to do later this afternoon, and Ginny has to leave early, so I'm afraid we'll have to be quick about this."

"No problem."

They walked around the town square and went into several of the businesses, where Anthony was welcomed with open arms. They had lunch at Flossie's, and Anthony reminisced about the days when he used to make a meal of Flossie's apple fritters. Then they strolled through the park. He seemed satisfied with what he saw, so Deanna said she needed to get back to her office.

"I'll walk you back before I head over to see Lori in City Hall," he said.

"That's not necessary," Deanna replied. "I can walk back on my own. You don't have time to waste."

He clenched his jaw, then gently placed his hand at the small of her back. "I don't consider walking you to your office wasted time. I left with you, and I'm taking you back."

Deanna's heart and mind collided, rendering her silent all the way back to her office. When they finally arrived at the door, she turned to thank him. He stood there waiting. The urge to kiss him was overwhelming. She took a step back.

"I look forward to doing business with you and your clients in the future," she said as she extended her hand.

He took her hand and drew her closer to him. She felt as if she were dreaming when he gently stroked her back and tilted her chin up to face him.

"I'm sorry, Deanna, but I can't deny my feelings for you anymore. I've tried, but I have to admit that yesterday, when you took off with Frank, I was eaten up with jealousy."

She gasped as she yanked away from his grasp. "Don't, Anthony. I can't. . ."

Anthony shoved his hands in his pockets and cast his gaze downward. She wanted nothing more than to be back in his arms, but it would only spell trouble for her later. Experience warned her that he wasn't a man who would stick around for long.

When he looked back at her, the angst-ridden expression on his face surprised her. He really had been affected—far more than she initially realized.

"I understand, Deanna," he said slowly, his voice hoarse. "I've been thinking about you day and night since before I even came back to Mistletoe, and I guess I just sort of imagined you'd be happy to see me again. Clearly, I was wrong."

"No, Anthony, you weren't wrong. I *am* happy to see you, but not—not in that way."

He remained still. Deanna knew then that she needed to voice her concerns.

"I can't allow myself to get too emotionally involved with someone who isn't likely to stick around." She half hoped he would argue.

"You're right. I can't make any promises." Anthony inhaled deeply. "And I understand."

She felt a deepening sadness as she realized he wasn't going to argue with her. Anthony obviously had no intentions of committing to remaining in Mistletoe.

He lifted his hands, took a small step back, and shifted his weight away from her. "Okay. I'll behave. We'll keep our relationship strictly professional."

Disappointment continued to shroud her being. "Thank you," she whispered.

"Well," he said as he reached back and rubbed his neck, "I guess this is where I need to say good-bye."

"Yes, I think so," she replied, still riveted to the spot.

"I'll be back for the festival."

She managed a smile. He looked at the door and nodded toward it, giving her a sign that he'd wait until she went inside.

With shaky fingers that she hoped he didn't see, she thrust the key into the lock and turned it, shoving against the door at the same time. When she got inside, she turned to say good-bye again, but Anthony was gone.

She wasn't prepared for what had just happened. She hadn't expected it. Suddenly Anthony seemed to want to head down the path she wanted to travel, but this time she knew better. She had to keep reminding herself that it would be a disaster to fall for him again. She didn't want to get hurt—but it was too late. She was still deeply in love with Anthony.

And then there was Frank. Dear, sweet Frank. Clueless Frank who needed boyfriend lessons. How difficult it seemed for Frank to juggle a career and a relationship, even though he seemed to want both. At least he said he did.

Deanna squeezed her eyes shut and prayed. *Dear Lord, I have everything worked out in my life—a good job, a nice house, a sweet boyfriend who won't go anywhere. I pray that I'll learn to appreciate what I have and stop wanting something I shouldn't have.* She glanced over at the picture of Frank and sniffled before closing her eyes again. *Thank You for all of Your wonderful blessings, Lord.*

Later that afternoon, Lori called. "I heard Anthony left town a few minutes ago. Thanks for spending so much time with him. It'll help our little town. Only I hope Frank isn't too upset."

"Why would Frank be upset?"

"Because, well, you know how it was after Anthony left. I figured Frank might think—"

"That was a long time ago. A high school crush. We're adults now, remember?"

Lori laughed. "True, but sometimes I don't feel like an adult."

Neither do I, Deanna was tempted to say, considering she'd allowed a teen crush to invade her present-day life. "Let me know if there's anything else I can help with, *Ms. Mayor.*"

They chatted a few more minutes until Lori said her appointment had arrived. After she hung up, Deanna thumbed through the stack of papers she needed to send to other organizations that had expressed interest in bringing groups to Mistletoe. Lori was doing an amazing job for the town as mayor.

After Anthony's near-kiss, Deanna did everything in her power to see Frank whenever he wasn't working. He always went along with whatever she wanted to do, but she sensed his mind was elsewhere. Finally, after wondering and not getting a clear picture, she asked him.

"Are you okay?"

He scrunched his forehead. "Yeah, I'm fine. Why?"

"You seem distracted."

He shrugged. "I'm just getting sort of frustrated about business. I've been trying to build my accounts, but the senior partner has all of the old Mistletoe businesses sewn up. Most of the newer people either have accountants in other cities, or they have software and do it themselves."

"I'm sure it just takes time." Deanna reached for his hand and squeezed it.

"When I was hired, I was told that I'd be doing some of the grunt work for the local clients but that eventually I'd be working solely on my own accounts. That hasn't happened yet."

"I have confidence in you."

Frank's lips curved, but his smile didn't reach his eyes. He obviously didn't share her confidence in his abilities.

"I'm working on bringing more groups to Mistletoe. Maybe some of the folks who come to visit will decide they like it here and stay."

"That would be nice," Frank said without emotion.

Frank's mood was much lighter the next time Deanna saw him, so she figured he'd just been in a slump and had found a way to pull out of it. As far as she could tell, other than when he was having his occasional distant mood, their relationship was moving along. She understood the pressure of business. Although she still didn't feel the same flutter in her chest as when Anthony was around, she kept telling herself that a remnant of a schoolgirl crush was nothing compared to the more mature love developing between her and Frank. She and Frank were two adults with a common goal.

But what was their common goal? She had a pact with her friends to find true love before they turned twenty-eight, but did Frank want the same thing? He seemed perfectly satisfied with maintaining the status quo in their relationship. Sure, he'd once said he wanted a family someday, but that wasn't enough for her to hang her hope on.

She needed to do something dramatic to kick their relationship up another notch. What she needed from Frank was a commitment—or at least the promise of a commitment.

With all of the excitement over the upcoming festival, Deanna decided to wait until it was over to start a plan of action. Lori had asked her to be on a committee, and that took up quite a bit of her time.

On the first day of the event, Deanna gave Ginny the afternoon off so she could enjoy some time with her husband. They needed to keep the office open because out-of-towners would want brochures about Mistletoe. Deanna kept her office door open and positioned herself to see the front door, enabling her to greet people as they entered.

She'd just settled into her work on a new brochure when the bell on the door sounded. She glanced up and spotted Frank as he walked in. She smiled until she saw who was right behind him.

Chapter 10

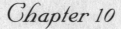

Deanna's pulse quickened. "Anthony!"

Frank's immediate frown made her feel awful for not acknowledging him first. "Frank, are you two together?"

"We met up in the parking lot," Anthony said as Frank glared at him. "I wanted to stop by to see if you had anything else for me to look at before I head over to check out the event."

Deanna shook her head. Frank remained in one spot, hands on his hips, his chin rigid. Clearly, he wasn't happy.

Anthony glanced back and forth between Deanna and Frank before taking a step back. "Well, since you don't have anything, I need to get going. This is a quick trip, so I don't have much time to waste. See ya later, Deanna." He turned to Frank and extended his hand. When Frank didn't reciprocate, Anthony pulled back and put his hand on the door. "Later, Frank."

The moment he was gone, Frank cleared his throat. "I can't remember you being as happy to see me as you were to see

Anthony just now, Deanna."

Feeling the heat of a blush creep into her face, Deanna managed a smile. "Of course I'm happy to see you."

"Good, good." Frank nodded, looking thoroughly unconvinced. "I thought I'd come by your place after work and we could go to the Christmas in July festivities together. But if you have plans. . ."

Deanna closed the distance between them and looped her arm in his. She felt his arm stiffen.

Whoa. That dude was fuming.

Anthony felt an unwelcome tug at his heart as he realized he had no business expecting to rekindle a relationship between him and Deanna. That truth hurt worse than he wanted to let on. If he'd gone on instinct, he would have told Frank to get lost. But what good would that do? Deanna had opted for safe—a man who could promise her he'd never leave Mistletoe. He couldn't make that promise. Or could he?

This isn't easy, Lord. Give me the strength to be the kind of man You want me to be and not some jerk who steals girls from nice guys.

Ever since he'd seen Deanna again, he knew he was a goner. Frank didn't seem like a good match for her, but what did he know? He wasn't in control of Deanna's life.

As he strolled toward the festivities, he mentally kicked himself for such thoughts. Why did everything have to be so complicated? If his folks hadn't needed him so much after he finished school, he would've hightailed it back to Mistletoe and never looked back. But life got in the way. He loved his family, and they had to come first. And he didn't have a single regret about being there for his mom during his dad's final days. But still. . .

"Hey, Anthony!" he heard from behind. He spun around and spotted a group of people he'd gone to school with, smiling as they joined him. At least he had something to take his mind off himself.

For the remainder of his stay, he found that it took every ounce of self-restraint to stay away from Deanna during his last fact-finding trip before putting the finishing touches on next year's tour brochures. Occasionally, he spotted Deanna with Frank; every time, he turned and went in the opposite direction. No point in making things worse for her—or himself.

Lori caught up with him as he reached the edge of the fairgrounds. "Hey, Anthony, one thing before you leave," she said breathlessly.

"What's that?"

"I appreciate all the work you're doing to bring more folks to Mistletoe."

He grinned back at her. "I'm more than happy to do it. Mistletoe is my favorite town in the world."

A strange look crossed her face. "Then what's stopping you from hanging your hat here permanently?"

He shrugged, although he felt a tug at his heart. "My business is in Boise."

"You can do something about that."

"You're probably right. Maybe I will someday."

She leveled him with a look that made him squirm. "*Someday* might be too late—that is, if you don't want to lose Deanna."

"What are you saying, Lori?"

She shrugged. "Just that if you want something, you have to be willing to take risks to get it."

He forced a laugh. "I'll try to remember that."

"Somehow, I think you already know that. Just look at you. You bought a floundering business, one of the biggest risks ever, and here you are."

"True, but that's different."

She paused, then tilted her head and studied him for a few seconds before nodding. "Have a nice trip home, Anthony. I look forward to doing business with you in the future."

Lori's words echoed in his head as he drove toward the town square. He'd always gone after what he wanted. Why did it have to be different now? All he'd been willing to risk before had been business related. Could he put his heart in jeopardy as he had his bank account? He seriously needed to think about the prospect.

When it was time to leave for Boise, he toyed with the idea of heading out without talking to Deanna, but that wouldn't be the gentlemanly thing to do. It would also make working with Deanna in the future uncomfortable.

Deanna looked weary when he stopped by her office. Hiding his feelings under an all-business persona, Anthony presented some last-minute information to her and agreed to e-mail her the final proofs before going to press with the literature. He stalled for a few uncomfortable beats, but Deanna's demeanor made it clear that their meeting had concluded.

Now that Anthony was gone, a surge of exhaustion overcame Deanna. Knowing he was in town had made it doubly hard for her to concentrate on her duties as tourism director and her relationship with Frank, which was strained anyway. At first, she suspected Frank was upset about Anthony, but as the festivities went on, she realized something else was bothering him. After their discussion about his job, she assumed Frank's coolness had to do with work, but in her heart she knew better.

Perhaps one of her friends could help her sort through the problem. Deanna picked up the phone to chat with Lori.

"She isn't here," Felicity, the receptionist, said, "but she'll be in first thing in the morning. Want me to have her call you then?"

"Sure, that'll be fine."

Deanna hung up and thought about what to do next. Time was passing quickly, and nothing much had changed between her and Frank. She sighed as she realized she might not be able to find true love—at least not with Frank.

She bowed her head. *Lord, please give me the knowledge to deal with matters of the heart. If Frank is the right man for me, make it clear. If not, please release us and give us a peace about it.*

Time passed quickly as Deanna and Lori teamed up to bring more groups into town. Things were looking up for Mistletoe, which gave Deanna a sense of satisfaction. She kept open communication with Anthony, and he made a couple of visits to Mistletoe, stopping by to see her each time. They had lunch appointments, which she looked forward to. Anthony fit in with Mistletoe so well it was almost as though he'd never left. But each time he had to go back to Boise, she felt the same deep sadness and the same fear that he'd forget to contact her while he was away.

Frank, on the other hand, grew more distant by the day. Finally, after Deanna couldn't keep her mouth shut about it any longer, she confronted him over dinner one Friday evening.

"What's going on, Frank? You don't seem like yourself lately."

He hung his head and sniffed before looking back at her. "I don't feel like myself."

"Are you not happy?" she asked. "With me, that is?"

Frank reached out, lifted her hand, and looked into her eyes. "You're a very sweet woman, Deanna, but I don't think I can be what you want me to be. I like you very much, but I'm—I'm not in love with you."

She swallowed hard. Although his words injured her pride, his admission didn't hurt as much as she thought it would. In fact, she admitted to herself, and then to Frank, that she felt the same way toward him. The strain she'd felt to honor the pact she had with her friends lifted, too.

They talked for hours before deciding to remain friends, but without the pressure of trying to have a romantic relationship. After he drove her home, she went to her room, knelt beside her bed, and prayed for guidance and clarity.

To Deanna's amazement, she was actually relieved. However, another emotion she needed to deal with wasn't so welcome. She was now positive that she was still in love with Anthony, and there was nothing she could do to change that, an irony she'd have to learn to deal with. Asking him to settle down in Mistletoe wouldn't be right when he obviously didn't want to stay in any one place for long. And she wasn't about to leave the only place she'd ever lived in and loved. Being strong and independent, she knew everything would be fine—however painful the outcome might be.

"Lord, I don't even pretend to understand any of this, so please just hold me up and help me work through this." The instant she whispered those words, she experienced an inner peace, but the sadness lingered.

Autumn had always been one of Deanna's favorite times of year. The air was filled with anticipation over the coming holidays. People in Mistletoe seemed lighter on their feet, and after several snowfalls, everyone was joyful and ready to celebrate the Savior's birth.

Deanna managed to put her relationship with Frank behind her, so when he announced to their singles' group at church that he was offered a position out of town and would be moving soon, she was happy for him. He approached her afterward. "I enjoyed every minute of my time with you, Deanna," he said tenderly.

"I had a wonderful time with you, too." For the first time in months, she saw true happiness in his eyes. "I wish you the very best, Frank."

Deanna could see that the Lord had His hand on her life, and things were out of her control. Rather than forcing what she wanted, she continued to pray for guidance. So what if she couldn't find *mutual* true love by the time she turned twenty-eight? Her friends would understand.

By the middle of November, Deanna was deeply involved in putting the finishing touches on her part of the Christmas tourism campaign. She'd arrived at her office early to see if she had any messages. When she pulled up her e-mail, she froze. There was another urgent message from Anthony.

About to click on it, she hesitated for a moment. Urgent, huh? What could be urgent about a tour bus company making a stop in Mistletoe? All sorts of cynical thoughts flitted through her mind.

Okay, Lord, please forgive me for being this way. Anthony didn't do anything intentional. It's my fault I let myself get all worked up over him back in high school. And it's my fault I carried a torch so long.

With a shaky hand, she clicked on the message that read, *Deanna, I'll be in Mistletoe in a couple of days, and I wondered if you could hook me up with a Realtor. Anthony.*

She quickly typed a return message to him, letting him know she'd do what she could. While she was still reading her messages, the bell sounded, indicating she had new mail. Anthony must be at his computer. She forced herself to finish reading the current message before clicking on Anthony's.

I'm interested in both residential and commercial real estate, so I'd prefer someone who handles both. Thanks! Anthony.

The word *residential* jumped off the screen. Her heart

hammered, but she quickly checked her emotions. She couldn't assume anything, or she'd wind up disappointed.

As if Mistletoe were big enough for a Realtor to specialize in one or the other. She remembered his comment about buying the old hardware store, but she'd gotten over her anger. If he bought it, at least it wouldn't be sitting there vacant. She responded with *Okay, I'll see what I can do. Deanna.*

She grabbed her phone and punched in the number of the most established Realtor in town.

After the pleasantries, Joan Hamerich said, "Anthony Carson? I heard he was in town not too long ago. Any idea why he's looking at real estate?"

"He mentioned wanting the old hardware store, but other than that, I have no idea," Deanna said. "Can you clear a couple of hours for him?"

"Sure thing. It's not like I stay booked this time of year anyway. All of my rental properties are occupied, and not many people plan to buy real estate right before the holidays, so this is actually a great time."

"I'll let him know. Thanks, Joan."

Deanna typed a message to Anthony, advising him that she'd lined up an appointment for him with Joan Hamerich. She sat there for a few minutes before she figured he was no longer at his computer.

Three days later, Anthony appeared in her office at the same time she did. "You're early," she remarked.

"I couldn't wait. Do you think Joan is in yet?"

"Come on inside where it's warm, and I'll call."

Joan answered the phone on the first ring. "Not only am I ready, but I have a dozen properties to show him."

Deanna relayed the information, and Anthony looked pleased. She told him how to get to Joan's office, then tried to settle into her own routine. But it was impossible. All she could do was wonder what was going on with Anthony and whether he had found what he was looking for.

She didn't expect to hear back from him that day, so she forced herself to do some busy work. Midafternoon, Ginny phoned. "Have you seen Anthony Carson yet?"

Seconds later, the door swung open, and Anthony walked in with an ear-to-ear grin on his face. "I'm moving to Mistletoe," he blurted.

Chapter 11

Deanna found her voice. "Huh?"

"I just put a down payment on a house and a store a block off the square."

"Are you sure that's what you want?"

Anthony's smile faded. "Positive. Joan even lined me up with a construction crew to renovate the house and fit the shop to my needs."

"Which house did you buy?" Deanna felt frozen to her chair.

"The old Pritchard house."

"The one that was in the Pritchard family for years? That place has been wrapped up in an estate dispute for as long as I can remember. You *do* realize it's historical, right?"

He nodded. "Yeah, that's part of the charm. It just needs a little updating."

"Updating? It's historical!"

"Yes, I realize that."

"I hope you don't think you can change it."

Suddenly his smile turned to a scowl. She saw his irritation, but she was just as annoyed with him. Who did he think he was, planning to make alternations to a historical landmark?

"The house needs to be brought up to code before anyone can live there, Deanna. Would you please at least try to get over whatever it is you have against me?"

She felt her shoulders sag. "I'm sorry, Anthony. I don't have anything against you. It's just that I love this town, and I. . ." She quit before she told him how she felt about him.

"I understand. Why don't you come by later, and I can show you my plans."

Deanna forced a smile. "That's not necessary. It's really none of my business."

Anthony studied Deanna as he backed away. Less than a minute ago, she looked as if she wanted to spit nails at him. And now she seemed resolved about his moving to Mistletoe. Something was going on in that pretty head of hers, and he wanted to get to the root of it. She obviously wasn't about to let on what it was, so he decided he'd have a talk with one of her friends.

He stopped in at City Hall, and Lori was quick to tell him that Deanna had trust issues with him because he hadn't contacted her when he'd left Mistletoe years ago. Lori concluded with a smile and added that he should go for what he really wanted.

Light on his feet and feeling better than he had in years, Anthony started working on a plan in his head. He shot up a prayer for reinforcement and the strength to carry it through. He couldn't let happiness slip through his fingers again, and he sure wasn't about to let Deanna go when he had her friend's blessing on doing whatever it took to bring her back into his life.

He managed to avoid Deanna the next week while he made arrangements with the construction crew to repair floors and walls. He headed over to his new commercial space and chatted with the crew he'd lined up to convert it into his new tour bus headquarters. With the type of business he owned, he could be based anywhere, and Mistletoe was centrally located, so why not here? He was fortunate to have a reliable assistant who could run the Boise office for the time being.

As soon as he had everything in place, he called Deanna and asked her to meet him at the house so he could show her the changes he planned to make.

"I'm busy right now," she said. "I hope you're not changing too much."

"Not too much," he said. "Just the color of the walls, inside and out, and moving the porch. That's all." He had to stifle a chuckle. If she realized he was teasing her, he wasn't sure he'd get her to drop everything to come over.

"You can't—" He heard her suck in a breath as if she might be fuming—exactly the reaction he'd wanted. "Never mind. I'll be right there."

Perfect. He told the head carpenter to let him know when Deanna arrived so he could meet her at the door.

Less than five minutes later, the carpenter hollered, "She's here!"

Anthony got to the door in time to see her storming up the sidewalk with a mission, her face set in determination. She was the same girl he'd known years ago, only more mature now. And he knew he still loved her with all his heart. "Stay with me, Lord," he whispered as he greeted her on the front porch.

"Okay, so what is it you plan to change?" She planted her hands on her hips and glared at him.

"Just a few things here and there." His heart beat so hard, his chest felt as if it might explode. "Maybe add a window here, and extend the porch over—"

"Hold it, buster," she said as she shook a finger at him. "You can't make major changes without approval. This house—"

He caught her finger in his hand and pulled her to him. He heard her breath catch in her throat, but she didn't resist. As he wrapped his arms around her, she relaxed and sighed. Then she tensed again.

"The neighbors will be upset—," she began before he gently put a finger to her lips, shushing her.

"Deanna," he said softly as he gently stroked her back, "since you feel so strongly about this place, why don't you be in charge?"

She pulled back and tilted her head. "What?"

"You heard me. You can be in charge of the renovations. Make this house like you'd want it."

"But why? You're the one who'll be living here. Or were you planning to rent it out?"

"I'm not planning to rent it out."

"Then what *are* you planning to do?"

He shrugged and pretended to be blasé. "I'll be living here—but so will you, if you'll marry me."

Anthony tightened his grip on her when her jaw dropped and her face flushed. "I—I don't think I heard you correctly."

He looked into her eyes and held her gaze as he relaxed his hold and lowered himself to one knee. "I guess I didn't do it right." Gazing up at her, he held both of her hands. "Deanna Moss, will you make me the happiest man in the world and become my wife?"

It seemed as if the whole world stood still the several seconds it took her to smile. Then she started laughing, and he laughed with her before he realized he didn't know what was so funny.

"Why are you laughing?" He stood to face her. "Is my proposal that corny?"

"No." She wiped a tear from her cheek with the back of her hand. "I'm just nervous and don't know what to say."

"Just say yes."

"Okay." She looked him directly in the eye. "Yes, Anthony, I'll marry you."

His heart pounded. "I'm glad I finally came to my senses and returned to Mistletoe."

"You and me both," she said softly, as he drew her into his arms and kissed her.

DEBBY MAYNE

Debby and her family live on the west coast of Florida. She enjoys writing romantic stories and sharing the lives of her faithful Christian characters as they fall in love. Her novels show God's love, grace, and mercy through His Son, Jesus Christ. Her characters are people with normal problems who must suffer through heartache and tragedy yet rely on their faith to get them through life's journey.

Under the Mistletoe

by Lisa Harris

Dedication

To my husband, who shares my memories of eggnog,
Colorado pine trees, ski trips, and mistletoe.

The name of the LORD is a strong tower;
the righteous run to it and are safe.
PROVERBS 18:10

Chapter 1

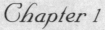

October

Joshua Dunkin had been in love with Madison Graham since the seventh grade—a lofty dream that had been reduced to fourteen years of friendship. Not that friendship was a bad thing, by any means. But neither was it a relationship that would end with a white picket fence and 2.5 kids.

Joshua eased the paintbrush across the engine of the miniature train in a final stroke, wishing that this day, of all days, didn't bring with it the constant reminiscing he tried to avoid. At least the day was almost over. Already, the sun was making its final pass across Glacier National Park toward Flathead Lake and the Kootenai National Forest, leaving in its wake the golden glow of another stunning Montana sunset.

Flipping on the wall lights and the string of white Christmas lights that framed the three front windows of the loft year-round, Josh sat back to examine his work. Madison would no doubt be pleased with his latest model for her Christmas shop, Under the Mistletoe. It never ceased to amaze him how the tourists continued to stream into the small mountain town in northwestern Montana. He had heard rumors, though, that the town that had "invented" Christmas—as the town fathers liked to say—had started to lose its Christmas spirit, and the number of tourists was down significantly. The mayor, Lori Compton, had implemented several new events in the past year to boost tourism, including the Christmas in July carnival and harvest festival, which had been a huge success. Hopefully, by the time December twenty-fifth arrived in another two months, the town of Mistletoe would be back on its feet again.

Josh dropped the brush into a jar of mineral spirits, then stood to stretch the muscles in his back that had tightened while he worked. The smell of Thursday night's meatloaf special and apple fritters drifted up from Flossie's Diner to mingle with the poignant scent of wood shavings that lay scattered beneath his workbench. Good thing it was dinnertime. He was hungry.

The phone rang. After a quick perusal of his workspace, he located it and lifted the receiver. "Josh here."

"Joshua. Hey, this is Madison."

Josh forced himself to control the offbeat tempo of his heart at the sound of her voice and erase the picture that flashed before him of the two of them eating dinner together at Flossie's.

"How are you, Madison?"

"I'm great. How are you?"

"Just fine." He ran his finger across the wooden caboose. "I just finished one of the train sets for you."

"That's terrific. I can't wait to see it."

Josh slowly wrapped the phone cord around his arm. *Stop the small talk and ask her, you fool. Simply ask her out. It will take all of five seconds.*

He gripped the cord with his free hand and reminded himself that dating Madison would never work. Their last, and only, date had ended with her plunging into Flathead Lake in the middle of winter and vowing she'd never speak to him again. No, it was better not to push his luck and just be thankful they had still managed to stay friends.

He cleared his throat. "So, what's up?"

"I'm on my way home from the airport after a trip to New York, and I wanted to see how you were doing."

New York?

She'd neglected to tell him about this trip, though the frequent-flyer points from Missoula to JFK airport were certainly piling up—and he wasn't sure all of the travel was due to buying excursions to stock the store. Maybe that's what had changed the most between them. Madison was enamored with life away from Mistletoe, and it wouldn't surprise him at all if she packed up one day and left. He, on the other hand, couldn't feel more differently. His small toy company might not ever bring him fame and fortune, but it made enough to support him comfortably in the beautiful mountains of Montana—a place he never intended to leave.

This train of thought brought him back to the question that had been haunting him recently. What did he, with his blue jeans and love for the open land, have in common anymore with Madison and her dreams of the lights of New York City? They had less in common now than a posh five-star hotel had with a "ride 'em, cowboy" dude ranch.

"Josh?"

He shook his head, trying to clear his mind. "Sorry, I'm a bit distracted today."

Who cares about New York? Just do it, man. Ask her out.

What did he have to lose? "Madison, I was wondering. . ."

The phone line crackled. She was using that handless thing-amajig again. The one guaranteed to lose any good connection between Kalispell and Mistletoe.

"The line's going. . .bad." Her voice drifted in again. "If I don't see you. . .I wanted to make sure that you knew I was thinking about you today with it being the anniversary of your parents' accident."

"You remembered?"

"Of course I did. Are you okay?"

"I am, but I appreciate your asking. The day always dredges up a few memories, but thankfully most are good ones, so I can't complain."

The fatal car wreck on the windy mountain road three winters ago had been as unexpected as his parents' subsequent deaths.

"They were. . .good. . .Will you. . ."

"Madison, I can't hear you." He pulled the phone away from his ear and groaned. Her words came across muffled, then he heard more static, and then the line went dead.

"Great." He hated for her to drive that long stretch of road by herself, especially at this time of day, and had told her so at least a dozen times. He'd even offered to pick her up at the airport, but Madison had to do things her way. If anything happened to her. . .

He held the receiver in his hand, then unwrapped the cord from his arm before hanging it up. The avocado green phone was a relic that had belonged to his grandparents, who'd used this loft above the diner as a dentist's office back in the seventies and eighties.

He still owned the family ranch outside of town, but at the moment it seemed more practical to rent out the four-bedroom house and live in the loft until he found someone with whom he could share the hundred acres of property. Something he'd yet to do. Dating had always been a challenge since the population of Mistletoe and the surrounding towns didn't add up to more than a handful of eligible women. And not one of them compared to Madison. But she had made it clear that friendship was all she wanted out of their relationship.

Still, he envisioned her honey-colored, shoulder-length hair, blue eyes, and determined chin.

On a sigh, he grabbed his jacket from the coatrack and stepped out onto the small landing. Madison might be softspoken, a tad quirky at times, and share with him a love for licorice, root beer, and country music, but that didn't mean she was the only girl for him.

It was time to bury the memories of the past, just as he'd been forced to bury his beloved parents three years ago. How Madison always managed to show up in the equation, he wasn't quite sure, except that his mom had loved her like a daughter, and some people in the town, himself included, had always assumed the two of them would eventually tie the knot.

But not all situations ended in "happily ever after" as in one of those sappy romance novels he'd caught her reading more than once.

The phone rang, and he stepped back inside the apartment and grabbed it. "Josh here."

"Josh, it's Madison." Her voice quivered.

"What's wrong?"

"Is there any way you can come get me? I'm still out here on the highway, and I—I've just hit a deer."

Chapter 2

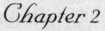

Josh jumped out of his Jeep and pulled up the collar of his jacket to block the icy wind. He hurried down the narrow highway shoulder toward Madison's two-door car. With the last light of the sunset having faded into darkness already, the temperature had dropped below freezing and the golden sky had turned into a sea of dark indigo. A sliver of moon was all that remained to light the highway that wound its way through craggy mountains and forests of red cedar.

He rapped on Madison's car window, trying to erase the memories of the night he found his parents' mangled vehicle. She jerked her head up, rubbing at the imprint of the steering wheel on her forehead.

"Joshua!" She fumbled with the latch, then pushed open the door, a smile lighting up her angelic face. "I think the only time I've ever been colder than this was when you pushed me into Flathead Lake two winters ago."

Okay, maybe not so angelic.

Josh folded his arms across his chest and shot her a wry grin. "That's a fine welcome for someone who just drove an hour to pick you up with a bag of apple fritters and a thermos of hot chocolate in the backseat of my car."

"With the tiny marshmallows?" She scrambled out of the car and stood in front of him with an old quilt wrapped around her.

He pulled the blanket firmly around her shoulders, thankful to see that she'd been somewhat prepared for a road emergency. "I didn't *push* you into the lake. You slipped. And, yes, there are tiny marshmallows."

"I didn't slip, but you're still forgiven because of the marshmallows." She stood on her tiptoes and wrapped her arms around his neck.

She had no idea what her nearness did to him. His heart seemed to have lodged in his throat, and his lungs couldn't take in another breath. Sometimes life just wasn't fair.

She kissed him on the cheek before taking a step back. "Thank you for coming to my rescue. You've always been my hero, you know."

He couldn't help but match her grin, but being a hero wasn't what he had in mind for their relationship. Not that he would be opposed to adding the role of hero to a romance. . .if they actually had one.

He tilted her chin up and caught her gaze, fighting the urge to return her kiss—this time squarely on the lips. "You're full of sarcasm tonight."

"I wasn't being sarcastic at all." The corners of her mouth

curled into a smile that reached her eyes. "I really do appreciate it."

"I know you do. Come on." He grabbed her suitcase from the backseat, then wrapped his free arm around her. "You're as cold as a Popsicle. Why didn't you leave the car running?"

"The engine died after I hit the deer and swerved off the road. Now it won't even start."

A wave of panic flooded through him. "You could have frozen to death out here. What if you couldn't get ahold of me?"

She dismissed his concern with a wave of her hand. "I'm okay, Josh. Really."

Her smile helped him relax as he held open the passenger door. "Get in. We'll have Taylor tow your car into town in the morning."

"Do you think it'll be okay out here all night?"

He leaned against the door frame. "If you're hinting that I, your gallant hero, should volunteer to stay with the car, forget it."

Madison laughed and motioned for him to get into the car. Within a matter of seconds, he had her luggage in the backseat and the heater running on high with all of the blowers aimed directly at her.

"Warm yet?"

"Getting there." She pulled off her hot pink knit hat and ran her fingers through her hair. "I owe you big-time for this."

Josh took one more glance at her. Something was different. The glow of the dashboard lit the car enough for him to realize what he'd missed at first. She'd cut her hair off. For several seconds, all he could do was stare.

Madison cocked her head. "What's wrong?"

"Your hair."

She shook the shortened locks that stopped at the nape of her neck. "Do you like it? I went to this hairdresser in midtown Manhattan, and before I knew it, the woman had talked me into cutting it and adding highlights."

He'd always loved the way her hair brushed against her shoulders and the way she swept it out of her face with the flick of her hand. "It's. . .different."

"You don't like it?"

"I didn't say that." Josh checked the rearview mirrors, then made a U-turn and headed back toward Mistletoe. "It's just so. . .short. It'll take some time to get used to, that's all."

"That's what someone told me about New York the first time I went there. I love it now. You'll get used to my hair, too." Madison poured a cup of chocolate from the thermos. "You know, you really should come with me on one of my trips, Josh. With outlets for your toys in one or two of the bigger stores, you could make some real money."

Josh grunted. "I do fine between your shop, a couple of outlets in Billings, and my Internet business. If I got any bigger, I'd have to find a way to cut corners to produce my products faster."

"What's wrong with that? With some upgrades on your woodworking equipment and two or three more employees—"

"It would turn into a factory, which would defeat the whole

purpose of hand-carved wooden toys." He slowed down to take the curve. All he needed was to run into a deer tonight, too. "I'm an artist who works with my hands. I don't want to give that up for an assembly line and a corner office in some fancy building."

"This is the twenty-first century, Josh."

"So?"

Madison dug into the bag of apple fritters and handed him one before nibbling on the corner of hers. His stomach growled, the smell of cinnamon and sugar reminding him he hadn't eaten dinner.

"So?" Madison held up her hand. "I can't keep your train sets in stock. If you were to up your inventory, you could double, even triple your sales. Take for instance this man I met in New York. Albert."

"Who's Albert?" He took a bite, then glanced at her, noticing the glow that settled across her face when she said his name. Albert. What kind of name was Albert? Sounded more like a bellhop than a suave New Yorker. Humph. Apparently he'd been right when he speculated that her trips to New York weren't solely for business purposes.

"Albert has a toy empire, as he prefers to call it, in New York. Maybe you've heard of AT Toys, which stands for Albert Tanner Toys."

"Cute."

"Cute? They manufacture action figures and more recently have moved into the video market."

"Or, in other words, into the twenty-first century?" Even the sweet apple fritter couldn't take away the bitter taste forming in his mouth. "And I suppose he runs this toy empire by pushing papers around in his high-rise office, and in the process makes five times what I make."

"Well, more than likely, yes."

"I'm an artist, Madison, not a paper pusher or a number puncher. I run a small business with three employees, and we do just fine."

"I know that. I'm just trying to think about your future. You could have so much more."

Josh sighed, not wanting to fight with her. "Did you ever think that maybe I don't want more? I have wonderful friends and live in one of the most beautiful places on earth. What else could I want?"

He squeezed the steering wheel and swallowed hard. Only one thing was missing in his life. He'd always thought it was Madison. At the moment, he wasn't so sure.

Madison brushed her hand across his forearm. "It's not that I'm unhappy here, Josh. I have wonderful friends, a church home, and everyone in my family lives within an hour from my house, but Mistletoe isn't—"

"New York?"

"Exactly." A dreamy look broke out across her face. "I've been to Broadway plays, eaten at five-star restaurants, and even gone shopping at Saks."

"With Albert?"

"Well. . .yes."

"I suppose even I couldn't make a case for Flossie's Thursday night special compared to dining at five-star restaurants."

"I'm not digging at Flossie's, or Harvey's Five-and-Dime, or any of the other fine establishments in our town, but there's something about the city that excites me." She dabbed the corners of her mouth with a napkin. "Mistletoe offers something different to the world, and I've always been a part of the year-round celebration of Christmas. I love the holiday with the lights, the music, and everything the season represents. I just need something. . .I don't know. . . something different. I want to take a risk and find that 'something more.'"

The muscles in Josh's jaw tensed. "Then I'm glad you found somewhere that will make you happy. Someone to make you happy."

Madison pulled her feet up beneath her and leaned back in the seat. "I wouldn't say that I've found someone."

Yet. Joshua heard the word, even though Madison didn't voice it.

Thirty minutes later, Joshua wound his way through town toward Madison's two-story home on Plum Tree Street. It was the house where she'd grown up, played basketball with him in the front drive, and challenged him to Monopoly marathons on rainy weekends. He pulled into the driveway and let the engine idle.

"We're here." He brushed her cheek with the back of his hand, then pulled it away.

Madison sat up and yawned. "Oh. . .Josh. . .I didn't mean to fall asleep. I guess I'm still on New York time."

"I guess so."

"Don't bother walking me to the door. I'll get my stuff." She jumped out of the Jeep before he could react and pulled her bag from the backseat. "I'm sorry I ruined your entire Thursday night."

"I don't mind."

"I know. That's why I appreciate you." She blew him a kiss, then lugged the suitcase up the narrow walkway.

At the front porch, she turned to wave at him before hurrying to open the front door. He needed to accept the truth. Broadway, Saks, and AT Toys. He couldn't compete with any of them. Madison was leaving Mistletoe behind. Leaving him behind.

Josh pulled away, missing the girl he used to know. The girl with shoulder-length hair and a love for Flossie's Thursday night specials.

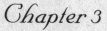

The next morning, Madison jiggled the key inside the lock, then pushed open the front door of Under the Mistletoe. At seven fifteen, the sun had barely begun to make its daily appearance, and the entire town square, including the decorated trees lining her storefront, still twinkled with their tiny white Christmas lights. In Mistletoe, nighttime always took on the glow of the holidays whether it was July or December. The three inches of snow that had fallen last night only added to the year-round festive atmosphere.

Inside, she flipped on the overhead fluorescent lights of her quaint shop and took in a deep breath of Christmas. Pine trees, vanilla, and cinnamon created the perfect aroma symbolizing the holiday for which Mistletoe was known. That was one thing the small town had on New York. She could redecorate the eight-foot-tall trees displayed in her shop's front windows, serve eggnog and apple cider to her customers, and play Christmas music over the shop's sound system year-round, and no one thought anything strange of it.

Making her way through the open front room, she couldn't help but smile at the improvements she'd made over the past three years since she'd bought the shop from Maggie Alexander. She'd arranged the front section of the store like a Victorian parlor, complete with antique mahogany couches, wing chairs, and tables displaying a vast array of unique decorations for sale. An arrangement of shelves held an eclectic variety of holiday gifts, ornaments, and toys for customers to browse through. And because of their popularity, she'd even created a center display for Josh's wooden toys, something every child would love to find waiting under the tree.

Picking up one of the green engines with its hand-painted details, she realized just how involved Josh had become with her business—and in her life. Beside the fact that he brought in a constant flow of customers interested in buying his unique pieces, he'd also helped her hang shelves and pictures and expand her online business with her own Web site. Because of his help, it now took two full-time employees to staff the shop and fill orders from around the world, something that gave her a sense of pride and put to use the business degree she'd earned at college.

But even that sense of pride couldn't squelch the restlessness she'd felt the past few months. An entire world was waiting for her out there, and she'd managed to spend her whole life within a fifty-mile radius. Even the welcome glow of the Christmas lights was beginning to fade. Setting down the train engine, she let a sigh escape. As much as she loved Mistletoe and all it stood for, she knew she didn't want to sell Christmas paraphernalia for the rest of her life.

Working to suppress her frustration, she stepped into the tiny back room she'd converted into a kitchen and storage area for extra inventory and grabbed the creamer and sugar out of the top cabinet. She needed coffee. Here was yet another thing Mistletoe lacked. In New York, every other corner had a coffee shop with signs boasting countless coffee flavors. Flossie's offered caffeinated or decaffeinated. Not exactly a cosmopolitan selection. Bending down, she rummaged through the lower cabinet for the coffee can that had been pushed toward the back of the shelf.

The front door jingled open. "Madison?"

She stood up and whacked her head against the cabinet door she'd left open above. "Ouch!"

"You okay?"

"I'm fine, Erik," she hollered into the other room, recognizing Mistletoe's postman's voice. "I'll be right out."

Rubbing the sore spot on the top of her head, she winced. Maybe she hadn't gotten enough sleep last night and simply needed her morning cup of java. Quickly dumping a scoop of grounds into the coffeemaker, she added the water and switched the machine on. Five more minutes and she'd be good to go.

Madison stepped back into the front room where Erik and his ever-present basset hound, Daisy, waited for her. Madison bent and scratched Daisy behind the ears. "Hey, girl. You're both out and about early."

"Thought you wouldn't mind. I've got a package for you that came in yesterday, but I didn't want to leave it outside in the snow. It looked. . .personal."

Madison smiled, forgetting the bump on the top of her head. Christmas or not, she'd always loved presents.

Erik set the box down, then leaned his tall frame against the counter. "Heard you hit a deer last night on your way home."

"News certainly does travel fast." Reaching for the package, her smile disappeared. One couldn't sneeze without the whole town knowing about it.

"This is Mistletoe, you know."

Yes, she knew. Small towns were notorious for news traveling faster than the speed of light, and Mistletoe was no exception.

Her smile returned when she spun the box around and noticed the return address: A. Tanner, New York. She hugged it to her chest. "Thanks for bringing it by. I appreciate it."

"Sure thing." Eric tugged on Daisy's leash to keep her from getting into a bowl of orange-vanilla potpourri on one of the lower shelves. "I thought normally you had your inventory sent Federal Express."

"Normally I do." While she didn't consider Erik one of the nosier residents in town, it couldn't hurt to keep the contents of the package, along with the identity of the sender, to herself.

He took a step backward and shrugged. "Well then, I'll see you later. Have a nice day."

Once Erik was out the door, she grabbed a pair of scissors from the counter, then slid the blade along the side of the box. Inside was a jumble of purple and gold tissue paper protecting a card and a small crystal ornament in the shape of a heart.

Fingering the ornament in one hand, she smiled. She didn't

remember telling Albert that she'd collected ornaments since she was nine, though maybe it was obvious considering she sold them for a living. Even she and Josh had exchanged ornaments every Christmas for as long as she could remember. She shook her head, not wanting to think about Josh right now.

Instead, she opened the card and read the message.

I miss you already.

Madison held the gift against her heart and wondered if this was what it was like to be in love. She and Albert had never actually talked about their relationship or where either of them wanted it to go. Even she wasn't sure. A relationship with Albert would mean moving to New York and leaving everything she knew here behind. He certainly wouldn't enjoy living a hundred miles from nowhere with nothing but Flossie's Thursday night specials and a night of karaoke for entertainment.

She walked across the carpeted floor, still holding on to the ornament, and stopped at the window overlooking the town square. The sleepy community was beginning to wake up. One of her best friends, Lori Compton, made her way toward City Hall to begin another day as mayor. Mrs. Pearson, who had recently retired after thirty-five years of teaching at Mistletoe Elementary, was walking her three poodles along the sidewalk bordering the small park in the center of the square. Even Dwight Tolbert, Mistletoe's barber for as long as Madison could remember, was letting in his first customer for the day.

Madison reached up to hang the crystal heart at the edge of one of the branches of the decorated tree. A flash of red turned her gaze back outside. Josh, dressed in blue jeans, a University of Montana sweatshirt, and a red baseball cap, was headed to Flossie's for breakfast. He waved to Henry Forester, who was shoveling last night's snow off the sidewalks in front of the Savings and Loan, then slipped inside the café out of the cold.

Turning away from the window, she fingered the ornament Albert had sent her. The truth was, she'd always loved the small-town values of Mistletoe despite the sometimes quirky nature of its residents, but with Albert in the picture, the ties that held her here were beginning to fray. Albert showed her all the city had to offer. A large apartment with a killer view, an executive position in his company. . .anything she wanted.

The problem was, if a move was what she wanted, why did her heart feel so conflicted?

Josh stepped out into the warming afternoon sun and took in a deep breath of the fresh Montana air. Madison could have New York with all its smog and pollution. Give him God's clear blue skies and the mountains, and he'd be content forever. After being cooped up working all morning, the crisp fall wind, a reminder of the coming winter, felt good against his face. Already, the snow from last night had begun to melt. Unless the skies brought another snowfall tonight, most of it would probably be gone by morning.

Deciding that a brisk walk around the town square would rejuvenate him enough to work the rest of the afternoon, he crossed the street, slowing down only briefly when he passed Under the Mistletoe. He glanced in the window for a sign of

Madison and saw her talking to some customers who were browsing through a display of ornaments near the front. She laughed, and the hair now framing her face bounced against her cheeks. She looked beautiful. She had been right, of course—he would get used to the new style.

Just like he would get used to the fact that Madison was interested in someone else and probably wouldn't stay in Mistletoe forever. It made him wonder what would have happened if he'd actually managed to ask her out yesterday. He certainly couldn't offer her the excitement of Manhattan, but he could offer her his heart.

Or rather, he could have.

Had he already forgotten she wasn't the same person he'd grown up with? Madison Graham was looking for something beyond the confines of Mistletoe, a city that could offer her the bright lights of Broadway and a shot at earning a lot of money. She wasn't interested in anything more than friendship with him.

The thought of her leaving made him want to fly to New York himself and check out this Albert. At least the guy had better be someone who didn't take Madison for granted and who was worthy of her giving up everything she knew—her family and friends, her church, and her shop.

He scuffed his foot against the ground, kicking at a patch of snow. That was one of the things that had drawn him to Madison in the first place. Never had he met such a hard worker or anyone more willing to sacrifice to make their dreams come true. Like Under the Mistletoe. She'd taken an old family business and put new life into it, managing to double the profit margin in less than three years.

And she put the same energy into her relationships as well. When anyone got sick, Madison was always one of the first to jump in and do what she could to help, whether it was bringing meals or just making a simple phone call. He'd found that out when he broke his leg two years ago. He'd ended up with enough spaghetti, meatloaf, and chocolate cake to last him a good two weeks.

Passing the Savings and Loan, he realized that he'd already walked the entire town square without really seeing anything and still felt as antsy as he had when he'd started. He'd make another round and add prayer this time.

Madison, with a bag of popcorn in her hand, was coming out of her shop as he walked by the second time, deep into a conversation with his heavenly Father.

She smiled. "Hey. How are you?"

Josh stopped and tugged on his baseball cap, feeling self-conscious all of a sudden. "I'm good, thanks. And you?"

"Fine." She popped a few pieces of popcorn into her mouth. "I needed a breath of fresh air and thought I'd sit down in the park for a few minutes. Rosemary's watching the store."

Josh worked to loosen his tongue, which seemed stuck to the roof of his mouth. This was crazy. This was Madison. Buddy and pal since second grade. Why did he suddenly feel tongue-tied? Albert had obviously just upped the stakes a notch, making him realize he was running out of time.

He cleared his throat and shoved his hands into his front pockets. "Do you mind if I join you?"

"Of course not." She pushed a strand of blond hair off her cheek and smiled again. "I'd like the company, actually."

They headed for the center of the town square, which had been made into a park complete with benches and a sixteen-foot tall Christmas tree in the center. An elderly couple sat together on one of the benches, throwing bread crumbs toward a half dozen cardinals, while a mother and her toddler watched the feeding frenzy.

Madison offered him a handful of popcorn, then slid onto one of the iron benches.

"How are things at Under the Mistletoe?" he asked, munching on the salty snack.

"Lori's plans to rejuvenate the town really have worked. Last month's sales figures were up a good 15 percent, and according to Deanna and her tourism stats, I'm not the only one seeing an increase in business. Of course, I'm just thankful to have made it through the past three years in the black. That's a miracle in itself." She leaned back and crossed her legs, the enthusiasm in her eyes obvious. "Albert says I need to be looking five years into the future so I can take a risk and expand my business, though I told him it's too early to think that far ahead."

"I suppose he might have a point. You can't gain anything without taking a risk." Josh clasped his hands together, wondering whether it was Albert or New York that bugged him the most. No—they were definitely both on an equal par. He tried to swallow his annoyance. "Either way, I really am proud of you."

"Thanks, Josh." She nudged him with her elbow. "Your

friendship and opinions have always meant a lot to me."

He tossed the last piece of popcorn into his mouth and frowned. Friendships were highly overrated. He'd always pictured the two of them together one day, but the timing never seemed right. Now Albert had apparently beaten him to the punch. Or he would if he didn't get his act together.

He glanced at Madison out of the corner of his eye, wondering how he'd been so naive to think that he had all of the time in the world to win her heart. Last night he might have managed to convince himself that he didn't have a chance to win Madison's affections, but with her sitting inches away from him, ignoring his heart was proving to be impossible. And since Romance 101 had obviously never been his best subject, he needed a strategy. Believing that friendship would automatically morph into love had been wrong, though his options at the moment seemed limited. For now, he'd start with a casual comment, reminding her of the positive attributes of Mistletoe, move on to a compliment, then go straight to a dinner invitation.

"The town is beautiful, isn't it? After the first snow, no town can compete with Mistletoe."

Madison nodded her agreement. "It's my favorite time of year."

On to step two. "By the way, I thought I should tell you that I've decided I like your hair."

"Really?"

He nodded, searching for the right descriptive word. "It suits you. It's very, um, cute."

"Is that your new word? Cute?" Madison jutted her chin, her

eyes wide. "Cute is my six-year-old niece in a fairy costume—"

"In a fairy costume?" He stammered as he shook his head. "I meant. . . What I meant was stylish and elegant—"

"Oh no. You're in too deep now, buddy." She jumped up from the bench with a broad smile, then scooped up a handful of snow and threw it at him.

"Starting a war, are you?" Josh laughed and brushed a few ice crystals off his pant leg. "You have horrible aim, you know."

"I have horrible aim?" She stood and grabbed another handful, this time forming the snow into a ball.

Madison whipped the snowball at him, and it landed square on his chin.

He winced at the cold and laughed. Now it was his turn to pack a snowball and throw it at her. His aim was perfect as it hit her collar. Snow tumbled inside her jacket, and she squealed as she tried to shake it out.

"Josh!"

"What? You started it."

"You're right. This is war."

A second snowball hit him in the ear, but he managed to lob another one that landed on the top of her knit cap and tumbled down her nose.

Josh was laughing so hard he could hardly breathe as she smacked him in the chest with another powdery orb.

"Truce. Please." She rested her hands on her thighs and tried to catch her breath. Her cheeks were rosy, and her blue eyes shone bright. "I don't remember the last time I've laughed so hard."

She took a step forward, then stumbled.

He moved to catch her, grabbing her arms to support her as she fell against him. His heart pounded inside his chest as she gazed up at him, and he caught the sparkle in her eyes.

Her face was close enough for him to kiss her. Only a breath away. . .

Neither of them moved, until the corners of her mouth turned down in a frown.

He broke the silence between them. "Are you okay?"

"Of course. I just twisted my ankle."

"Do you want me to look—"

"No, it doesn't even hurt. It just startled me, that's all."

Madison stepped out of Joshua's arms and managed to keep her balance this time, still not sure what had happened. Her heart was beating too fast, and she couldn't seem to catch her breath. Maybe it was because she could still feel his arms around her, warm and secure. Or maybe because she couldn't help wondering what it would have been like for him to kiss her.

She blinked and shook her head. This was crazy.

Turning away, she reached down to pick up the empty popcorn bag she'd dropped during their snowball fight, confused at the range of emotions that flooded through her. This was Josh. The boy she'd known since she was eight years old.

Except he wasn't a boy anymore.

Not able to stop herself, she looked up once more and caught his gaze. She didn't remember his eyes being so blue or his smile so bright. But falling for Josh...

No. She had New York in her sights—and Albert. She just needed to remind herself that while Josh might be handsome, and at the moment utterly irresistible with his baseball cap, dimpled chin, and crooked smile, she didn't plan to live the rest of her life in this small town. Not since she'd discovered there was more beyond the confines of Mistletoe, Montana.

She brushed snow off her jacket for all the diversion was worth. "I—I've really got to get back to work, Josh. I'm sorry. I'll see you later."

Madison hurried across the street toward her shop without looking back, all the while trying to ignore the question that seemed to pound through her pulse. What would have happened if Joshua Dunkin had kissed her?

Chapter 4

W ell?"

"Well, what?" Madison looked up from the account ledger at one of her best friends, Deanna Moss, and frowned. She looked far too inquisitive as she shoved a lock of her strawberry-blond hair out of her eyes.

"New York, Albert. . .I want to hear all about it."

"There's really nothing to tell." Madison tapped her pencil against the counter. "Not yet, anyway."

"Come on, Madison." Deanna's hand smacked against the counter. "I want details."

"Okay. There's a chance. A slight chance." She slammed the ledger shut and tried to curb her jumbled emotions at the thought of moving to New York. "I really don't know yet. We haven't talked specifically about where our relationship is headed."

"At least tell me what you think about him. All I know is that he's handsome and rich." She sighed. "And on the downside, he lives entirely too far from Mistletoe."

Madison ignored Deanna's last comment and instead tried to envision Albert with his toffee-colored eyes and short brown hair, always cut perfectly just above the collar of his expensive suits. But all she could see was. . .

Josh?

She squeezed her eyes shut and tried to shake the image of Josh throwing a snowball at her. Josh's dimples as she laughed beside him. Josh close enough to kiss her.

Madison frowned. She couldn't picture Albert throwing a snowball at her or laughing with her until her sides ached. Albert preferred an intelligent conversation over a three-course meal or an evening at a classical concert performed by one of the leading talents of New York.

"Come on, Madison." Deanna sipped hot apple cider from a mug Madison had poured for her. "Lori and I haven't even seen a picture of this guy."

Madison shrugged and realized she didn't have a photo of Albert. How had that happened? She had an album full of pictures of her and Joshua together. She searched her mind for a change of topic. "Don't you have something to—to direct?"

As director of tourism for the town of Mistletoe, Deanna did a far better job directing tourists than her friends' love lives.

"I try not to work on Saturdays." Deanna frowned. "And you're impossible."

Madison cringed at the words. Her friend was right. She'd woken up on the wrong side of the bed this morning and didn't even know why. Albert was planning to call her today, business had been brisk, and another two inches of snow blanketed the town square. Life was good.

At least it should be.

"I'm sorry." Madison started straightening a display of Christmas cards on the counter. "I guess I'm just nervous about the relationship. Albert's a good man, and he loves God, but we still don't know each other well enough for me to make a final judgment."

Deanna frowned. "Meaning he doesn't take your breath away and make your heart pound when he's near you?"

"I think it's more because this is a long-distance relationship, which complicates things and has made me a bit hesitant."

Madison moved to straighten a display of red and green Christmas candles. Of course Albert's presence took her breath away, made her heart pound, and every other romantic cliché Deanna might come up with.

"I'm sorry." Deanna squeezed Madison's hand. "You know I'd never bug you over a guy; I'm just interested."

"I know, and I really do appreciate it. I just need to sort it all out myself and determine if I'm ready to take that leap of faith."

The bell on the front door jingled as Deanna turned to leave. "Hey! Morning, Josh."

Madison's head bobbed up from the candles, and she felt a hot blush rise up her cheeks. She bit her lip and wished he didn't look so good in his blue jeans and long-sleeved T-shirt and plaid shirt jacket. She didn't remember ever seeing Albert in a pair of jeans, or plaid for that matter, though no doubt he'd look just as good if he did wear them.

"Morning, Deanna. . .Madison." Josh balanced an armload of boxed trains, his smile broader than usual.

"Hi, Josh." Madison swallowed hard and went back to her display.

"Oh, Madison, I almost forgot." Deanna turned back to her friend. "Are we still on for pizza and a movie tomorrow night at your place?"

"Yeah, that sounds great."

"I'll call and remind Lori."

Madison looked at Josh as he set the trains down on the counter; she wondered why her heart was pounding so hard. She'd heard that a nasty strain of the flu was going around. Except she didn't have time to be sick.

Frowning, Deanna looked at her. "Are you okay?"

Madison dipped her chin. "Of course I am."

"You look a bit flushed, though I didn't notice it earlier." Deanna checked Madison's forehead like an overprotective caregiver. "You're not coming down with something, are you?"

"No, Deanna, I'm fine. Really." She squeezed her hands into fists at her sides.

"Okay, then I'll see you later." The door jingled again as Deanna exited the shop.

"You're sick, Madison?" Josh leaned against the counter and looked at her, his eyes heavy with concern.

She placed her hand against her chest and struggled to catch her breath. "Of course I'm not sick. Can I get you some apple cider?"

"Well, I can't stay long, but that would be nice, actually." He rubbed his hands together. "It's getting cold out there."

Grateful for the distraction, Madison grabbed a cup and poured from the thermos. Her hand brushed his as she gave him the drink, and her knees suddenly felt weak. She was definitely coming down with something.

Madison hurried behind the counter. She had money for Josh, which she should have given him last week. She'd give him his check and he'd leave. She was just nervous about her future with Albert and the possibility of leaving behind Mistletoe, her family, and the shop. All perfectly normal feelings for anyone getting ready to embark on a new and exciting venture. Maybe taking that risk was exactly what she needed to do.

"Madison?"

She looked up at him and smiled apologetically. "I'm sorry. I must have missed what you just said."

"Are you sure you're not getting sick?"

"No, I guess I'm just a bit distracted, that's all."

Madison took in a deep breath and the spicy scent of Josh's aftershave filled her senses, making her head reel. She blinked and focused on the train cars he'd brought. They were a new model, green with black lines. The kids collecting his line would love them.

Josh focused his gaze on the new model train car he'd just brought into the store. He wasn't sure what to think, but Madison was acting more nervous than a greenhorn trying to mount a wild bronco. Maybe whatever had passed between them in the park yesterday had affected her. He knew it had done something to him. Just the thought of her sent his heart racing like a runaway train and convinced him that he wasn't going to give up just because Albert—the suave toy maker—had popped onto the scene. "What do you think?"

"About what?" She looked up at him, her face still flushed a rosy pink.

"The trains."

"They're perfect. As always." She cleared her throat and began stacking them on the display set up in the middle of the room. "I'll need at least this many more, though, and some of those wooden puzzles, as soon as you can finish them."

"I'm already working around the clock, it seems, but I'll have them by next week."

"Oh, and I have a check for you." She hurried around the counter and opened the till, avoiding his gaze.

"Thanks." He pocketed the check, then glanced at his watch. It was now or never. "I was wondering if I could ask you something."

She looked up at him finally. Expectant? Hopeful? "Of course."

"Yesterday, I—we had—"

The phone rang.

Madison glanced at the phone, hesitating before picking it up. "Under the Mistletoe; how may I help you?"

Josh strummed his fingers against the counter as a smile spread across her face.

She covered the receiver with her hand. "I need to take this call. You don't mind, do you?"

Albert.

"No." Josh forced a smile and shook his head. "I'll talk to you later."

He hurried out the door, the bells jingling as the shop door slammed behind him, and wondered if the fact that he'd taken his own sweet Montana time to get around to pursuing a relationship with Madison was going to cost him the woman he loved.

Thirty minutes later, Madison hung up the phone and tried to calm the flutter of butterflies in her stomach. It was perfectly normal for her to be nervous and even to harbor a few reservations about the situation. All the same, she'd made a decision.

She, Madison Graham, had lived her entire life following the rules, but even Josh had told her that she wouldn't gain anything without taking a risk.

And there was something else she wanted in life.

Albert.

This was exactly why she was going to sell Under the Mistletoe and move to New York.

Chapter 5

adies, I have an announcement." Madison held up her glass of lemonade and tapped it with her fork, addressing Lori and Deanna, who sat beside her on her living room floor eating deep-dish pepperoni pizza and garlicky cheese bread.

Lori tapped her mouth with her napkin and leaned forward. "Your eyes are sparkling. What is it?"

Madison raised her chin and added an extra dose of determination to her words. "I'm moving to New York."

There. She'd done it. Announced to the world—okay, to her two best friends—that she was moving. Saying it out loud made it seem real. And wonderful. New York had everything she wanted. A new career, hundreds of blocks of shopping and restaurants, and most important, of course, Albert.

"You're moving to New York?" Deanna's eyes widened in apparent disbelief. "You can't just pop up and say you're moving to New York."

"Why not?"

"Why not?" Lori shook her head as if she couldn't believe the statement required an explanation. "Because New York is two thousand miles away, and Mistletoe is your home. You have a shop to run, and us—"

"This is because of Albert, isn't it?" Deanna interrupted Lori's ramblings.

Madison sighed. This wasn't going as planned. They were supposed to be happy for her. "Have you already forgotten our marriage pact? Married by the time we're twenty-eight? I'm running out of time, ladies."

Lori's lips thinned. "Not if it means marrying the wrong man. You barely know this guy. And besides, moving to New York was never part of the pact."

"I know Albert enough to realize that I want to pursue our relationship. He called yesterday and told me that his sister needs a roommate. He wants me to move in with her so we'll have a chance to give our relationship a try." With her head spinning over the possibilities, she hoped she was making sense. "But this is about more than Albert. This is a chance for me to spread my wings beyond Mistletoe. I get to work for his company and make three times what I make here—"

"Living in New York will cost that and probably a whole lot more."

Madison shook her head at Deanna's comment. If she couldn't convince her best friends of the legitimacy of her plan, she'd never convince her family and her church friends. . .or Josh. No! This was not the time to bring Josh into the picture.

Someone would buy her business, and Josh would continue to sell his trains as always. Nothing would really change.

Madison cleared her throat. "It's time I took a risk with my life. I thought the two of you, more than anyone else, would understand."

"Go skydiving, swim across Flathead Lake before it freezes over in the winter, add one of those giant talking snowmen to your inventory. . .whatever. I don't care." Lori's voice cracked with emotion. "But don't move to New York just to try to prove something."

Madison squeezed back the tears. "You don't understand. I've lived in Mistletoe my whole life, and while things are good, something's missing in my life."

"And you think Albert is the answer?" Deanna asked.

"You both would love him if you met him. He's good-looking, funny, smart, and he loves me."

"Are you sure?"

"What do you mean, am I sure?" Madison's frustration at making her friends understand was quickly turning to irritation. She wasn't eighteen anymore. She could make her own decision despite what everyone else seemed to think. "Of course he loves me. He asked me to move to New York, didn't he?"

"And do you love him?" Lori caught her gaze.

Madison stared down at her pizza and picked at the crust.

"You're hesitating."

"Okay. I'm not sure. I've never really been in love before."

Deanna grabbed Madison's hand and squeezed. "We're just worried about you, that's all. Things are different in New York, and what if things don't work out between the two of you? Then what? You've sold the business, and you'll have nothing left. It all just seems so sudden. . .and drastic."

Madison blinked back the tears that threatened to erupt. "I don't know what will happen, but at least I will have tried it. And I'll still have a job in New York."

"If things go sour between the two of you, don't be so sure about that." Lori took a sip of her flavored water and shook her head.

"I still want something else. I can't see myself living in Mistletoe for the rest of my life, selling Christmas ornaments, candles, and wooden trains."

Deanna shoved her plate away from her. "Mistletoe and the shop weren't beneath you a year ago. Before you met Albert."

"Albert's not the only reason I'm selling the shop. It's something I've been considering for months."

Lori stood up and planted her hands on her hips. "Girl, you might be fooling yourself, but this has *everything* to do with Albert."

Josh strode down the sidewalk past Flossie's, thankful to be finished with his work, which had taken up every waking moment of the past ten days. During that time, his mind had been preoccupied with thoughts of Madison. Their encounter in the park, the moment he'd almost kissed her. And then Albert's call.

The smell of hamburgers and fries wafted from the diner and made his stomach rumble. Dinnertime might have arrived, but at the moment, he had something even more important than his appetite to take care of.

He frowned as he crossed the quiet intersection at the town's only stoplight. Between an unexpected trip to Billings and a rush order for a client, he and Madison had ended up playing phone tag the past few days. He'd considered simply leaving her a message, but what he had to say couldn't be said to an answering machine. He had to let her know how he felt, but he hadn't wanted to talk to her with a paintbrush in one hand and a bouquet of flowers in the other.

Stepping up onto the curb, he checked his watch. Five minutes before five. If he was lucky, he'd catch her before she left to go home for the day. If he missed her, he planned to show up on her front doorstep with dinner and a prayer that she would at least be open to what he had to say. He'd waited long enough.

Josh grabbed the door handle of Under the Mistletoe, then stopped. Something was wrong. The trees in the front window were decorated with their familiar ribbons and bows. The welcome sign on the front door hung slightly askew, but that wasn't the problem, either.

He took a step back and looked again into the shop's front window. There it was. A FOR SALE sign.

Josh squeezed his eyes shut, then opened them again. Something wasn't right. Not only would Madison never sell her store, she certainly wouldn't do so without telling him about it.

She did try to call a half dozen times in the past week.

He'd been the one to take his phone off the hook during the day and leave messages for her at odd hours when she was

219

obviously out or had her cell phone turned off. Josh shoved his hands inside his front pockets, knowing there had to be a simple explanation as to why Gladys Mercer had one of her real estate signs hung in Madison's store window.

"Josh. Are you all right?"

Josh spun on his heels. Lori Compton stood behind him. With her knack for organization and fresh new ideas, she'd turned out to be the perfect mayor for Mistletoe. Then again, he'd thought he'd make the perfect suitor for Madison—a notion that was obviously farfetched.

Lori took a step forward. "You've been standing here for the past two minutes. I just thought—"

"Madison is selling the place?"

Her brow lowered. "You didn't know?"

"She didn't talk to me about it. I don't understand. That's not Madison."

"She left three days ago for New York. She's moving in with her boyfriend's sister. She and Albert are going to see if they can make a go of their relationship." Lori tugged on the chain of her necklace. "You didn't know about any of this, did you?"

"Just about Albert and that she was hooked on New York, but selling the store? I can't. . ." Josh ran his fingers through his hair, certain he was going to be ill.

"She insisted that even if things didn't work out with Albert, she still wanted to make a go at a new career in New York."

"I can't believe I didn't know about all of this."

Lori's gaze swept the sidewalk. "I'm afraid that might have been my fault. Mine and Deanna's."

Josh cocked his head. "What are you talking about?"

"When Madison told us she was leaving, we were pretty hard on her."

He still didn't understand. He probably would've been even harder on Madison than her two friends. "I'm glad you were. You should have been."

"But I think that discouraged her from making her move common knowledge in the town, though I think most people do know about it by now, especially with the sign up." Lori frowned and shot him an I-really-feel-sorry-for-you look, as if he were some loser who'd just lost his last dime. "So she didn't even call you?"

"Actually, she did try to call me. Several times, in fact, but we kept playing phone tag. I've been swamped with work and—"

"She wanted to tell you in person."

"When will she be back?"

"Christmastime. Even she couldn't miss Christmas in Mistletoe with her family."

Josh shrugged. There was really nothing else he could do. He'd been such a fool. Albert had offered her New York. He could hardly blame her for choosing the guy. But now she was gone. He'd have to keep telling himself, because at the moment, the sign was the only proof that he'd just lost his heart for good.

Lori pulled her scarf tighter around her neck. "You're in love with her, aren't you?"

"With Madison?" He let out a deep sigh. "Since the seventh grade."

221

"Then why didn't you say something to her?"

"I don't know." He shrugged. "We've always been such good friends. I suppose I assumed that our friendship would eventually turn to love. It just never did."

"A girl wants to be wooed, Josh." Lori held up her hand. "I'm sorry. It's really none of my business."

"No, you're right. I've been a complete fool, and in the process I've lost her forever."

"I really am sorry, because believe me, I much rather would have liked to see the two of you together than her and that Albert."

"There's no use being too hard on her." Josh shoved his hands into his jacket pockets, feeling completely helpless. "She's big enough to decide who she loves and where she wants to live. I just hope she's happy with him."

"I hope you're right, Josh. I really hope you're right."

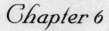

Chapter 6

Madison zipped up the new black boots she'd bought on sale at Macy's, then glanced at the clock. Katie, Albert's sister, had already left on her date, and Albert was twenty minutes late, which seemed strange. Albert was never late. The symphony started in forty-five minutes, and if they didn't leave soon, they'd be late because of traffic. She tugged to straighten her calf-length black skirt and examined her outfit in the full-length mirror. Maybe she should have stuck with the blue sweater. . .or the green one?

Madison let out a groan at her ridiculous display of indecision. The red sweater was fine. Besides, she didn't have time to change again. Turning away from the mirror, she stifled a yawn and arched her back to loosen the muscles that had grown tight from sitting at a computer all day. While she missed the chance to deal one-on-one with customers, at least she was catching on to the dynamics of her new job. But between ten-hour workdays and dates with Albert in the evenings, she was exhausted. Ever since her arrival in the city three weeks ago, he'd taken her out nearly every night, insisting that it was good publicity for the company for them to be seen with the right people.

While she'd met dozens of his friends, there were times when she'd begun to feel like just another ornament attached to his arm. Tonight, though, he promised it would be just the two of them. A welcome relief after playing the role of a social butterfly in front of far too many of his uppity friends. She shook her head, knowing she had nothing to complain about. Albert was kind, considerate, and always a gentleman. Besides that, he was driven and focused, two of the qualities she admired in him, and the main reason his business was thriving. Others might look at those traits and see him as ruthless and unfeeling, but his high-profit margin proved the value of his unswerving commitment.

Looking out the window of the fourth-floor apartment, she hummed along with the jazzy rendition of "White Christmas" that played on the radio and told herself to stop acting as though she needed to convince herself she was happy. It was natural for a relationship to take time to grow and develop. In the meantime, she needed to simply relax and enjoy being spoiled.

A taxi blared its horn as it passed in front of the apartment, and Madison jumped. No matter what time of day it was, yellow taxis rumbled down the streets amid pedestrians, street vendors, and other traffic. With Thanksgiving only three days away, New York was already starting to glow with strings of lights on every corner, while silver bows and brightly decorated packages seemed to fill every crowded storefront.

The coming holiday season had become a constant reminder of home.

Madison pulled a tube of lipstick from her purse and moved back in front of the mirror to apply a layer of red that matched her sweater. One thing struck her as a complete contrast between Mistletoe and New York. Here in the big city, Christmas had become a commercialized business. And while she loved the excitement that buzzed in the air, competition between shops was intense as stores did everything they could to draw in customers. Instead of love and good cheer, the streets seemed to be filled with harried pedestrians sloshing through the snow in search of one more gift.

Closing her eyes, she could picture Mistletoe's town square. Every December, framed in a halo of white lights, stood a nativity scene depicting the birth of Christ. On Christmas Eve, the church choir would sing carols such as "O Little Town of Bethlehem" and "It Came upon a Midnight Clear," reminding them that this holiday was more than a way to lure tired shoppers in for one more purchase to add to their already extended credit limits.

Madison sighed and dropped the lipstick into her purse. She was just homesick. That was it. Still, it seemed as if New York had forgotten the true meaning of Christmas.

Or perhaps she had.

The doorbell rang, and, pushing aside the thought, she grabbed her long coat and hurried toward the door. Swinging it open, she hesitated, then took a step backward. Albert stood between two of his employees, whom she recognized;

the three men were surrounded by the undeniable stench of alcohol. "Albert?"

Dressed in black-and-white suits like a trio of penguins, all three men stared at her. Then Albert wrapped his arms around his buddies. "Aren't you going to invite us in?"

"Of course, but the symphony—"

"I know we're late, but the symphony can wait. I have good news." Waving to his friends to follow him, he sat down on the leather couch, then propped his feet up on the coffee table.

His buddies followed suit.

Madison reeled around and sent up a prayer. How well did she really know this man? Obviously not as well as she thought she did. Or maybe she only knew the things he wanted her to know.

He patted the seat beside him and motioned for her to sit down. "You know Phil and Gary, don't you? From the office?"

"Phil. Gary. How are you?" She nodded her head but remained standing.

"Tonight, Madison, we're going to celebrate."

Her brow narrowed. "Celebrate what? We were supposed to go out, and—"

"We've just signed a multimillion-dollar contract for the production of that video I told you about, and we want to celebrate."

The growing knot in her stomach twisted. "I'd say you already have been celebrating. You're drunk, Albert."

"Come on, Madison." He slapped his hands against his thighs. "We've been drinking, but I'm not drunk. Besides, I think I've played the good boy for you long enough. There's nothing wrong with a little fun now and then. Loosen up."

Madison's eyes widened. "I have nothing against fun, but—"

"Good." He grabbed her arm and pulled her onto the couch against him. "Gentleman, I say we skip the symphony and catch that comedy act on Fifth Street after dinner. It's supposed to be a riot."

Phil—or was it Gary?—nodded.

Albert stood and staggered toward the kitchen, pulling her with him. "What do you have to drink, sweetheart? And I'm not talking about hot chocolate and marshmallows."

A picture of Josh bringing her hot chocolate flashed in front of her. How could she have been so blind? The signs had been there for weeks, but she'd let the bright lights of the city blind her to the fact that Albert wasn't the kind of man she was looking for in a relationship. And she'd managed to throw everything away for a glimpse at a better life, which hadn't proven to be better after all. Madison leaned against the wall and tried to control her rapid breathing. She was no better than the prodigal son Jesus had spoken of in one of his parables. She'd spent the past three weeks convincing herself that she could be happy here, only to discover that happiness had been in her grasp all along in a sleepy little town called Mistletoe.

It was time for the prodigal to go home. If it wasn't too late.

In twenty-four hours, Madison managed to break up with

Albert, quit her job, and book a flight back to Montana. How could she have been so foolish? She'd thrown away everything she knew and loved for the lure of superficial happiness. Standing outside Lori's house, she cringed, knowing she'd lost Under the Mistletoe in the process. Four days ago, she'd signed the faxed papers Mrs. Mercer had sent her, surprised that the store had sold so quickly. But as long as her friends and family still wanted her to come back home, she'd be happy. She could always get a job in her father's plumbing company, a plight far better than another day working for Albert.

She knocked on Lori's door, needing to see another familiar face that would welcome her back with no questions asked. The door opened, and before Madison could take another breath, Lori squealed and wrapped both arms around her.

"I can't believe it. You're back! I thought you weren't coming until next month."

"I couldn't miss Thanksgiving with my best friends." Madison scanned the room. "I'm back for good, Lori. No more New York, or Albert, or—"

"What?" Lori squealed again and pulled her into another embrace. "This is fantastic."

Madison slipped her wool hat off her head and frowned. "Go ahead. You can say what you're really thinking. 'I told you so.'"

"Told you so? Never. All I care about is that you're back." Lori led Madison into the foyer and out of the brisk night air, then helped her take off her coat.

"You're freezing. Do you want something to drink? I just

made myself some hot chocolate, and I could make you a mug, as well."

Madison rubbed her hands together and shivered. "I'd love some. Thanks."

"Good. Then I want to hear everything." Lori hung up Madison's coat on the antique coatrack. "Have you seen your parents?"

"I stopped by and had dinner with them on my way into town. They were so happy I was back." Madison glanced around at Lori's familiar great room with the stunning wall of windows overlooking the sleepy town of Mistletoe. "I know it's crazy, but I never thought I could miss a place, and its people, so much. But I did."

"You belong here, Madison." Lori squeezed her shoulder. "I'll be right back with some hot chocolate, and you can tell me everything."

Madison stood by the fireplace, warming her hands in front of the crackling flames and scanning the framed photos that filled the stone mantel. There was one of Lori, Deanna, and her skiing. Another photo of the three of them with Kathy before she moved to California. Lori's parents. Lori and Russell's engagement picture. Lori and her sister. Her and Josh.

Her and Josh?

Madison took the wood-framed photo off the mantel and ran her finger across Josh's face. She'd forgotten about this photo Lori had taken two summers ago when the singles' group had spent the day at Glacier National Park. They'd had so much fun that day, picnicking, hiking, and playing volleyball.

How could she ever have compared Albert to Josh? Or compared anything of what she had here with the bright lights of the city? Instead of recognizing her blessings, all she had been able to see was that Albert was more successful with his own company, and the city had more to offer than her small hometown. Mistletoe, Montana, might not be able to compete with the rest of the world on certain levels, but now she realized it had everything she needed.

And she'd also realized what she didn't need. Albert had turned out to be nothing more than a chameleon with the ability to become what others around him wanted. She'd thought she needed a knight in shining armor to take her away from Mistletoe and show her the excitement of the city. And he'd done that very thing for her. Except all too quickly she'd learned that shopping, Broadway plays, and five-star meals could never fill the empty corners of her heart. Nor could success be measured by dollar amounts.

"He's in love with you, you know."

Madison spun around at the sound of Lori's voice. "Who?"

"Joshua."

Madison shook her head. "Since when?"

"I believe he said 'since the seventh grade.'"

Madison set the photo back on the mantel. "What are you talking about? Josh and I have always been friends. Great friends, but. . ." She swallowed hard. "He told you that he was in love with me?"

"Yep." Lori handed her a mug of hot chocolate. "He told me the day he found out you were selling Under the Mistletoe."

A cloud of guilt swept across her heart. "I never told him I was leaving."

"I know. He found out the hard way."

"I tried to call him. I really did. But we kept missing each other, and before I knew it, I was gone, and then. . .I don't know, it just seemed too late. Too cold to tell him over the phone." Tears began to form in the corners of her eyes. "And then there was the shop. I knew Rosemary would handle things until the store sold, which it did. Last Friday to some entrepreneur from. . .I don't know. I can't believe I didn't even tell Josh about the shop."

"Madison—"

"My store belongs to some stranger." Tears began to flow freely down Madison's cheeks. "Can you believe what I've done? I've been a complete idiot."

Lori pulled Madison into a tight hug, then told her to have a seat on the couch. "You have to try not to be too hard on yourself."

That would take time, and now she had the added confusion of trying to work her mind around the idea that Josh was in love with her. "He loves me?"

"You could give him a call."

Madison stared into the twinkling lights of the Christmas tree in the corner of the room. Josh had always been there for her. Whether it was a plumbing problem in her kitchen, a stroll through the town square, or a ride to church. Could it be that true love had been right before her eyes, and she'd thrown it away?

"You really think he loves me?"

Lori nodded and smiled.

Madison's own smile wilted into a frown. *"Loved" me might be a better way of phrasing it.* "Even if he did love me, he can't anymore. Beside, I'm through with men until I can trust myself to make right choices. Albert turned out to be a complete disappointment. I don't know how I fell for him."

"Trust me, you're not the first person to find yourself interested in someone whose character is questionable. The good thing is that you didn't marry the guy."

"So what do I do now?"

"I think it's time you told Josh everything. If nothing else, you owe him that much."

Madison strode around the town center, careful to avoid the slick patches of ice on the sidewalk. Pulling the thick collar of her coat around her neck, she sat on one of the benches facing the street and forced herself to look across the street at Under the Mistletoe. Except for the SOLD sign in the window, nothing had changed. Not that she had expected the new owner to do anything in only a week, but she was glad that for now the evergreen trees in the window still twinkled with their white lights, and the fancy packages she'd set underneath their branches still shimmered in the afternoon sunlight.

She hadn't asked Mrs. Mercer what the new owner intended to do with the store, though the contract included all merchandise yet unsold. The only good thing to come out of the sale was that she would make a nice profit once the transfer of funds was complete. But even that fact didn't ease the sting of regret that seemed to jab her at every turn.

What had she been thinking?

She'd always been the sensible one in her family. The one who refused to jump into something just because it looked good on the surface. It had taken her six months to decide that the shop was a solid investment. And after three years of hard work, Albert had stepped into her life, and all she'd been able to see was what New York had to offer and what Mistletoe lacked. In the end, what had been lacking had been something inside of her and nothing money could buy.

Not that any of this was Albert's fault. She'd made her own decision to sell the shop, throwing it all away for some happy-ever-after fairy tale that didn't even exist. If she just would have stopped once and evaluated what life would be like with Albert instead of getting caught up in the glamour of how she thought things would be, she would have saved herself a lot of heartache. Madison gnawed on her bottom lip. King Solomon had been right when he wrote that all was meaningless under the sun, and apparently, she wasn't too old to learn that difficult life lesson. She'd be sure to think twice the next time some handsome stranger popped into her life, seemingly too good to be true.

Madison shoved her gloved hands into her pockets and wondered how much she'd thrown away in her quest to find happiness. Her heavenly Father would welcome her back with open arms, but what about the town of Mistletoe? What about. . .Josh?

She glanced up at the window to his apartment above Flossie's Café and wondered what he was doing. Her fingers found her cell phone inside her pocket, and she pulled it out. She could call him now—should call him—but feared his response. It wasn't as if she expected him to be in love with her still, but she couldn't bear the thought of throwing away their friendship. At the least, he deserved an apology.

Listening to "O Holy Night" play in the background, she closed her eyes, wishing she could simply erase the past few months. But that could never happen. From the time she was three or four, her mother had taught her the reality of consequences. Unfortunately, now that she was almost twenty-eight, the consequences had become much greater than doing a stint in time-out or having to miss her favorite TV show.

"O night divine, O night, when Christ was born. . ."

Tears welled up in Madison's eyes as the words of the song bore a hole through her heart. All of the false dreams she'd been fighting to hold on to dispersed into the crisp afternoon air, leaving behind a sense of renewal and hope. None of them compared with the incredible gift of God, her Creator, in sending His only Son to this world to bring life to a fallen world. That night *had* been divine. And in her focus on her new life in the city, she'd forgotten the true meaning of Christmas. She'd forgotten the significance of Jesus' birth and what He had done for her by dying on the cross.

Madison clasped her hands together and rested her elbows against her thighs. "Oh Lord, I can't believe how little it took for me to forget my commitment to You. The rare times I spent in prayer with You over the life-changing decisions I've been facing. . . How could I ever have thought that I could make these decisions without You?"

She wiped away the tears with her gloved hands and drew a deep breath. Admitting her mistakes didn't completely erase the pain. Leaving Albert and New York had been easier than she'd thought once she realized how foolish she'd been, but Albert had probably already found someone else to take her place. Madison sighed. That thought couldn't help; it could only hurt. Albert and New York didn't matter anymore. It was time to make a fresh start. This time with her heavenly Father in charge again.

"Hey, girl."

Madison looked up as Lori slid onto the bench beside her. She handed her a steamy cup of coffee in a Styrofoam cup. "I saw you out here from my office window and thought you might need something to warm you up. I know it's not from one of those fancy East Coast coffee shops, but my assistant does make a pretty good cup."

Madison took a sip and smiled. "It's perfect. Thank you."

"So what are you doing out here by yourself?"

Madison laughed, surprised at the measure of peace she felt from renewing her relationship with her Savior. "I'm contemplating my life and the number of people I owe an apology to. Josh in particular. I have this feeling that things are never going to be the same between us again."

"Do I sense a spark of interest after all these years?"

"Yes. . . No. . . I don't know." Madison focused on her coffee. She wasn't ready to think about romance again. Still, what if there was a chance for love to come her way with someone she'd known her whole life? "All of this is about more than Josh.

I guess looking at all that New York *wasn't* showed me all the good that Mistletoe has to offer. Maybe it's simply one of those cliché-ish situations when one discovers that the grass isn't really greener on the other side of the fence."

Lori leaned back against the bench and nodded. "I'd say that's a lesson all of us have to learn at one time or another."

Madison fiddled with the rim of her cup. "I learned something much more important, as well."

"What's that?"

"In all of this, I shut out the most important One in my life—Jesus Christ. I made decisions based on feelings and never spent time praying about what I should do."

"So what now?"

Madison took another sip of her coffee. "I've got a few things that need to be made right. Then I suppose I'll ask my dad for a job until I figure out what I want to do."

"You're going to work at your father's plumbing store?"

"Thanks for the vote of confidence." Madison ignored the distaste in her friend's eyes. There were worse things than going from business owner to toilet saleswoman.

Lori nudged Madison with her elbow. "You could always open up another shop in town. I've been thinking that Mistletoe needs a good coffee shop with a Christmas theme. You could serve peppermint, gingerbread, eggnog, and pumpkin year-round, along with dozens of other mouthwatering flavors."

"I don't know." Madison held up her cup and grinned. "Are you trying to tell me you're getting tired of plain ol' black coffee?"

Lori grinned. "Just think about it."

Madison shook her head. "Not probable, but I will pray about it. First, though, I've got a call to make."

Madison dropped her empty cup into the trash bin and walked to the edge of the street. She fixed her gaze on her shop one last time—her *old* shop. She might not be able to make everything right, but it was time to try.

Josh glanced out the window of his apartment and lifted his arms to stretch the tight muscles in his back. He'd spent too many hours hunched over one of his popular 3-D wooden puzzles. The snow covering the town square sparkled in the late afternoon sunlight, and dark clouds roiled in the western skies. Yesterday had brought an inch of snow, and the weatherman predicted another two inches tonight; perfect conditions for the singles' yearly ski trip scheduled for this weekend.

About to turn away from the window, a flash of pink caught Josh's eye. A woman stood at the edge of the park, staring across the street toward the vicinity of Under the Mistletoe.

"Madison?" he whispered.

Blinking his eyes, he moved closer to the cold glass pane. No. It couldn't be her. Madison was two thousand miles away—with *that guy*. Albert the suave New Yorker and toy factory owner.

Not convinced, he took another look just as the woman turned her head. Josh frowned. It was her. Madison stood on the sidewalk, the wind ruffling the edges of her coat while she stared at her shop.

Josh turned away from the window and felt his jaw tense.

That was just like her—the new Madison, anyway—to show up in town and not have the decency to call him. He wasn't worried about his business, but he had thought they were friends.

He pulled off his sweatshirt, then dropped onto the bench press in the corner of his apartment and began doing a bicep curl. Concentrating on his breathing, he did twenty reps before switching to his other arm. He might have lost Madison, but he still had his friends, his church, and the town. He'd been wrong to think he was missing something in his life without her. The truth was, he didn't need her in order to be content. Not that he hadn't valued her friendship, but Sunday's sermon had reminded him just how important it was to allow God to be the One to fill the empty spots in his life with His presence. Josh couldn't rely on someone else to do that job. People would let him down, but God never would.

He gently set the weights down, then reached for a towel to wipe off the back of his neck. While he did long for a wife and family—someday—right now he was determined to be thankful for what the good Lord had given him, which was plenty. If he couldn't be content with what he had, then he'd end up being miserable.

The phone rang. Josh started in on his daily quota of pushups and let the answering machine pick it up. After the obligatory "I can't answer the phone right now" message, he waited, listening for the caller.

"Hey, Josh."

His mouth went dry. It was *her*.

"It's Madison. Are you there? We need to talk."

Chapter 8

Josh swallowed hard. There was no need for her to call him. It was too late for apologies. And what did she expect, anyway? To sweep back into town for a few days and make everything right so she could clear her conscience before whisking herself back to the big city? Albert could have her for all he cared. Let her work for some huge toy factory in the Big Apple where they mass-produced video games and other worthless toys that zapped every ounce of creativity from a child's mind.

Josh squeezed his eyes shut for a moment.

I'm sorry, Lord. That was uncalled for.

He smacked his fist against the bench press. He had no right to judge her decision, or Albert for that matter. He was probably a great guy who could offer more than Josh would ever be able to on a small-town artist's salary. And Madison deserved that. Still, he didn't want to talk to her. The only thing it would accomplish was to crush the already broken pieces of his heart into fine bits. It was his fault for never telling her how he felt. He'd have to live with those consequences. But he didn't have to talk to her.

"Josh? Josh, are you there? Pick up if you are."

Groaning at her persistence, he hesitated before crossing the room, then swiped the phone off the hook. "Yeah, I'm here—"

"Oh, good." He could hear her breath of relief. "Listen, I'm back in town, and I'd really like to see you. I–I've missed you."

"You missed me?" Josh clenched the cord of the phone between his fingers. She loved Albert, not him, and he wasn't going to forget it.

"I owe you an apology, Josh. I never said good-bye or told you about the shop. I tried to call, but that's no excuse. We were in business, and the new owners might do things differently." After a long pause, she cleared her throat. "It was wrong of me not to involve you in the decision."

So this was all about business. Of course. What had he expected with Albert in the picture now?

"Listen, Madison, it really doesn't matter. I'll still have a place to sell my toys—"

"But it *does* matter, Josh. I was wrong. If we could sit down and talk over a cup of coffee at Flossie's—"

Someone knocked at the apartment door.

"Listen, someone's at my door. I need to go. Best of luck to you with New York and Albert."

"But—"

"Bye, Madison."

Josh hung up the phone, hating the fact that she affected him as much as she did. He'd known the moment he saw that wistful gleam in her eyes when he'd first heard her say Albert's name, she'd lost her heart to someone else. And it hadn't been him. He'd been a fool to imagine their friendship would magically transform into love one day. And handling love like a laid-back, small-town boy had made him lose her to a fast-paced city slicker.

He moved to answer the door. None of that really mattered now, because it was over. Madison would stay for a few days before returning to New York. And one day he'd find another girl willing to live a quiet life with him on a hundred acres of land in the Montana mountains.

Madison snapped her cell phone shut, trying to process Josh's response. Snow began to fall in the square, large white flakes that made the decorated town look like a Christmas snow globe. She wiped an ice crystal from her cheek and blinked back her tears. She'd known there would be consequences to her actions, but never had she dreamed that Josh would refuse to see her. And it wasn't as if she'd expected him to proclaim his undying love to her, but not to want to see her at all? Not to let her finish apologizing for what she'd done?

One thing was certain—he wasn't in love with her anymore. Which was fine. Really. It wasn't as if she was in love with him. After just breaking things off with Albert, she wasn't ready for a rebound relationship, even if Josh was a friend she'd known forever. Lori never should have given her that ridiculous notion that Josh was in love with her.

Madison tilted her chin. She only wanted their friendship back.

Besides, now that she was renting her parents' house in town again, he wasn't going to be able to avoid her forever. Thursday nights at Flossie's, the singles' group at church. . .they were bound to run into each other, and she wasn't going to be able to stand it if their relationship continued along this awkward vein.

Crossing the street, she headed for Under the Mistletoe. At the curb, a car sped by, sending a wave of slush across the legs of her black pantsuit. She stepped onto the sidewalk, then reached down to assess the damage. Great. Now she was depressed *and* wet.

She pushed open the door to the familiar sound of jangling bells at the entrance of Under the Mistletoe. Rosemary was busy with a display of teddy bear ornaments near the counter. A quick glance around the shop confirmed there weren't any customers at the moment. Good. She'd be able to talk to Rosemary in private about the new owner.

"You're just in time. I was just getting ready to close up the shop." The blue-eyed teenager greeted her with a smile. "Welcome home, by the way."

"Thanks. I can't tell you how good it is to be back."

"How long will you be in town?"

"I'm staying, actually." Madison smiled at the declaration. "New York didn't. . ." She shrugged. "Well, it just didn't work out for me."

The young woman flashed a toothy white smile before flicking her ponytail off her shoulder. "That's wonderful news, though I can't blame you for wanting to see the rest of the world. Once I finish school in May, I'm heading for California. I want to be an actress."

Madison nodded in understanding, but she prayed that Rosemary wasn't searching for something that could never be found in money or fame. "Just keep in mind that sometimes the bright lights of the city never end up comparing to the warm, soft lights of home."

"Maybe, but I'm still determined to at least try to leave my mark on the world."

Perhaps Lori had been right when she said that everyone had to discover for themselves that life wasn't always greener on the other side. "I wanted to ask you about the new owner. Have you met them?"

Rosemary dusted off the front counter with a rag. "I think it's someone from out of town, though I'm not sure. The good thing is that they don't want any changes made, so at least I don't have to worry about losing my job."

Madison winced at Rosemary's words. Another name to add to the list of people affected by her rash decision. "I'm really glad to hear that. I'm sorry if you've been worried."

"I can always get a job working tables at Flossie's, but I enjoy working here."

Madison laughed. In her mind, working tables was one step up from selling toilets at her dad's store. "Trust me, I understand the feeling."

"Can I get you something? We're serving fresh eggnog today."

"No, I—I just finished some coffee." Madison bit her lip as she glanced around the shop. She'd put her heart and soul into each and every display. From the packages with their silver bows in the windows to the holiday wallpaper on the walls. She was going to miss it.

Stopping in front of a display of red Christmas stockings, she made a decision. "I would like to buy an ornament, though, before I leave."

"An ornament?" Rosemary giggled. "Well, this is the perfect place. I believe my former boss once boasted that the shop carried over a thousand unique ornaments."

Madison smiled at the comment and moved to a row of baskets filled with new ornaments that had come in since she'd left. "All I need is one today."

Ten minutes later, Madison took the wrapped ornament from Rosemary and moved toward the front door.

"Stop by again when you can."

"You know I will, Rosemary. Thanks."

For the first time all morning, Madison had a smile on her lips and a song ready to burst from her heart like a 1950s musical. Her plan might not work, but then, that really wasn't up to her.

Josh pulled open the door to his apartment. "Mrs. Robertson, I . . ." He quirked an eyebrow. It wasn't his elderly neighbor standing in the hallway, but the mayor. "Oh, Lori. Hi."

"I'm sorry. If I'm interrupting—"

"No, I just thought it was my neighbor. She was by for some sugar awhile ago and promised to bring the container back. Do you want to come in?"

"I can't stay." Lori pulled off her gloves, shoved them into her coat pockets, and stepped into his apartment. "I just needed to. . .well, in all honesty, to butt my nose into something that's not any of my business."

Josh couldn't help but laugh at her blunt statement. "Nothing like an honest politician. What's up?"

"It's about you and Madison."

Josh shook his head and held up his hand. "Wait a minute. There is no *me and Madison*."

"I know. Just hear me out." Lori took up his previous offer and plopped herself down on his couch. "Please?"

He sat across from her on his worn recliner. "I suppose."

Lori crossed her legs and caught his gaze. "Madison's back in town."

Considering he'd just talked to her thirty minutes ago. . . "I'm aware of that."

"Did you know that she's back to stay?"

"Excuse me?" How had that subject not come up in their conversation? "I just talked to her, and she never mentioned staying."

"Did you give her a chance?"

"Oh. I. . ." Josh's gaze dropped to the tiled living room floor. He felt guilt rush through him. He'd cut her off because he hadn't wanted his heart broken again. How could he have been such a jerk? "Does she know you're here?"

"No, but someone has to clear the air between you two."

"So you decided to play the role of matchmaker." Josh frowned. "I liked you better as the nosy politician."

"I thought you said honest politician."

Josh ignored the comment. "It's really none of your business, Lori."

"I told you up front that I was butting in. What can I say? I'm a romantic at heart."

Josh slapped his hands against his legs, stood, and walked to the window. "I don't know about Madison and me, but I'd like to know about Albert and New York. What happened? I thought she was happy."

"Sometimes happiness is right before your eyes and you don't know it until you lose it." Lori got up from the couch and moved to the door. "If you still love her, don't give up on her, Josh."

Lori slipped out the door, leaving Josh to wonder what had just transpired. Was Madison really in love with him? Or was this a matchmaking move by Lori to keep her friend in town?

Crossing the room, he sat down at his desk, slid open the top drawer, then pulled out a small box. He shook his head and dropped it back inside the drawer.

No. This was crazy. Just because Madison was planning to stay in Mistletoe didn't mean she was interested in him. Surely Lori knew that. He'd only end up letting Madison sweep away the remnants of his heart. He didn't have a shot at romance with Madison.

Josh stood up and whacked his leg against the corner of

the drawer in the process. *Ouch!* He sat back down, rubbing the sore spot. Wasn't that the same excuse he'd used over the past few years? Madison would never love him as more than a friend? He only had his heart to give. . . .

He picked up the box again and slid off the lid. He'd heard the longing in her voice when she called but had tried to ignore it.

Maybe his heart was enough.

Maybe Lori was right and he shouldn't give up on a relationship with Madison. At the least he owed her a cup of coffee at Flossie's. From there, only God knew what was going to happen next.

Chapter 9

Madison headed down the sidewalk toward Main Street and Flossie's, then stopped at the curb. This was crazy. Josh had made it clear he wasn't interested in her words of apology, nor should he be, and no gift was going to make a difference. She'd blown it with him. End of story. Why should he forgive her? She certainly didn't deserve it.

Fingering the small package in her pocket, she debated what to do. The light turned green, giving pedestrians the go-ahead, but she still didn't move. She could see Josh's loft up ahead, the white Christmas lights lining the windows. The traffic light turned red, and she forced herself not to turn around and run back to her house past the other side of the square. The truth was that Josh had every right to be mad at her. All she wanted, though, was another chance to talk to him. It wasn't as if he were one to hold grudges. Far from it. Unlike Albert, Josh's Christianity wasn't something he used when convenient. He'd forgive her. Eventually.

The light turned green again. Sucking up her courage, Madison stepped off the curb onto the street. A figure walked toward her, blurred by her tears that threatened to escape.

She blinked and stopped in the middle of the street. "Josh?"

"Madison, I—I saw you down here earlier and thought I'd try to catch you." He combed his fingers though his hair, looking almost as nervous as she felt. "I believe I owe you a cup of coffee. . .and an apology."

"You owe *me* an apology?" Her eyes widened in disbelief. "Why in the world would you think you owed me an apology?"

"Because you wanted to talk to me on the phone, and I was wrong to cut you off."

"You weren't wrong." She looked up into his blue eyes and felt as if her legs were about to melt into the pavement. "I'm the one who's supposed to be apologizing."

"Okay, then which would you prefer?" He flashed her a smile. She was definitely a goner. "Flossie's or a walk in the park?"

Madison's heart swelled at the invitation. She couldn't resist the crisp, sunny, late November afternoon—or his company. "Definitely the park—"

A car honked. She felt Josh's hand against her elbow as he steered her out of the middle of the street and toward the town center. Madison tried to control her breathing, but she couldn't think straight. What was wrong with her—and with Josh? Thirty minutes ago, he had refused to speak to her. Now he had his hand around her elbow and was leading her protectively across the street. Her pulse raced, her cheeks became flushed, and her insides felt as if they were trembling. Why was it that every time she was around him, she felt as though she was...in love?

In love?

But that was impossible. She wasn't in love with Josh. She couldn't be in love. All she needed to do was apologize for the way she had acted, then they would both go their separate ways. He'd sell his wooden toys in the new owner's shop, and she'd sell plumbing equipment to the three surrounding counties. No one ever said life was always fair—or full of happily-ever-after endings.

Her feet crunched into the snow as they crossed the edge of the park toward the bench where they'd had a snowball fight only a few short weeks ago. Where she'd laughed until her sides had ached. She took another peek at his dimpled smile, and the truth hit her. She did love him. Joshua Dunkin who had always been there for her. Who knew she loved hot chocolate with marshmallows, root beer, and licorice. Who knew how to make her smile—

"I should have brought something hot for you to drink." He wrapped his arm around her. "You're shaking."

She shook her head, still reeling at her heart's revelation. The cold weather wasn't what had her trembling. "It's really not that cold. I'm just..."

In love with you, Joshua.

"Just what?" His gaze seemed to penetrate her heart.

Madison sat down on the bench and shoved her hands into her coat pockets. Before she attempted to figure out what had happened between Main Street and the park bench, she had to make things right between them. "Josh, I called earlier because I needed to apologize. It was wrong for me to leave for New York without talking to you. I got caught up in a world that didn't exist, and I learned the hard way that what I had here was something worth holding on to. In my impulsiveness, I almost lost everything. My friends, family, a good church home...and you."

He sat beside her, his gaze affixed to her face. "What do you mean, 'and me'?"

"I mean..." Madison blinked and looked away. Her insides felt like mashed potatoes. How could she tell him that she loved him? Needing to clear her head, she started to stand up, but he grabbed her hand and pulled her back down beside him.

"No. Don't leave, Madison. Please." He didn't let go of her hand. "I have my own confession to make."

"What do you mean?"

"I've loved you since the seventh grade, if you can believe that."

So Lori hadn't embellished on that line. "Why didn't you ever tell me?"

"I don't know. You made it clear that you only wanted to be friends, and I guess I hoped that someday our relationship would turn into something more serious. Then Albert came along."

Albert... New York... She'd been such a fool. "You should have told me."

"Would I have been enough to keep you here?"

"I don't know, but. . ." She lowered her head, avoiding his

gaze. Experiencing New York had opened her eyes to what she had right here in Mistletoe. If she hadn't gone, she might have always wondered. Gathering her courage, she turned to look at him. "You're enough to keep me here now."

Josh felt the warmth of Madison's hand in his and tried to grasp what she had just said. He was enough to keep her here? Was it really possible that Madison felt the same way about him that he felt about her? She sat beside him, her lips slightly pursed... and perfectly kissable. Josh looked up at the branch above him, smiled, then, unable to resist, reached out and ran his thumb down her cheek. "Do you know where we are?"

"Mistletoe? The town square?"

He shook his head.

Her eyes widened as she looked at him. "Then what do you mean?"

He pointed at the clump of mistletoe hanging above them from a tree branch. "I think it's a sign."

"A sign?"

Her soft laugh encouraged him to do what he should have done years ago. Josh cupped her face in his hands and kissed her. The sweetness of her mouth against his was enough for him to want to kick himself over what he'd been missing out on all these years.

Josh pulled back after a moment, hardly believing that he'd just kissed Madison in the middle of the town square. He brushed a snowflake off the tip of her nose, grabbed both of her hands, and pulled them against his wildly beating heart. "Madison, you know I can't give you the city and all the excitement of New York. I'm just a hardworking artist from the mountains of Montana."

"There's no place in this world that I'd rather be than right here. Right now. With you." She pulled something out of her pocket. "I have something for you."

He opened the small box she'd handed him and held up an ornament of the state of Montana that read HOME IS WHERE THE HEART IS. Maybe his dream of their relationship ending with a white picket fence and 2.5 kids wasn't so out of reach after all.

"Where's your heart, Madison?"

Madison looked up into Josh's blue eyes, realizing for the first time what it really felt like to be in love. And true love had always been right before her eyes. God had taken away what she never needed in the first place and had given her something far better.

She swallowed hard. "I think I just lost my heart."

"Keep that thought, because I have something for you, as well." Joshua handed her a wrapped box from his own pocket, the smile never leaving his face.

Inside was a key on a ribbon, not the ornament she'd expected. She looked up at him. "I don't understand."

"Come with me."

Taking her hand, they hurried toward the edge of the park

toward the shops. "Where are we going?"

"You'll see."

Under the Mistletoe loomed straight ahead as they crossed the quiet street. "The store is closed. . . ." Madison stopped in front of her old store and let her words fade into the chilly afternoon. The key. . .the new owner. . .Josh. "You're the new owner?"

He nodded. "I know we normally exchange ornaments every year, but I was hoping this year we could do things differently."

"But the shop?"

"Unlock it."

Trembling, Madison pushed the key into the lock and opened the door. The familiar bouquet of cinnamon and vanilla filled her senses.

Josh stood in the doorway and took her hand. "I thought we could run the store together. Maybe even add a coffee shop specializing in Christmas flavors."

"You've been talking to Lori." She let out a merry laugh. Apparently, she owed her friend a lot. "I can't believe this. You bought my store."

"Our store, Madison." He grasped her hands. "I want you to be my wife."

She pulled him into the shop, away from the chilly breeze, and wrapped her arms around his neck. "Yes. Yes, I'll marry you."

Suddenly everything was clear. She was the lost child whose heavenly Father had welcomed her home, then showered her with gifts far beyond her wildest dreams. And He'd shown her that the best gifts of all don't always come in big, flashy packages. Like the King of kings being born in a stable because there was no room for Mary and Joseph at the inn. Like her longing for something beyond the radius of the small town and realizing that everything she'd ever needed was right here in front of her.

LISA HARRIS

Lisa is a wife, mother, and award-winning author who has been writing both fiction and nonfiction for the Christian market since 2000. She and her husband, Scott, along with their three children, live in northern South Africa as missionaries. To learn more about her other books, please go to www.lisaharriswrites.com.

All I Want for Christmas Is. . .You

by Kim Vogel Sawyer

Dedication

For Kathy A., who lent me Daisy;
and for Kathy H., who took me on the Sausalito ferry.
Love you both muchly!

Thanks be to God for his indescribable gift!
2 CORINTHIANS 9:15

Chapter 1

December

Kathy Morgan clung to the railing of the Blue and Gold Fleet transport ferry. A cold, salt-scented breeze tugged at the long knitted scarf she'd tied over her hair. The scarf's dancing tails whipped the underside of her chin, and icy water droplets spritzed her face, but she remained at the rail rather than retreating to the reading lounge where it would be dry and warmer.

For once the ever-present winter fog had decided to hover well above the water, giving Kathy a limited view of Sausalito's houses climbing the side of the mountain. It had always seemed to her that the city rose from the water, and today the sight brought vivid memories of another body of water, another mountain view. How long had it been since she'd thought of Mistletoe?

A wave of homesickness struck, surprising in its intensity. For the past five years, Sausalito and San Francisco had been her world. She'd given little thought to the small mountainside community of her childhood. Since Mom's death four years ago, she'd had no reason to visit Mistletoe, preferring instead to use her vacation time to travel to Hawaii, Las Vegas, the Florida Keys... So why now this longing for Mistletoe?

Sighing, she turned and leaned against the railing. The cold of the metal seeped through her jacket to her hips, and she shivered. Hugging herself, she closed her eyes and conjured pictures of the place that had been home from the time of her birth until her graduation from the college at nearby Kalispell.

Images of Christmas filled her head. A snow-frosted park and massive cedar trees glistening with twinkle lights. A life-size nativity in the center of the town square. Idyllic shops, as if plucked from an English village—their windows draped with evergreen boughs and crimson velvet bows. The scent of cinnamon and spice filling the air. And everywhere, hanging in every doorway and from the corner lampposts, clusters of mistletoe, inviting romance to bloom at a moment's notice.

Her eyes popped open. Romance... Was that the source of all this reminiscing? Her twenty-eighth birthday had passed only three weeks ago. Her girlhood friends, who still resided in Mistletoe, had sent their annual birthday card. In it, Lori had scrawled a teasing message beneath her signature: *Hey, time's up, Kath. Have you found your Mr. Right?*

Kathy whirled and wrapped her fingers around the railing. The rush of chilly air in her face made her eyes water. Or was something else causing moisture to blur her vision? She blinked rapidly, refusing to acknowledge the lump that filled her throat.

It had all sounded so perfect back when she, Lori, Madison, and Deanna made the pact. They'd been so young, so idealistic.

Suddenly she had the desire to return to that simpler time, the slower pace. But Mistletoe was a lifetime ago. One couldn't recapture the past.

The ferry's horn blasted, alerting her to the journey's end. She snatched up her briefcase and joined the handful of other passengers disembarking at Fisherman's Wharf. The bus ride to Montgomery Avenue should give her just enough time to clear her head and get her focus back where it belonged.

She hopped out at the corner stop and wove between the many briefcase-carrying pedestrians to reach the doors of the towering glass and mortar building that housed the Andale Advertising Agency. She swished her identification card through the security reader and, at the prompt, entered her password. A buzzer sounded, approving her entry. The heels of her fashionable boots clicked on the marble floor as she moved briskly toward the elevators. She rode to the sixth floor, waved to the receptionist, and stopped at the refreshment center. Inhaling the pleasant aromas, she poured a cup of coffee and doctored it with two packets of sugar and a splash of mocha creamer.

In her windowless cubicle, Kathy propped the briefcase on top of the credenza and hung her scarf over the cubicle wall. Sitting in her black leather executive chair, she popped the lid off the paper cup and took a cautious sip. The aromatic steam pleased her senses, and she took a second, longer draw on the coffee, letting the flavorful brew warm her from the inside out after her chilly ride across the bay.

The coffee washed the odd yearnings of the early morning away, and she felt ready to start the day. Placing the coffee cup on an ironstone coaster bearing Andale's logo, she reached beneath her desk to boot up her computer. She had no sooner pushed the button than someone pulled her executive chair backward slightly and delivered a kiss on the top of her head. The scent of British Sterling cologne wafted past her nostrils. She spun around in the chair. "Chad! Don't sneak up on me like that."

He laughed, his eyes flashing. "Then how would you like for me to sneak up on you? Name the way, and I'll do it. Anything for you, baby."

His impish grin coupled with the teasing tone made Kathy laugh despite the start he'd just given her. She and Chad Cole had begun their employment at Andale at the same time. As new employees, they'd banded together to offer each other moral support, and in a short time a friendship had developed. Lately, though, she'd gotten the impression Chad wanted more. *Time's up, Kath!* She wondered. . . Was it time to allow Chad to be more than a friend?

Rocking in her chair, she gave a mock scowl. "Shouldn't you be getting ready for your presentation to Murphy on the Feline Fritters account?"

Chad groaned. He often complained about the presentation side of his job, saying it was too much like public speaking—the only fear he admitted possessing.

"Aren't you prepared?"

"My part is ready to go." He cocked one eyebrow. "What about you? Do you have the jingle written?"

Kathy resisted echoing his groan. She loved writing advertising jingles—capturing the essence of a product in a concise, attention-grabbing series of words—but this particular account had tested her ability. Nearly every idea she'd come up with had seemed absurd rather than appealing. "It's written."

"Let's hear it." Chad perched on the edge of her desk, crossed his ankles, and then folded his arms. He looked at her attentively.

She pressed her lips together for a moment, then shrugged. It would be public before long anyway. Perhaps a practice run with Chad wasn't amiss. She sang, "Give your kitty a tasty treat; Feline Fritters just can't be beat. Chicken, beef, and seafood, too—your feline friend will meow, 'Thank you.'" She waved both hands beside her face and warbled, "Mee-yow-ow-ow."

Chad stared at her, his lips twitching for several long seconds before he burst out laughing. "Your feline friend will meow, 'Thank you'?" He held his stomach and laughed harder.

She bumped his leg with her foot. "Hey, knock it off. It rhymes!"

"It sure does!" He continued to chuckle, shaking his head. "Kathy, you are priceless."

She turned her chair around to face the computer screen.

Chad caught the chair's back and gave it a spin so she faced him. "Did I offend you?" To his credit, he looked truly remorseful—an emotion not frequently seen in his teasing eyes.

She sighed. "I know it's a little...goofy. But it's hard to come up with something serious when you're talking about cat food."

"Actually, I think it's cute." He smirked, tapping the end of her nose with his finger. "Just like you."

She twisted away from his touch, grimacing. "Chad, please. . ." His affectionate gestures, while endearing at times, weren't appropriate in the office, as she'd mentioned many times before.

He backed up. "Tell you what—I'll make it up to you. I'll buy you lunch. Anywhere you want to go."

She bit the inside of her cheek, fighting a smile. "Anywhere?"

"Anywhere," he reiterated.

"Even Callieban's?"

Chad raised both brows. "Callieban's!" The most exclusive café near the bay, Callieban's was known for twenty-five-dollar appetizers and forty-dollar lunch plates. He huffed. "You don't play fair, babe. But. . ."—he braced his hands on the arms of her chair, bringing his face only inches from hers—"for you. . . Callieban's."

Pressing herself against the back of the chair, Kathy put both palms against his chest. "Then it's a date. But for now, scoot. I have work to do."

He pushed off from the chair and gave a mock salute. Then, whistling the tune to her Feline Fritters jingle, he headed around the corner.

Kathy looped her scarf around her neck and made her way toward the elevators. Chad had called midmorning to say he had an errand to run before lunch, but he'd reserved a table and would meet her at Callieban's at twelve fifteen. She glanced at her wristwatch as she waited for the elevator. Even though she'd worked right up to twelve, she'd still make it on time if she caught a cable car.

The elevator opened at the same time a voice called, "Ms. Morgan!"

She turned from the elevator and spotted the company's president, Mr. Andale himself, approaching. Her heart thudded when he stretched out his hand in greeting. "Mr. Andale." She could count on one hand the number of times in her years of employment she'd spoken directly to the head of the advertising agency. Normally he stayed sequestered in his top-floor office and allowed the various managers to deliver messages.

After giving her hand a brief, impersonal shake, he said, "I'm sure you're on your lunch break, so I'll only take a minute of your time. Do you recall the jingle you wrote for California Cruisin'? It has been awhile—a year ago March, I believe."

Kathy nodded. "Yes, sir." She'd been particularly proud of the jingle for the largest cruise line in the state. Set to an island beat, the jingle played not only in radio ads, but also at the end of every television commercial. Rumor had it the cruise line's private band used it as an opener to on-deck concerts.

"I received a royalty check this morning from California Cruisin', and I had the payroll clerk cut your portion." He slipped it from a hidden pocket in his jacket and placed it in her hand. "I believe you'll see it's quite substantial."

A glance confirmed his statement. Kathy's stomach trembled when she counted the zeroes. "Wow. . ."

Mr. Andale chuckled. "I've been in the business a long time, and even I'm not accustomed to seeing royalties like that. But the line of commercials has been very popular, and your jingle was a big part of their appeal. Congratulations."

She gulped. "Thank you, sir."

"In addition to that check, I held a quick telephone conference with the board of directors earlier this morning. We agreed we would like to reward you for your extraordinary efforts by giving you some additional vacation time."

Kathy stared at him, mute.

He raised one finger. "But there's a catch. You've got to take the days prior to the first of the year. It's already December 3, so you'd need to make plans quickly."

She licked her lips and nodded. "That won't be a problem."

His laughter made her smile. "Congratulations again, Ms. Morgan. Enjoy your lunch, your bonus, and your vacation."

"Oh, I will!" Kathy watched him stride back toward the corner of the floor where his private elevator waited, but she remained rooted in place for several minutes, barely able to believe the good fortune that had just befallen her. Wouldn't Chad be pleased!

Chapter 2

Kathy waited until the waitress took their order before surreptitiously showing Chad the check from Mr. Andale.

Chad released a low whistle. "Whoa, baby, that's a lot of doggy biscuits!"

Grinning at Chad's pet term for "dollars," she gave a nod. "I know." She slipped the check back into her purse. "It will fund that extra vacation I've just been given."

Chad sat back in his chair, pinching his chin between his thumb and forefinger. The gleam in his eyes sent a niggle of discomfort through Kathy's chest.

"What are you thinking?"

He caught her hand and stroked her knuckles with his thumb. "Do you suppose we could make that vacation something extra special?"

She wasn't certain when *her* vacation had turned into *their* vacation. "What do you mean?"

His thumb traced a circle around the knuckle of her ring finger. "How long have we been dating?"

Although she had viewed their time together more as friends hanging out than as boyfriend and girlfriend dating, Kathy shrugged. "Five years, I guess."

"Five years, four months, and eleven days." He scowled slightly. "I've been extraordinarily patient, waiting for our relationship to go to the next level."

She opened her mouth to speak, but he held up his hand, forestalling her response. "And I'm not complaining. I decided a long time ago that you're a woman worth waiting for, and I accept your values, even if they are a tad outdated." His smile softened the perceived reprimand. "But I say it's time for us to think. . .next step."

Her hand, where his thumb continued to draw lazy circles, tingled. She slipped it from his grasp and scratched the skin.

He leaned toward her, his expression fervent. "Kathy, listen. We could fly to Vegas and spend a week or two really getting to know each other. Maybe the check you got was meant for that purpose—to give us an excuse to move our relationship forward."

"Married?" Kathy drew back, her hand pressed to her pounding heart.

Surprise flashed across his face, but it disappeared so quickly that she couldn't be sure she'd read him correctly. "Sure, why not? If that's how you want it."

"Just like that—get married?"

He snorted. "It isn't *just like that*. After as long as we've been together. . ." He took a deep breath and captured her hand again. "Sure, married. Why not? I'll be thirty in another three months. It's about time to settle down." Was he speaking to her or himself? "I think we'd be happy together. Don't you?"

Kathy considered his question. She got along well with Chad, even if she thought he was a little too flippant at times. Still, a person could consider that facet of his personality charming and lighthearted. They had a comfortable relationship—she genuinely liked Chad. In the back of her mind, the line from her birthday card replayed: *Have you found your Mr. Right?* She searched Chad's face. Was he her Mr. Right?

"Kath?"

She realized he still awaited an answer. She opened her mouth to say something—anything—but the waitress returned, carrying a tray with two bowls of steaming clam chowder and a basket of cheesy biscuits. Kathy nearly heaved a sigh. *Saved by the bell. . .er, bowl. . .*

That evening, huddling in the reading lounge of the ferry as it chugged beneath the Golden Gate Bridge on the return trip to Sausalito, Kathy replayed her lunch date with Chad and his unexpected proposal. When they had finished lunch, she promised to consider his proposal, but she asked him to allow her a few uninterrupted days of thought. The disappointment in his eyes nearly prompted her to blurt out an agreement, but something had stopped the words.

Now she wondered. . .why hadn't she accepted Chad's proposal? *Have you found your Mr. Right?* The question haunted her. How could she know for sure? She hugged her purse to her stomach, and she remembered the check Mr. Andale had given her. Nibbling her lower lip, she considered Chad's suggestion. Then she balanced it against her first thought, which had been a private vacation. Suddenly the idea of getting away—someplace where she could think about her future and whether or not Chad should be a part of it—became an overwhelming desire.

Why not go to Mistletoe?

The question seemed to slip from the fog and into her brain. But unlike fog, which eventually dissipated, the idea didn't drift away. The morning's longing rose again, stronger than before—to explore her childhood haunts, laugh with her high school girlfriends, examine the shops, walk through the park, and put wreaths of holly on her parents' graves. To experience Christmas—the Christmas she remembered as a little girl. And nowhere else on earth could she do that except Mistletoe, Montana.

The ferry's blaring horn awakened her from her musings. She tugged her jacket collar up around her chin as she left the ferry and climbed the hill to the Victorian home that had been turned into an apartment she shared with three other single women. It would be even colder in Mistletoe, but she owned sweaters. If she needed to, she'd use some of that royalty check to buy more. Then she'd pack all of them, stay in the bed-and-breakfast inn run by old Mrs. Flanagan, and give this idea of marrying Chad some serious thought.

Surely, in Mistletoe, where there would be no distractions, she'd be able to discover the truth of whether Chad was her Mr. Right.

Kathy paid the taxi driver, smiled her thanks, and stepped onto the curb. With the price of the tab from the Missoula International Airport to Mistletoe, she could have made the down payment on a vehicle. Not for the first time, she considered renewing her driver's license. But as always, remembrance of the cause of her mother's death—an automobile accident—immediately squelched the idea.

Chad had often reasoned that people died crossing the street, too. And that all of her walking could have deadly consequences. But Kathy made no pretense of making sense of her fear of driving. She just knew it existed.

After the taxi pulled away, she stood for a moment and looked up and down Main Street. Nostalgia washed over her, bringing a rush of memories in such rapid succession she could barely grasp one before another started. Why had she gone so long between visits?

Her heart pattered high in her chest, excitement filling her. Even though no one met her to offer a personal welcome, she felt completely drawn in simply by standing on the same sidewalk where she had stood as a child, holding a dripping ice cream cone while her mother laughingly mopped her face with an embroidered handkerchief.

Tears welled, and she sniffed hard. It felt so good to come *home*.

After a few minutes of reflection, she pulled up the handle of her suitcase and headed for the corner. If she remembered correctly, Mrs. Flanagan's Bed-and-Breakfast was on the corner of Maple and Second, just a few blocks away. The gentle *bumpity-bump* of the suitcase's wheels on the bricked sidewalk reminded her of the little red wagon she used to pull around town, hauling her teddy bears and dolls. The memory brought yet another smile. After she settled in at the B&B, maybe she'd take a walk to Elm Street. Her street.

When she turned the corner toward Maple, she spotted the yellow and white Queen Anne house, and her heart skipped a beat when she saw the little scrolled VACANCY sign attached to the bottom edge of the B&B's decorative placard. The house's yellow paint appeared to have faded, but the abundance of white gingerbread trim remained the same.

As a child, Kathy had always wanted to climb the rose trellis on the far side of the wraparound porch, but fear of being pricked by thorns had kept her feet on the ground. Probably for the best, she concluded. Now, in December, the trellis bore no roses, but Mrs. Flanagan had wound plastic holly vines with bright red berries through the lattice. Christmas everywhere, just as she'd remembered.

A little note on the door encouraged her to walk right on in—so different from San Francisco!—and she did so after twisting the key to ring the brass bell mounted on the inside of the carved oak door. Even before she had the door latched behind her, a wrinkled, white-haired woman scurried from the far end of the hallway, hands outstretched, beaming a smile that brightened the entire foyer.

"If it isn't Kathleen June Morgan, as I live and breathe!"

Kathy found herself wrapped in one of Mrs. Flanagan's famous hugs. The old woman still smelled of sautéed onions. Kathy clung to her, eyes closed, savoring the warm welcome.

"How did you know it was me?" she asked when they finally pulled apart.

"Why, who could forget that flamin' red hair and those darlin' freckles?" Mrs. Flanagan clucked and shook her head, her pale gray eyes sparkling. "No other girl in all of Mistletoe could hold a candle to your bright hair."

Kathy grimaced. There were times she'd cheerfully trade her trademark hair and freckles for the anonymity of blond hair and a creamy complexion.

Mrs. Flanagan laughed, tweaking Kathy's nose. "Now quit that scowlin'. Your mother, bless her soul, wore her flamin' hair proudly, and so should you." She sighed, fondness underscoring the release of breath. "Your mama was a beauty, Kathy. And you are, too."

Tears stung again. Although Chad told her on a regular basis she was attractive, somehow it held more meaning coming from this woman who'd known her since infancy. "Thank you, Mrs. Flanagan."

The woman propped her small fists on her bony hips. "And are you stayin' in my inn?"

"If you have room."

"If I have room, she says! As if she'd come into Bethlehem instead of Mistletoe." Mrs. Flanagan clucked again, shaking her head in mock dismay. "I'd put myself on the porch and give you my room if need be, but thankfully enough I won't need to." She snorted, then winked, gesturing for Kathy to follow her up the winding, spindled staircase that led to the second floor. "You follow me, darlin'. You are stayin' in the Christmas suite. Just this mornin' the reservation got canceled, and I'm thinkin' now it was the good Lord's doin'. At the time, though, I confess I fussed a bit."

They passed two closed doors and came to the end of the hall, where Mrs. Flanagan removed a silver skeleton key from her pocket and turned it in the brass lock. "Do you remember the Christmas suite, my dear?"

Kathy stepped into the room and let out a delighted gasp. "Oh, Mrs. Flanagan, it's lovely!" She perched on the edge of the antique white iron bed, which wore a red-and-green calico Irish chain quilt, and let her gaze rove the room. Trailing green vines of ivy climbed the wallpaper. Strands of silk holly with plastic red berries served as valances over the lace-covered windows. Rising, she crossed to the dresser, where a pitcher and bowl painted with poinsettias stood proudly on an embroidered dresser scarf. She pressed her finger to a cluster of tiny knots that formed berries in the midst of holly leaves stitched into the linen runner. Her brows pinched together. Why did it seem so familiar?

"Aye, it's one your mother made," Mrs. Flanagan said, as if in response to her unspoken question. "As are the pillow covers, and the charmin' quilt on the bed, and the framed needlework hangin' above the bed. Always handy with a needle, she was." Tears winked in the woman's eyes. "So will you be comfortable in here, darlin'?"

Kathy dashed across the room to give Mrs. Flanagan an impulsive hug. "Oh, Mrs. Flanagan, being here with Mother's handiwork is as good as being in my own house on Elm Street. Thank you."

The thin arms tightened around Kathy's back. "Thank you, darlin', for comin' home. How my old heart has missed your mama. . .and you. Havin' you here makes my Christmas complete."

Tears stung Kathy's eyes. "Mine, too."

Mrs. Flanagan gave Kathy a quick pat on the back, then let go. She bustled toward the door, calling over her shoulder, "Get yourself settled in. You've got a private bath, so take a long soak in the tub if you like. Use the telephone to call old friends. Make yourself at home. And, oh!" She paused in the doorway, pointing a gnarled finger in Kathy's direction. "This is a bed-and-breakfast for everyone but you—for you, it's a bed-and-breakfast-and-lunch-and-supper, so I'll expect to see you in the kitchen at six tonight."

Kathy laughed. "It's a date."

Mrs. Flanagan winked once more, then disappeared down the hallway. Kathy closed the door, her words echoing in the Christmas-themed room. She'd made the same comment to Chad just two weeks ago, when he'd promised to take her to Callieban's. *"It's a date."* The words brought him to the forefront of her thoughts.

She sank into a red velvet chair in the corner of the room, and her gaze shifted to the tiny carved table beside the chair. A French Provincial rotary-dial telephone awaited her use. A little drawer in the table revealed the Mistletoe telephone book. Mrs. Flanagan had said to use the phone to catch up with old friends.

Lifting the book to her lap, she flipped it open to the *C*s. "Lori Compton..."

Chapter 3

After the second ring, Kathy heard a voice chirp, "Hello?"

"Hello. Is this Lori Compton?"

"Yes. Who is—wait! Kathy?"

Kathy smiled, hugging the receiver to her cheek. How good it felt to be recognized. "Yep, it's me."

The happy squeal made Kathy cringe, but she laughed. "And guess what? I'm in Mistletoe."

"You're not!"

"I am."

Another squeal nearly pierced Kathy's eardrum. She briefly explained her unexpected bonus and the snap decision to spend Christmas in Mistletoe. "I hope to spend at least a little time with you while I'm here. I know you're busy as *mayor*."

"And getting ready for the wedding," Lori reminded her. Kathy could picture her friend's impish grin. "I'm sure I sent you the newspaper article announcing my engagement."

"Well . . ." Kathy hedged, guilt striking. She had received an invitation to Lori's wedding and had intended to mail a gift, but she had set it aside, thinking she'd get to it when she wasn't so busy. Only the time had never come.

"Since Deanna, Madison, and I are engaged," Lori went on, apparently unaffected by Kathy's evasive answer, "the pact is nearly complete."

The expectant note in her voice opened the door for Kathy to share about Chad's proposal. She opened her mouth. And closed it. Opened it again. Closed it. What should she say?

"Kath? You okay?"

"Yes." Kathy forced a glib tone. "I'm fine—just a little tired from my trip. Maybe the four of us could get together for lunch."

"That would be wonderful! How about next week, on Monday? I'm tied up this week between wedding plans and helping Russell prepare for the Christmas program at church."

"I'm free," Kathy said. She had no set plans other than exploring, remembering, relaxing. And deciding whether or not to become Mrs. Chad Cole. . .

"I'll call Madison and Deanna and make the arrangements. How about Flossie's, right at noon?"

Kathy's mouth watered at the suggestion of the little café where she and her friends used to gather after football games. "Do they still have their famous apple fritters?"

"Complete with two thousand calories each."

Kathy laughed. "Perfect!"

"Great. We'll see you then. And, Kath?"

"Yeah?"

"Welcome home."

Kathy hung up with a smile on her face. She drew in a deep breath, replaying Lori's comment about the pact being nearly complete. Why hadn't she told Lori about Chad?

Maybe because she wanted Chad to know first.

Her heart thumped. Wouldn't it be fun to end the year with a wedding celebration? Then all four friends would have honored the pact. The romance of the idea brought a nervous giggle. All it would take was a quick e-mail, and Chad could start planning their Las Vegas wedding. A glance at the old-fashioned telephone let her know she wouldn't find Internet service in Mrs. Flanagan's inn, but the public library should have access.

She jumped up from the chair and reached for her coat, but as her hands closed on the tweed fabric, her gaze fell on an antique secretary tucked in the corner behind the bed. She walked slowly to the secretary. Pulling down the desktop, she located a smorgasbord of lined and unlined paper, calligraphy pens, rubber stamps and ink pads—everything she needed to custom design a special missive.

A smile tugged at her lips. How much more romantic would it be for Chad to receive a hand-written acceptance rather than an impersonal e-mail? She pulled out the pressed-back chair, sat, and chose mottled ecru paper. She carefully stamped a red rose at the top left-hand corner, then uncapped a black, wide-nib pen. Using her best cursive, she wrote, *Dearest Chad, I've decided all I want for Christmas is. . .*

A half hour later, the letter—which Kathy considered a work of art—was complete. She folded the paper into thirds and slipped it into a matching envelope. Using the same pen, she scripted his name and address, choosing the agency's address rather than his apartment's. He only checked his apartment mail once a week, and she wanted her letter to be opened as quickly as possible. Her heart gave a double beat, and for a moment Kathy wondered if fear or excitement had caused the reaction.

She shook her head, frowning at her nervous thought. Excitement, of course!

Glancing at her wristwatch, she reasoned she could walk to the post office and be back by six o'clock if she hurried. She slipped on her coat and headed outside, turning at the end of the sidewalk in the direction of town. She'd go to the post office and purchase a stamp, and in a day or two Chad would have his answer. Recalling his aggravation when she'd told him she'd be going to Mistletoe alone instead of to Vegas with him, she felt a pang of regret. Maybe she should have just agreed to his plan rather than insisting on this trip down memory lane.

But then she wouldn't have enjoyed Mrs. Flanagan's warm hug or Lori's enthusiastic welcome. She wouldn't have experienced the joy of homecoming. Even if it delayed her wedding, she couldn't regret coming back to Mistletoe.

Ahead, in the middle of the sidewalk, she spotted a red and blue postal box, and her heart gave a leap. Maybe she wouldn't have to go all the way to the post office after all. Eager to get her letter on its way, she jogged the last few feet and pulled down the drop door. With a whispered, "Here it goes," she slipped the letter inside and gave the door a slam.

And then she clapped her hands to her cheeks and cried, "Oh no!"

An empty leather pouch swinging on his shoulder and his basset hound, Daisy, lumbering along beside him, Erik Hoffman exited the back door of the post office. He had one more task to complete for the day—emptying the postal service collection box that stood at the far corner of the town square. The box was used mainly by tourists to send postcards purchased in one of Mistletoe's many shops. Lately the number of cards had increased, which indicated the town's declining economy was on the upswing. *Thank You, Lord.*

Erik smiled as Daisy trotted ahead, leading him in the right direction. People sometimes laughed at a postman accompanied by a dog instead of running from one, but he enjoyed the basset's company. Plus she was so social, if he did encounter a dog that might be tempted to bite his leg, Daisy would completely defuse the situation by sheer friendliness. He couldn't think of another place where he would be allowed to take his dog to work on a daily basis. Only in Mistletoe. . .

Although relatively new to Mistletoe, having transferred from Helena two years ago, he'd fully adopted the quaint town as his home. Up in the mountains, Mistletoe had managed to escape much of the political correctness of big-city life. The nativity scene in the center of the town square, not only accepted but openly lauded by the community, gave evidence of the town's unique attitude. Now that he'd experienced the wonder of Mistletoe, he couldn't imagine living anywhere else.

Up ahead the postal box waited, and Erik unfastened the flap of his pouch in anticipation of transferring mail from the box to his bag. Suddenly Daisy halted, bounced on her front feet, and released a low-pitched woof.

"What is it, girl?" Erik's steps slowed, and he squinted ahead. Despite the sporadic streetlamps, the late afternoon shadows cast by the mountain peaks made it difficult to make out details, but he noticed a strange, bobbing...something...on the far side of the postal box. Red and green, somewhat round in shape, it bounced in an offbeat pattern. Had a child tied a balloon to the box?

He gave Daisy's head a reassuring pat. "I'm sure whatever it is, we aren't in mortal danger. Let's go check it out, huh?" The dog lunged forward, yanking the leash from Erik's hand.

Daisy rounded the box and immediately began leaping, tongue lolling, while releasing intermittent yelps of joy. A shriek sounded in response, and Erik realized the bobbing object wasn't a balloon, but a head. Based on the pitch of the shriek, a woman's head. When she sent a panicked look over the top of the box, his breath caught. She was an exceptionally attractive woman.

Another series of deep-throated woofs spurred Erik to action. He captured the dog's leash, pulling her away from the wide-eyed woman. "Hang on a minute. Daisy won't hurt you, unless you consider being licked to death painful. Let me get her tied to the lamppost over here. Just stay put." He scuttled sideways, dragging the resisting Daisy with him. Forty pounds of ecstatic basset attempted to make a new friend.

"I don't have much choice." The woman crouched behind the box in an awkward position, only her head visible. A green knitted scarf tied in a knot beneath her chin covered much of her hair, but what Erik could see was deep red. His first thought was *She looks like Christmas*. His second thought was *Why is she hiding behind the postal box?*

While he tied Daisy's leash in a knot strong enough to hold the bouncing canine, she said, "I'd forgotten how quickly it gets dark here in the winter." Her comment indicated she was familiar with the town, but he'd never seen her here. He'd have remembered that hair. Maybe it was the combination of dusk and streetlights, but he'd never seen such red hair before.

"I've been worried I'd have to spend the night out here."

Daisy continued to leap in the air and bark with glee. Erik put his hand out and ordered, "Daisy, hush!" With a whimper, the dog obediently laid down. He turned to the woman. "It's safe now. You can come out."

"Um. . ." He could have sworn she looked sheepish. "No, I can't. I'm stuck."

Erik rounded the corner of the box, then reeled back in surprise. Her arm was buried to the shoulder in the drop-down door. No wonder she couldn't stand up straight. His lips twitched as he tried to swallow his smile. "I've never known this box to attack any other patrons. What did you do to provoke it?"

Her cheeks flooded with pink. "I was trying to get a letter out."

Erik shook his head, grinning. "This is a drop-off box, not a retrieval point."

Her huff sent out a cloud of condensation. "I know! But I dropped my envelope in before I remembered it didn't have a stamp. I hoped to pull it back out, but the box is too deep, and—" Her expression turned pleading. "Can you please get me loose?"

Suddenly Erik remembered he was still on duty. He leaped to attention. "Yes, sure. I'll unlock the back." He followed his words with action. "And I should be able to push your arm free." The box's gray interior made her pale hand appear almost ethereal. A green mitten, matching her scarf, lay on the small tumble of postcards in the bottom of the box. He slipped it over her hand before taking hold of her arm. "Okay, let's ease you out of here, okay?"

He tried to shift her arm upward, but it refused to budge. Frowning, he slid his hand along her arm. "Aha!" Her coat had caught on a bit of sharp metal inside. He unhooked the fabric, and she pulled her arm out with a sigh of relief.

"Oh, thank you." She stood upright and rubbed her arm, beaming at him from beneath a tangle of mussed bangs. "When some life returns to this limb, I'll shake your hand and introduce myself."

He shuffled through the mail and located an envelope without a stamp. The name and address were written in a neat-looking slanted script. He held it up. "Is this what you were after?"

Still massaging her arm, she nodded.

He scratched his head. "Well, technically, since it was in the box, it's the property of the postal service. Mail without a stamp is always returned, postage due, to the sender. But"—he tapped the envelope on his palm—"this doesn't have a return address, so it would have to go into the dead letter file."

"It *would have* to go into the dead letter file?" She peered at him with hopeful wide eyes, her thick lashes sweeping up and down.

He melted. This was Mistletoe, after all. "Here." He placed it in her mittened hand. Her smile provided all the thanks he needed. He turned toward Daisy, who waited with her head on her front paws, watching with mournful eyes. "Well, I'd better get these *stamped* postcards to the post office."

"Wait!"

He turned back.

She held out her hand. "My arm's awake now. I'm Kathy, with a *K*."

He took her hand. "And I'm Erik. . .with a *k*."

Laughing softly, she nodded toward Daisy. "And does your dog's name have a *k* in it, too?"

Crouching next to the dog, he began loosening the knot. "No, this is Daisy with a *D*, but there's a capital *K* at the end of *lick*, when it pertains to her. Hey, girl! Knock it off!" He angled his head away from Daisy's swiping tongue.

With another laugh, Kathy knelt beside him. "Let me help. C'mere, Daisy with a *D*." She kept Daisy occupied with pats and head rubs until Erik managed to work the knot free. The humans straightened to their feet and Daisy danced between them, tangling her leash around Erik's ankles. Kathy laughed at his failed attempts to catch the leash and bring the happy animal under control.

Over Daisy's occasional growling woofs, Kathy said, "Thank you again for helping me, but I need to scoot. I was expected for dinner at six, and I'm late."

For some reason, Erik deflated at her words.

She added, "Mrs. Flanagan will worry if I don't hurry back."

His disappointment fled as quickly as it had struck. "You're staying at Mrs. Flanagan's B&B? Great choice."

"I know." She bent over to pet Daisy. "She's an old family friend. It's great to see her again."

Ah, so she'd grown up in Mistletoe. "Where's home now?"

Her hand on the dog's ears, she tilted her head and smiled. "The San Francisco area—I live on Sausalito."

He resisted releasing a whistle. "Snazzy area."

She shrugged. "I suppose."

Normally he wasn't nosy, but she intrigued him. "What do you do in the San Francisco area?"

"I'm in advertising, specializing in commercial jingles."

Part of the television industry. Erik took a step back, dragging Daisy with him.

Chapter 4

Kathy watched Erik withdraw. What had caused the sudden chill in his demeanor? She stood.

"Hey, it's been good talking to you, but like you said—you're expected for dinner, and I'm still on the time clock, so. . ." He backed away, his expression suddenly leery, but Daisy continued to offer a wide doggy smile.

"Thanks again for getting my letter—and my arm—out of the mailbox," she called to his retreating back.

Although she heard a brief chuckle, he simply raised his hand in a backwards wave and kept going. On the walk back to Mrs. Flanagan's, she puzzled over his strange about-face. As she expected, the old woman was watching from the front window. She opened the door when Kathy came up the walk.

"Did you get yourself lost in your own hometown?"

Kathy stepped through the door and removed her scarf, laughing. "Not lost, but almost swallowed." She explained the predicament into which she'd gotten herself and her subsequent rescue, finally concluding, "He was a very nice man, but a little weird."

Mrs. Flanagan escorted Kathy to the kitchen, where the savory scent of stew filled the air. "If he had a dog with him, you're speakin' of Erik Hoffman, and I would never call him *weird.*" The gentle disapproval in her tone made Kathy smile.

"Well. . ." Kathy sat at the scarred table in the center of the homey kitchen while Mrs. Flanagan filled two bowls with stew. "If not weird, then confusing. He was so talkative and pleasant until I told him about my job." Her brows crunched. What had she said that would make such an impact?

Mrs. Flanagan joined Kathy. "Darlin', I'm guessin' when he spotted your bonny face, he felt an attraction. But then when he found out you were just visitin', he decided it would be best to make a hasty exit rather than riskin' his heart."

Kathy released a brief snort of laughter. "That's flattering, but doubtful. I can't imagine anyone falling for me that quickly."

A hint of sadness flitted through her elderly friend's eyes, but a soft smile wiped it away. "Whatever it might have been, it isn't worth frettin' about. And our stew's gettin' cold. Let's pray and eat."

Kathy bowed her head and listened to Mrs. Flanagan offer a prayer of thanks for the food. Her heart tilted sideways at the rush of remembrances brought by holding the warm hand and hearing familiar words of gratitude uttered in a sincere voice. Mom had always prayed before they ate, but since moving away, Kathy had slipped away from the practice. Suddenly she felt as though she'd been missing something precious.

"Amen." Mrs. Flanagan ended her prayer.

Kathy echoed, "Amen."

The old woman's eyes twinkled. "Eat up. There's plenty. And I fixed cherry crisp for dessert."

Kathy groaned with pleasure. "I haven't had a decent cherry crisp since I moved to California. You'll spoil me!"

"A little spoilin' is good for the soul," Mrs. Flanagan said firmly.

For some reason, Kathy suddenly wondered if there were other things here in Mistletoe that would be good for her soul. . . .

Erik fed Daisy her supper before heating a can of chicken noodle soup for himself. By the time the soup was hot enough to eat, Daisy had finished and stretched out in front of the fireplace in the small living room for her evening nap.

Erik sat in a recliner beside the dog and absently rubbed her belly with his stockinged foot while eating his soup. His gaze latched onto the Christmas tree in the corner of the room. In bachelor fashion, he'd hung a dozen glass balls out of Daisy's reach and called it good. The tree's green boughs dotted with red brought a reminder of Kathy's green scarf and tousled hair.

A smile tugged his lips when he remembered her flushed cheeks and flashing eyes. Twenty-nine years old and it had finally struck—the zing his older brother had warned would hit him one day. At the time, Erik had laughed at Trev, but now he understood. The moment he'd looked into her tawny brown eyes, he'd felt an electrical current zing up and down his spine.

With a grunt of displeasure, he reminded himself the zing was wasted. She was only here for a visit. She'd be returning to California. *To the television industry.* The idea filled him with disdain.

With the thought came an automatic prayer: *Lord, bring a man worthy of Susan's heart into her life.* The entire family had suffered through his sister's heartbreak when, shortly before his move to Mistletoe, a television crew had filmed a low-budget film near Canyon Ferry Lake, and Susan fell head over heels for one of the cameramen. She had claimed it was God's divine intervention that had placed her at the lake with a group of junior high girls from church at the same time the crew was there. But when the cameraman left without a good-bye, Susan's heart—and her faith—crumbled.

Two years later, his little sister had managed to recapture her faith in God, but her faith in men hadn't yet been restored. The experience had left a bitter taste in Erik's mouth, as well. The entertainment industry was one of selfish greed. That zing he felt when he looked into Kathy's eyes surely was misplaced. He wouldn't trust someone involved in television.

His soup bowl was empty. He carried it to the kitchen and rinsed it, then stood staring out the small window above the sink into the dark backyard. Someday he'd like to stand in that backyard and play catch with his son. Or—he smiled—his daughter. Didn't matter, really. God had a woman chosen for him. He'd been praying for the unknown someone ever since his senior year in high school when he'd taken a marriage and family class. He always figured God would let him know when he'd found her.

But isn't that what the zing was about?

He shook his head, dispelling the thought. That made no sense. Kathy was only passing through. *But still*, his mind pressed, *the zing had to mean something.* Maybe there was some other reason he'd been zinged. Maybe there was something she needed that he could give.

Daisy awakened from her nap with a squeaky whine. She trotted to his side and peered up with round brown eyes. The flutter of her lashes brought to mind another set of thick lashes, another pair of brown eyes.

With a snort of derision, he muttered, "You've got it bad, Hoffman, when you're seeing a woman's face in Daisy's fuzzy mug." He took Daisy into the backyard for her evening romp, but his mind kept drifting three blocks over, to Mrs. Flanagan's, to the visitor from California. Whether he liked it or not, she had managed to capture his attention. But now what to do about it?

The Christmas social.

Of course! Perfect! The church Christmas social—with cocoa and cider and popcorn balls and a hayride through the middle of town followed by caroling and a reading of the Christmas story at the nativity in the town square. A celebration of the true meaning of Christmas, the church's social was exactly what a girl caught up in the greedy, selfish, shallow world of advertising needed.

"Daisy, c'mon, girl!" He herded Daisy back into the house,

settled her on her pillow in the corner of his bedroom, and then picked up the telephone book. He'd offer Miss Kathy-from-Sausalito an official invitation to the Christmas social, and maybe he'd have a chance to get to the source of that crazy zing.

The jangle of the telephone interrupted Kathy and Mrs. Flanagan's conversation. The old woman snatched the receiver from the hook. "Mrs. Flanagan's Bed-and-Breakfast." Her face lit up. "Erik!"

Immediately Kathy's heart ping-ponged against her ribs. She set down her teacup and pressed her hand to her chest.

"Why, certainly. She's sittin' right here enjoyin' a cup of apple-cinnamon tea. Here you are." Mrs. Flanagan held the receiver toward Kathy.

Kathy raised her brows high. "For me?"

Mrs. Flanagan's grin turned teasing. "And why would he be callin' for me? I don't have lovely red curls and endearin' freckles on my nose."

Kathy felt her cheeks fill with heat as she took the telephone and pressed it to her ear. "H–hello?" *Don't stammer!*

"Good evening. I'm sorry to disturb your tea party."

She smiled. He sounded more like the man who'd discovered her half buried in a mailbox. "You aren't. What can I do for you?"

"This coming Saturday night, our church is hosting a Christmas social. I wondered if you might like to attend."

Kathy bit down on her lower lip as guilt wiggled down her spine. Although she had attended regularly with her mother while growing up, it had been far too long since she'd been in a church. "A—a social?"

"Yes. It's something our new minister planned. We'll eat ourselves silly, go out in groups to carol, take a hayride around the square, and then have an outdoor service to finish the evening. It should be a lot of fun. I thought. . ." Suddenly he sounded uncertain. "I thought you might enjoy a little small-town celebration. I'm sure many of your old friends and neighbors will be there."

Although Chad would probably think a church social outdated and backward, Kathy admitted a desire to partake in everything Mistletoe had to offer. "That sounds like fun, Erik. Thank you for thinking of me."

A *whoosh* sounded on the other end, as if he'd been holding his breath and let it out all at once. It made her smile.

"Good. It starts at six, so I'll swing by and pick you up around five forty-five."

"I'll be ready."

"And dress warm. A lot of the evening we'll be outdoors. The forecast predicts snow."

"I'll dress warmly."

"Okay. Well. . .good-bye." A click signaled the disconnection.

Kathy handed the telephone to Mrs. Flanagan. She answered the old woman's querying look. "He invited me to the church social."

"A date?"

Kathy gave a start. She hadn't applied that term to the invitation, but in reality that's what it was. A date. She blinked twice, her mind racing. "I—I guess so."

"Mmm-hmm." Mrs. Flanagan sipped her tea, a speculative gleam in her eye.

Kathy lifted her cup to her lips, but she couldn't swallow. A question pressed at her heart. Why had she accepted an invitation from Erik when she planned to accept a marriage proposal from Chad?

Chapter 5

At exactly five forty-five Saturday afternoon, Erik climbed the wooden porch steps to Mrs. Flanagan's B&B. He read the little note inviting people to come right in but decided it applied to guests, not someone picking up a guest, so he twisted the key to ring the old-fashioned doorbell.

The door swung open almost immediately, which told him Kathy had been waiting. The thought pleased him.

"Hello, Erik." She looked adorable with the green scarf tied over her bright hair and her tweed coat buttoned clear to her chin. The porch light illuminated a crooked row of three freckles on the left side of her nose. The pale brown speckles gave her an innocent appeal that was nearly irresistible.

The zing returned.

He cleared his throat. "Hi. I see you're ready to go."

She stepped out, closing the door behind her. "Yes." Her gaze shifted past him to the dusky street. "Where are those snowflakes you predicted?"

He took her arm, guiding her down the steps. "Oh, I didn't predict them—the forecasters did. But look at the sky." They paused at the end of the sidewalk and peered upward. Their breath came in puffs that mingled then vanished. "See how milky it looks? That's cloud cover. We may get those snowflakes yet."

She smiled.

Zing.

Putting his hand at the small of her back, he gave a gentle nudge. "Let's get going, huh? The cider will go fast, and I'll want at least two cups."

She laughed softly, the sound pleasant. They walked side by side, hands in their pockets, and made small talk. Along the way, other Mistletoe residents joined them, the crowd growing as they neared the town square and Living Word Chapel. Once at the chapel, Erik had to make few introductions. Most people remembered Kathy, and many greeted her exuberantly. He experienced a pang of jealousy when reminiscing began to take place. He had no part of Kathy's past. And as much as he hated to admit it, the fact bothered him.

They broke into groups for caroling, and he made sure he was in her group. She had a sweet soprano, and she seemed to enjoy singing. Walking to the next house on their list, she tipped her head to look up at him. "This is really fun. I haven't sung Christmas songs in ages."

He chuckled. "Why not? Don't you have Christmas in California?"

"Of course we do. It's just. . .different."

"Different how?"

But the group burst into "Hark! the Herald Angels Sing," so the question went unanswered. By the time they moved on, it felt awkward to broach the topic of California Christmases again, so he let it go. Yet he couldn't help wondering if Kathy had been leaving Christ out of Christmas.

He watched her face while Pastor Brown read the account of Christ's birth from the book of Luke. At times he thought he saw a glimmer of tears in her eyes, but her quick blinks always erased the moisture before he could be sure. At the end of the reading, the reverend offered a prayer, and then the service ended with everyone singing "Silent Night."

In the middle of the second verse, two tiny puffs of white drifted past Erik's nose. His voice stilled; his gaze lifted. More dots made their way toward the earth. Snow! He bumped Kathy's elbow and pointed, but she was already looking skyward, awe lighting her eyes.

Erik forgot about the snowfall, the social, and the dozens of townspeople whose voices still serenaded them with the gentle strains of "Silent Night." For Erik, all that existed was Kathy. His gaze roved slowly, memorizing the sweet upward curve of her lips and the velvety depth of her wide brown eyes. Her cold-reddened cheeks and nose gave her an elfin appearance. Snowflakes landed on her head, shimmering like diamonds on her satiny hair, and a picture flashed through Erik's mind—of slipping a diamond ring onto her finger.

The zing shot from his spine to his scalp and tingled like an electrical current.

He shook his head. No, it couldn't be. Not that fast. He couldn't possibly be falling in love.

Kathy lay beneath the Christmas patchwork quilt and stared at the dark ceiling. Hours had passed since Erik walked her back to Mrs. Flanagan's, but sleep wouldn't come. Something had happened tonight. Something magical. Something unexpected. She swallowed. Something scary.

It must have been the dancing snowflakes that made her heart patter. Or the songs. Or the Bible reading. Yes, that was it. In the park, under the stars, with the life-size figures of Mary, Joseph, and baby Jesus huddled together in the little wood stable just a few feet from where she sat with the residents of Mistletoe, the story of Christ's birth had taken on a meaning she hadn't explored since she was a little girl. Something inside of her had come alive tonight.

But it wasn't Erik. It couldn't be Erik. Because she was in love with Chad.

Wasn't she?

Her heart pounded harder. If she truly loved Chad, why hadn't she immediately accepted his offer to fly to Vegas? If she truly loved Chad, why hadn't she found the time to buy a stamp and mail the letter that still lay on the secretary, right where she'd put it when she returned from her walk Friday evening? If she truly loved Chad, why had she gone to the social this evening with Erik?

The desire to talk to someone—her mother, Lori or Madison

or Deanna, Mrs. Flanagan—weighed on her chest. If she could share these troublesome thoughts, maybe she would finally be able to sleep. But Mom was gone, and her friends were all sleeping. She was alone with her worries and fears.

And then—as gently as a snowflake drifting downward—a thought descended on Kathy's heart. Why not share them with God? Hadn't she been taught He was always there, always listening? Mom had believed it. Mrs. Flanagan believed it. She suspected Erik believed it, too.

But she pushed the idea away. God wouldn't want to listen to her. Not after her years of neglecting Him. The thought crept back. *Try. Just reach out.* Eyes wide and unblinking, Kathy stared at the dark ceiling and tried to envision God's face. What came to mind was the infant Jesus, sleeping peacefully in a manger.

Sleeping peacefully. . . She smiled. What a lovely picture. *"Rest in Me."* The soothing words enveloped her in warmth. Her eyes fluttered. *"Rest in Me".* . . . In moments she drifted away.

A knock at her door awakened her from a sound sleep. She opened her eyes, then slammed them shut, shocked by the light that flooded the room. Morning already? Forcing her eyelids open, she threw back the covers and padded to the door. She inched it open to find Mrs. Flanagan in the hallway.

"I wondered if you'd like to be goin' to the mornin' service with me?"

Kathy surmised by the woman's robe and slippers that the service wouldn't start for a while yet. "Yes, ma'am, I would."

Mrs. Flanagan beamed. "Good." She held up a finger. "One hour. Hurry."

Kathy nodded, closed the door, and dashed to the bathroom. Fifty-five minutes later, she and Mrs. Flanagan made their way up the neatly swept sidewalk of Living Word Chapel. The same sense of homecoming she'd experienced when she'd stepped out of the taxi three days ago washed over her again. It carried her through the service, and by the time the "Amen" to the closing prayer sounded, Kathy knew she needed to make some changes.

In the foyer, she spotted Lori, and she wove her way through the crowd to her friend's side.

"Kath!" Lori gave her a warm hug. "Are we still on for lunch tomorrow? Both Deanna and Madison said they could make it."

"Of course. I plan to skip breakfast so I'll have room for two fritters."

Lori laughed. "As if Mrs. Flanagan will allow you to skip breakfast."

How well everyone knew the dear old woman! Kathy shrugged. "Well then, I'll just have to suffer." They shared another laugh, and then Kathy said, "I'm glad it will work out for all of us. There's so much I want to talk to you about."

Lori's eyes twinkled. "Does it have anything to do with the pact?"

Heat crept up Kathy's cheeks.

Lori squealed. "It does! You've got a beau, don't you?"

Kathy waved her hands, trying to quiet her boisterous friend. "We can talk about it tomorrow, okay?" She glanced around, noting Erik stood just a few feet away. Although he wasn't looking at her, he was close enough to hear if he wanted to. The heat in her cheeks increased.

"At least tell me his name," Lori prodded. "Some little morsel to satisfy me until tomorrow."

Kathy sighed. Lori always had been the most persuasive of her friends. "Okay, okay. Chad. But that's all I'm saying now." She hoped her friends would be able to offer advice concerning what to do about Chad.

"Darlin'?" Mrs. Flanagan touched her arm. "Are you ready to go? I left a roast in my oven, and I'm not fond of burnt offerings."

"Yes, ma'am." Kathy gave Lori another quick hug. "See you tomorrow."

Lori waved, and Mrs. Flanagan caught Kathy's elbow and propelled her across the floor. Kathy hid her smile. For an older woman, she had an amazing amount of energy. As they passed Erik, she let her gaze flit in his direction. His blue eyes met hers, but he didn't smile. Before she could process his serious expression, Mrs. Flanagan hurried her out the door.

Chapter 6

Erik walked slowly toward his bungalow, his thoughts churning. Along the edges of the cleared sidewalks, dirty clumps of piled snow taunted him. Last night, under the pure white snowfall with Kathy, everything had seemed so perfect. But now the memory was soiled thanks to the name he'd overheard.

Chad.

The letter he'd pulled from the mailbox had been addressed to a Chad Someone. He recalled the carefully formed letters. She'd gone to a great deal of care penning his name. A woman didn't do that for someone unimportant. Chad obviously meant something to Kathy.

He gave a gray clump of snow a kick and watched it shatter, showering the toe of his shoe with dingy mush. What difference did it make to him if she had a boyfriend? Hadn't he decided he didn't want to care for someone like Kathy—someone who was involved in a money-grubbing industry and who would only be here for a few days and then leave? It was pointless! Caring about Kathy would only lead to heartache, and after watching Susan suffer, he had no desire to walk that path.

He'd seen a flicker in her eyes last night that told him something important was taking place under the surface. He prayed that "something" was an igniting of desire for God in her heart. If that was the result of his time with her, then it hadn't been in vain. He didn't need to make things personal.

Let Chad have her, he told himself firmly as he entered his house and closed the door, sealing out the cold. He only wished it were that easy to seal out his thoughts of Kathy.

Deanna and Madison waved one more time before heading out of the café. Kathy wished their lunch could have gone on forever, but her friends had jobs and responsibilities—it was selfish to keep them there just for her entertainment. Besides, they'd have time to catch up later. Her vacation wasn't even half over.

But their time together—and the lengthy conversation concerning her relationship with Chad—had convinced Kathy she had no business getting married on a whim. Although her relationship with Chad was long in years, it was short in depth. Before accepting a marriage proposal, she should be well acquainted with the man under the surface.

Lori remained in the booth across from Kathy. The cell phone in her pocket made her accessible to whomever might need her, so she said she could stay and chat as long as Kathy wanted.

Kathy propped her elbows on the table and raised her eyebrows. "So now that we've decided I'm going to be the pact breaker and let Chad know I can't marry him, tell me how to avoid feeling awkward around him when I return to work."

Lori sighed. "Oh, Kath, avoiding awkward is hard. Especially when the relationship has lasted as long as it has."

Kathy puffed her cheeks and blew out a long breath. Facing Chad with a refusal would be the hardest thing she'd ever done, yet she knew deep in her heart it was the right thing to do. "I really don't look forward to going back."

"So don't go."

Kathy sat up straight. "I have to. My job is there."

Lori waved her hand, dismissing Kathy's words. "Your job is writing jingles. Do you have to be *in* San Francisco to write jingles? I thought writers could write anywhere."

"Well, I suppose they can, but—"

"But nothing," Lori insisted. "This is the technological age! We have computers with Internet access, fax machines, and the ability to carry on conference calls with people who live on different continents. You could work for Andale and live anyplace in the world, if you really wanted to."

Kathy stared at her friend.

Lori chuckled. "Close your mouth, Kathy."

Realizing her jaw hung open, Kathy snapped her mouth shut.

"I'm not trying to tell you what to do, I'm just trying to give you some options. You aren't tied to San Francisco, Kath, unless you want to be. So the question is, do you want to be?"

Kathy sat back and nibbled her lower lip. She knew of

several employees from Andale who worked out of their homes rather than coming in to the office, but they were parents who wanted to be home for their children. Being single, she'd never considered it an option for herself. "I have no idea what my boss would think."

"And you won't know unless you ask." Lori leaned forward, placing her hand over Kathy's. "I just threw you a curve ball, so don't swing blind. Think about it—pray about it. It would be a huge change, and it shouldn't be done lightly. Okay?"

Kathy's heart pounded. Pray. . . She hadn't prayed for years. She managed a nod.

"Good." Lori grinned. "Now, we've been sitting here for at least thirty minutes since the waitress took our plates. Are you ready for another fritter?"

Kathy burst out laughing. "You bet!" The thinking and praying could wait until later.

When Kathy and Lori finally left Flossie's, it was nearly five o'clock. Kathy's belly ached—partly from too many fritters, partly from so much laughter. She couldn't remember the last time she'd laughed so hard or so often. Old friends truly were best. If she did return to San Francisco, she would make it a point to visit Mistletoe at least once a year.

After one more hug, she headed toward Mrs. Flanagan's B&B. When she encountered the mailbox in which she'd caught her arm, she slowed her steps. Was it only four days ago she'd tried mailing that meticulously crafted letter to Chad, telling him she would be his wife? What a silly, romantic notion it had been. After having shared the details of her relationship with him with her longtime friends, she clearly recognized the futility of trying to carve out a life with Chad.

She and Chad might be alike in their career goals, but that was all they had. Two people needed a lot more than a common workplace to make a relationship work. There should be mutual respect, a willingness to support each other, and—as Madison had wisely pointed out—a common faith at the base of the relationship.

Thinking about the times Chad had ridiculed her old-fashioned values, she wondered why it had taken her so long to realize she didn't want someone who would make fun of her deepest beliefs. Thank goodness she'd never allowed him to convince her to betray her conscience. That kind of regret would be hard to bear.

Leaning on the mailbox, she recalled Deanna's comment: "You just got used to being with him. It got comfortable, and it's hard to cast off 'comfortable.'" What a relief to know she had discovered the truth in time. If she'd managed to send that letter, the results would have been disastrous.

Recalling her attempt to mail the unstamped envelope, she chuckled to herself. She could only imagine how silly she'd looked, all hunched over with her arm stuck in that box. But Erik hadn't laughed at her—he'd just helped. *Such a nice man.*

Kathy propped her chin in her mittened hand, lost in thought. After such a short acquaintance, she already felt at ease with Erik. He was easy to talk to. And easy to look at. His taller-than-average frame was muscular—probably from hauling bags of mail all over town. His eyes were as blue as the Montana sky, his hair as golden as the leaves on an aspen tree in late October—a winning combination, as far as she was concerned. When he smiled—which he did often—the dimples in his honed cheeks could make a girl go weak in the knees.

"Hi, Kathy. Stuck again?"

At the familiar voice, she jerked upright. An embarrassed flush warmed her face. She clapped her mittens to her cheeks. "Oh, Erik. You startled me. I was just thinking about—" Fortunately, she stopped herself before she said "you." Clasping her hands together, she finished lamely, "I was just thinking."

His lips twitched, and he gave a slight nod. He wore a furry cap that covered his ears—the type of cap old men wore to go ice fishing—but he even made that look good.

What am I thinking now?

Flustered, she crouched and patted her thighs. "Hi, Daisy. Come see me, girl."

Daisy, tail gyrating, bounced over and gave the underside of Kathy's chin a swipe with her tongue.

Laughing, Kathy rubbed the dog's floppy ears and grinned up at Erik. "She's really sweet."

"Yep. She loves everybody." He unlocked the back side of the mailbox and scooped out the mail.

"How long have you had her?"

He dropped the pile of letters into his bag. "A little over three years, I guess."

"I bet she's good company. I can't have a pet in my apartment in Sausalito."

He stood and gave Daisy's leash a gentle tug, drawing the dog to his side. "Not even a goldfish?"

Although the words were teasing, he didn't meet her gaze, and his tone lacked its usual warmth.

She forced a light laugh. "I can't imagine a goldfish being as much fun as Daisy."

"No, I suppose not. Well"—he lifted his hand in a wave—"I've got to get these letters back to the post office for sorting. Have a good evening, Kathy." He strode away without a backward glance.

Kathy frowned. What had happened to Mr. Friendly? Then she shrugged. Everyone was entitled to an off day, she decided. She headed again for the inn, but before turning the corner, an idea struck. She hadn't yet visited her old house. It had sold shortly after Mom's death, so she wouldn't be able to go in, but she could stand in the yard and remember.

She checked the clock on the bank's tower. Mrs. Flanagan didn't expect her for another thirty minutes. That was adequate time for a quick memory jog. She turned her feet toward Elm Street.

Chapter 7

Eric, led by Daisy, turned the corner to his block, his mind running through the items in his refrigerator that could be quickly crafted into the semblance of a meal. He was capable of cooking—he'd lived on his own for a half dozen years—but he didn't necessarily enjoy it. Tonight he had a hankering for a full-blown supper—something hearty like meatloaf or Salisbury steak or stroganoff.

His mouth watered, thinking about his mother's homemade stroganoff—tender chunks of beef, mushrooms, and onions, smothered in a thick, creamy gravy flavored with sour cream, poured over a mound of steamed white rice or—even better—homemade noodles. He groaned, earning a whine from Daisy. After thinking of stroganoff, there was no way he could eat a grilled cheese sandwich.

Daisy whined again, and he said, "What's wrong, girl? You hungry, too?" Daisy was astute, but he couldn't imagine she had the ability to read his mind. The dog bounced on her front legs, straining at the end of the leash. Erik looked ahead and squinted.

In the waning light, he made out a small form on the sidewalk in front of his house—someone sitting on the cold ground. And that someone wore a green scarf tied over her bright red hair. He frowned. What was Kathy doing outside his house?

Daisy woofed, yanking so hard that Erik stumbled forward two steps. Kathy turned her gaze from the house to him. She straightened to her feet as Daisy led him directly to her side. Her bright smile chased away thoughts about stroganoff.

"You keep finding me in weird places." She laughed, brushing the seat of her blue jeans with both hands. "You probably think I'm a nut."

No, he thought she was too cute for her own good. Certainly too cute for *his* good. "Not at all, but this is an odd place to rest. A little frosty, I would think."

She laughed again, her eyes sparkling. "Yes, I'll need to thaw out when I return to Mrs. Flanagan's. But it was worth it." Turning her head, she looked wistfully toward his house. "I've been sitting here remembering. Lots of memories in that house."

Erik's shoulders jerked. He pointed. "*This* house?"

"324 Elm Street." She flashed a quick grin. "I grew up here."

He took a backward step and almost tripped over Daisy. "You're kidding!"

She tipped her head, puzzlement creasing her brow. "No. Why? Do you know who lives here?"

Shaking his head, he released a disbelieving chuckle. "You

might say so. I bought it when I moved to Mistletoe."

Her eyes grew wide. "But—but—I sold it to a family from right here in town!"

Erik shrugged. "All I know is the father was being transferred out of state. I've lived here a little over two years." How strange to think he'd been living in her childhood home, creating memories. Somehow it made him feel as if their lives crossed. The idea both pleased and perturbed him.

She stared at the house. Tears glittered in the corners of her eyes. She blinked rapidly.

Erik's heart melted. He touched her sleeve. "It's awkward, isn't it, thinking of someone replacing you in your home."

One tear spilled down her cheek. She swiped it away with her mitten and gave a quick nod. "I didn't expect it to be so hard. Obviously, I knew someone else was living in it. I did sell the house, after all. But I was just sitting here, wishing I still had it so I could. . .I don't know. . .visit it whenever I wanted to."

"You can." He blurted out the words before he thought the idea through. Did he really want her just showing up on his doorstep? It was hard enough separating himself from her out here on the sidewalk. Seeing her in his house would no doubt cement her into his mind. Yet when he saw her face light up, he couldn't regret the impulsive invitation.

"Oh, Erik, thank you!" She backed down the sidewalk, her hands clasped beneath her chin. "I have to go now—Mrs. Flanagan is expecting me, but could I come back? In an hour or two? Just for a quick tour, nothing more. I won't be a pest."

Oh, she was a pest all right, but not the way she meant it.

He forced his lips to form a smile. "Sure, Kathy. That's fine."

The gratitude shining in her eyes gave Erik's heart a lift. Daisy danced around his feet, eager to get in out of the cold. He murmured, "Down, girl," but what he really meant was "Down, boy." His heart was doing a dance the likes of which Daisy could never accomplish.

Hugging a plastic butter tub to her front with one hand, Kathy raised the other to knock on the front door of her—of Erik's house. Her heart pounded. She would be stepping into her child-hood home. The place she'd lived with her parents until she was six, and then with her mother until she was twenty-two.

The house was nothing fancy. Just a boxy wood-sided bun-galow with shingles sporting heart cutouts, crafted by her father shortly before an aneurysm unexpectedly claimed his life. Those shingles were now painted a deep evergreen instead of the slate blue her mother had chosen. But, she acknowledged, the dark green looked nice against the eggshell siding, and everything was neatly kept. Erik took pride in the house—that was evident—and it pleased her that her home was well cared for.

The door opened, and Erik and Daisy stood framed in the doorway. Daisy woofed hello, and Erik's gaze fell on the container. With a smile, she plunked it into his hands. "A thank-you for letting me come. Leftover supper—Mrs. Flanagan's beef stroga-noff. I already mixed it with the noodles, so I hope it won't be soggy."

Erik's eyebrows shot up. "Stroganoff! But how could you. . ."

Then he shook his head and gestured with one arm. "Come on in. Welcome to my. . .er, your humble home." He laughed, sounding self-conscious.

She stood on the tiny patch of linoleum that served as a foyer, peering up at him. "This is awkward for you, too, isn't it?"

With a light chuckle, he nodded. "A little. But I think we'll survive. Here, let me take your coat." He held the stroganoff container in one hand and hung her coat on a doorknob-studded board mounted behind the door. Daisy complicated the procedure by weaving back and forth between Erik's legs.

Kathy touched a tarnished brass doorknob. "This wasn't here before."

Erik headed for the kitchen, Daisy trotting along beside him. "When I moved in, it hung on the back of the bathroom door— for towels or robes, I guess." She heard a refrigerator door open and close, followed by a click she didn't recognize. "I use the coat closet for my hunting gear, so I needed a guest coatrack." He returned to the living room, his hands empty and Daisy missing. "It's come in handy there."

Kathy nodded, a lump in her throat. "My dad made it for Mom for Christmas the last year he was alive. She had seen one similar to it in an antique store, so Daddy found a bunch of old doorknobs at garage sales and made it for her."

Just touching his handiwork made her feel connected to her father. She gave the knob a loving rub, then turned to face Erik. "Okay, give me the tour."

She allowed him to guide her through the house, even though she could have found her own way easily. From the living room to the kitchen—where Daisy lay mournful but quiet in a wire kennel—and down the hall to the bedrooms and single bathroom. The tour took less than ten minutes, but during those minutes Kathy relived twenty-two years of life. When she finished, she felt drained.

Without asking, she sank onto the center cushion of Erik's sofa and released a sigh. "They say you can't come home again, but this trip has proved that wrong."

He seated himself in a recliner next to the fireplace. "How so?" He sounded genuinely interested.

"I don't know if I can explain it." Kathy tapped her lips with one finger, gathering her thoughts. "From the moment I stepped out of the taxi, I've had this feeling of. . .belonging. Acceptance." She threw her arms wide. "Coming home!" She laughed at his grin. "I'm staying in a bed-and-breakfast, yet I feel as though I've come home."

"That's a good thing, isn't it?"

His hesitant question made her pause and carefully consider a reply. Finally, she sighed. "Yes, I think so. It feels good, but it sure makes it hard to think about leaving again." Her conversation with Lori flitted through her mind. Could she possibly work from Mistletoe, using the computer and telephone to communicate with Andale Agency? Could she, as Lori said, write jingles anywhere?

Without effort, a line—a lyric—formed in her mind. *Christmas isn't Christmas till it happens in your heart. . .* She closed her eyes, allowing inspiration to carry her away. *Mistletoe, Montana, is the place where Christmas starts. . . .* Her heart joined the words with a lilting melody, inviting in its simplicity. *In the quaint Christmas square, joy and gifts abound; so make your way to Mistletoe—where Christmas lives year-round.*

It was rough, but with some tweaking, maybe Deanna would like to use it as a theme song to promote tourism. And if she changed the third line to—

"Kathy?"

She jolted, her eyes popping open. She met Erik's worried gaze.

"You drifted off. Were you thinking about leaving?"

No, she was thinking about staying. Forever. She jumped to her feet. "I'm sorry. I didn't turn out to be very good company."

He stood, too. "No, that's fine." Was he relieved that she headed for her coat? "I need to take Daisy out for a romp, anyway. And I might eat some of that stroganoff. All I had for supper was a PB&J."

"Yuck." She wrinkled her nose, then laughed. "Of course, back in Sausalito—" Why hadn't she said "back home"? Her heart pounded. Sausalito was slipping further and further away. "In Sausalito, I ate a lot of peanut butter and jelly, too. I don't really like cooking for one." She buttoned her coat and tied her scarf over her head.

"Well, enjoy Mrs. Flanagan's cooking while you're here. And tell her thanks for me, would you?" Erik held the door open for her.

"Will do. Good night." With a quick wave, Kathy bounced down the steps and made her way down the sidewalk toward the inn. Black wrought-iron streetlamps lit her pathway and highlighted the snowflakes that whirled toward the earth. As she walked, she scanned yards for FOR SALE signs. If she were to move here, she'd need a place to live. She laughed out loud when she realized what she was doing. Apparently her mind was made up—Mistletoe would once again be home. Her heart sang. She'd had such a happy childhood here. Of course, she needed to contact Mr. Andale and arrange to work from a computer. And she needed to contact Chad.

For a moment, her euphoria wavered. Telling Chad she wasn't in love with him would be hard, but it had to be done. She couldn't wait another minute, either. She hoped he would take it well.

She skipped the final few feet to reach the inn's porch. Inside, she found Mrs. Flanagan in the parlor having tea with some of the other guests. The old woman waved her over. "Sit down and have a cup with us, darlin'. I've been tellin' Mrs. Langvardt and Mrs. Huston here all about your work in the big city."

Although Kathy would have preferred to go upstairs and make that phone call to Chad, she accepted the teacup offered by Mrs. Langvardt. "It really isn't anything all that special." She hoped her nonchalant statement would discourage further conversation and she could slip away.

But Mrs. Huston's interested look destroyed that hope. "I understand you write commercial jingles. Would I recognize any of them?"

Kathy sat down and named a few of the products advertised with her jingles. The woman's eyes widened with admiration.

"My goodness! Well, I would very much appreciate spending

some time talking with you. My youngest son, John—he's a freshman in college"—her face glowed with pride—"is quite interested in advertising. Maybe you could give him some pointers?"

Kathy shrugged. "Sure."

Mrs. Flanagan cut in. "And advertisin' is not her only talent. She also does beautiful pen-writin'. What is that called?" She pursed her lips. "Oh yes. Calligraphy."

Kathy smiled at her elderly friend. "How did you know I do calligraphy?"

Mrs. Flanagan took a sip of her tea. "Why, darlin', I saw it on that envelope you left in the secretary in the Christmas room when I did my cleanin' Saturday mornin'." She took another sip, then added, "I noticed it was missin' a stamp, so I stamped it and set it out in the box for you."

Kathy's heart leaped into her throat.

"Oh yes." Mrs. Flanagan nodded, smiling at the guests. "The young man who receives that letter will surely be impressed with Kathy's pretty writin'."

Chapter 8

Tuesday and Wednesday, Kathy stayed—*hid* might be a more accurate description, she acknowledged with derision—at the inn and worked in her room. If she were going to convince the board of directors of Andale Agency to allow her to work from home—in a home that was hundreds of miles away from San Francisco—then she needed to have proof she could handle it.

In her laptop's hard drive, she carried files of the current accounts entrusted to her. She wanted to be ready to send off at least two to-die-for jingles before she made her request. She admitted to having some difficulty focusing on the task. Her thoughts kept drifting to the letter she'd written.

If it had been mailed Saturday, it would have reached Chad by Monday the earliest, Wednesday the latest. Her fingers stilled on the keyboard, her mouth going dry at the thought. How she wished she had thrown it away rather than leaving it lying around! It would have been so much easier to tell him she couldn't marry him if he hadn't already seen her acceptance. But she couldn't roll back time and change the outcome.

That letter would reach Chad's hands. The minute he got it, he would call her, and then she would gently tell him she'd made a mistake. But until that call came, she had work to do. With a huff of annoyance, she prompted herself, "Get busy!"

Satisfied with the jingle for Jerri Ann Cosmetics, she turned her focus to one for Plank City Motors. Cars would test her creativity more than cosmetics, she knew, but if she could write a car jingle from Mistletoe, she could write any jingle from Mistletoe. Deep in thought, she nearly jammed her fingers through the keyboard when someone knocked on the door.

"Yes?" She didn't get up.

"Kathy, darlin', I wondered if you'd be comin' down for dinner." Mrs. Flanagan's voice.

Kathy glanced at the clock. Six fifteen already! She massaged her temples and got up from the bed. Opening the door, she faked a smile. "I'm sorry. I lost track of time."

Mrs. Flanagan looked past her to the rumpled bed and the open laptop. She scowled. "Are you workin'? This is supposed to be your vacation."

"I know." Kathy closed the door and followed Mrs. Flanagan toward the stairs. She wasn't ready to share her idea about staying in Mistletoe until she had all of the arrangements made, so she couldn't tell her friend why she was working. "But I like what I do so much, it doesn't feel like work."

Mrs. Flanagan snorted. "Well, you're a rare one, then, not thinkin' of work as workin'. Much as I love this inn—and I wouldn't think of doin' another thing than what I do—it still taxes me. If I had vacation, I wouldn't spend it makin' beds and sweepin' floors."

Kathy laughed. The kitchen table was set for two, and covered pots waited. A wonderful smell filled the room. Hunger struck. She slid into her seat and folded her hands, waiting for Mrs. Flanagan to offer the blessing.

The old woman fixed her with a pointed stare. "I've been blessin' this food every meal since you arrived. I'd say it's your turn."

Kathy swallowed. "My turn?"

"Yes." Mrs. Flanagan bowed her head and closed her eyes.

Kathy stared at the top of the older woman's white hair and the pink scalp peeking through.

After a long moment, Mrs. Flanagan lifted her head and looked at Kathy. "Well, are you goin' to pray or not?"

"I—I—"

The woman's scowl changed from impatient to concerned. "Kathy, what is it, darlin'?"

"I don't remember how."

For several seconds, Mrs. Flanagan simply looked at her, an unreadable expression in her faded eyes. Then she gave a nod, bowed her head, and asked the blessing. Not until the meal was finished did she pin Kathy with a serious look.

"Darlin', what you said about not rememberin' how to pray." She paused, sighing. "That's a sad state in which to find oneself. Do you know how you got there?"

Kathy pushed her empty plate aside. "Not really. It happened so gradually. When I lived here with Mom, praying was a part of our daily lives. God was. . .there. But then I moved to California, and I got caught up with work and new acquaintances, and I just kind of quit. Quit going to church, quit praying, quit making God a part of my life."

The sadness in the old woman's eyes brought a sting of tears to Kathy's. "Well, maybe that's why you've come back to Mistletoe—to find God again."

Kathy thought about the evening of the Christmas social and the feelings that had swept her away when the minister read the story of Christ's birth. She had felt as though something was being reborn inside of herself. Maybe that was her heart finding its way back to God.

"I'll be prayin', darlin', for your heart to open to Him. He doesn't want to leave you driftin' far from His love and care." Mrs. Flanagan rose and began clearing dishes.

Kathy, still seated at the table, nodded. A simple line ran through her mind—a jingle she'd written over a year ago for a Christmas ad campaign for a major jewelry store. Just one line—*All I want for Christmas is. . .*—and then the camera had panned to a sparkling display of exclusive diamond jewelry.

Now, as Kathy played the line through her heart—*All I want for Christmas is. . .*—her mind's eye fixed on the manger from the nativity in the town square. She whispered, "All I want is You again, Lord."

Erik dropped the mail for Mrs. Flanagan's Bed-and-Breakfast

through the mail slot in the front door. He took his time sifting through the stack of letters in his hand, making sure he had the deliveries for the next two houses in order. His gaze shifted sideways to the lace-covered window near the door, hoping to see a shadow that indicated someone was coming to retrieve the mail.

He hadn't seen Kathy since the evening she visited her old house. Although he'd watched for her downtown, she'd never shown. And when he asked Lori, she said she hadn't seen hide nor hair of Kathy, either. Erik was starting to wonder if she'd headed back to San Francisco without saying anything to anybody. That was pretty much what his sister's cameraman had done, but Erik hoped better of Kathy.

No one moved around inside the house. Daisy whined, eager to move on. Erik sighed. "All right, I'm going." He thumped off the porch and headed to the next house. Wind whistled down from the mountain and crept beneath his collar. He tugged his hat a little more securely over his ears and continued his route.

He resisted the urge to look over his shoulder to find out if Kathy watched from a window. Something in his heart hoped for one more glimpse to add to his storehouse of memories. If she weren't gone already, she would be by the time he returned from his family Christmas get-together in Helena.

Only last night, in an e-mail, his brother, Trev, had teased, "Hey, brother, when are you going to bring home a girl to meet the folks? Maybe you need to arrange a mail-order bride!" Erik had seen no humor in the comment. He'd found the girl of his dreams with her arm stuck in a mailbox, but now he had to let her go.

Kathy had a boyfriend waiting in San Francisco. She was a temporary guest in town. His acquaintance with her could be measured in hours. He recited the facts to himself for the tenth time that day, but one fact overrode them all: She was important to him. He couldn't explain why. He only knew it was true.

For the past three days, every time he'd looked for her without success, he'd offered a prayer: *Grant her the desires of her heart, Lord, and let her greatest desire be You.* He couldn't remember ever praying that for anyone else, yet he felt led to offer that request. Again and again, the same prayer winged from his heart. It happened again now, as he headed down the block on his mail route.

A part of him wanted to add a postscript: *And let her second greatest desire be me.* But he recognized the selfishness of the request and managed to squelch it before it became a real prayer. If she already had a relationship, he had no business creating conflict. It was best Kathy never discover his fascination with her.

Kathy massaged the back of her neck with one hand and pulled the curtain aside with the other, peering out at the dismal day. Down below, through the leafless tree branches, she spotted a blue uniform and a black-and-brown-spotted dog. Erik and Daisy. Her heart doubled its tempo.

She quickly released the curtain and stepped back. He must have left the mail. Just knowing he'd been on the porch created a jolt of reaction. Her legs trembled, and she sank into the chair beside the window. Odd how a man she'd known for only a few days could affect her so strongly.

His back-and-forth behavior from friendly and warm to friendly and cautious had her completely baffled. She liked the friendly and warm Erik best. But how to keep him that way? There was something about her that made him keep his distance, but she was certain he didn't really want to distance himself from her. She had seen too many glimpses of longing in his eyes to believe otherwise.

Or maybe it was just wishful thinking. After all, there was that silly pact hanging over her head, her recent decision to break things off with Chad, and complete upheaval over her future living arrangements. Maybe she was simply rebounding, and Erik was the first good-looking man to show her some attention. She banged her fist on the chair's padded armrest and released a huff of irritation. How could she know whether her interest in him was something worth pursuing?

Why not pray about it? The thought came out of nowhere, making Kathy catch her breath. The suggestion made perfect sense if she truly wanted to restore her relationship with God. How could she have a relationship with Him if she never talked to Him?

Slipping from the chair, Kathy knelt and placed her linked hands on the chair's seat. Closing her eyes, she licked her lips and began. "God. . ." She took a deep breath. Just saying the name brought a rush of peace. "God. . .my heavenly Father. . ." Tears pressed behind her lids. "You sent me to Mistletoe, didn't You? You wanted me here to—like Mrs. Flanagan said—find You again. Thank You for bringing me home.

"If—if it's Your will, I'd like to stay here. If I'm meant to stay here, then please let Mr. Andale approve my working from Mistletoe rather than living in California. Please help me find a place to live. And please. . ." She swallowed hard. "Please help me build a family, Lord. I've been so lonely since Mom died. I tried to fill the loneliness by spending time with Chad, but I know now that was wrong. Thank You for letting me see the truth before I made a serious mistake."

Her eyes squeezed tight, she finished on a sigh. "Bring into my life the love You've chosen for me. Thank You for caring enough to bring me back to You. Amen."

Chapter 9

Early Saturday morning, Erik threw his duffle bag into the trunk, gave Daisy a boost into the passenger seat, and climbed behind the steering wheel of his vehicle. The little blue two-door sports car only got used when he left the community of Mistletoe, but he took it in for regular service checks and oil changes, so he felt secure aiming the car south toward Highway 83 for a lengthy drive.

Going home for Christmas... He looked forward to a full week with his family. In the two years since leaving Helena, he'd made several weekend trips, but it seemed more time was spent driving than visiting. This time, though, he'd have five uninterrupted days of talking, laughing, catching up. Since last Christmas, a new nephew had joined the family, bringing the grandchild count to three. Unless—Erik smiled, rubbing Daisy's head—you threw the granddog into the tally.

As Erik glided along the aspen-lined highway, he let his thoughts drift ahead. Mom always cooked up a storm, and homemade cookies, pastries, and candies would be waiting for him. His mouth watered thinking about peanut brittle and rich date bars and fluffy divinity.

Dad would keep a fire crackling in the massive stone fireplace, and when the grandkids came over, he'd pop popcorn over the flames in the heat-scorched iron popper that was older than Erik. Little Travis and Ashley would clap their hands and beg, "Faster! Pop it faster!" just like he, Trev, and Susan had begged when they were preschoolers.

Carols would play constantly from scratchy albums on an old phonograph—no CD player in the folks' house—and the tree would be encircled by packages Mom had been storing from after-Christmas sales last year. An old-fashioned, traditions-filled Christmas awaited him, and the miles couldn't pass fast enough for him to get there.

Remembering Trev's last e-mail, he wondered when he would be able to start forming his own family Christmas traditions. That thought immediately brought to mind an adorable red-haired commercial writer who'd invaded his community. . . and his heart.

He glanced at the car's digital clock and snorted. "Well, Daisy, I didn't even last a half hour before I had to think of Kathy." Scratching the dog's ears, he sighed. "I think I've got it bad. . . But"—he squared his shoulders—"this week away ought to cure me. Out of sight, out of mind, and by the time we return to Mistletoe, she'll be back in California and we can get back to normal."

Daisy released a short whine, put her head on her paws,

and peered at her master with a woeful expression Erik was certain mirrored his own.

Kathy yawned, stretched, and rolled her head sideways to peek at the alarm clock on the bedside table. Not quite eight o'clock. Mrs. Flanagan served breakfast between seven thirty and nine, so she could indulge in a few more minutes of laziness.

She'd gotten spoiled in her week of living in the bed-and-breakfast inn. Not once had she cooked a meal, washed towels or sheets, or scrubbed a toilet. Mrs. Flanagan had refused to accept payment for the room Kathy used, insisting as a long-time friend she would be insulted to be offered money. Yet she acted as though Kathy were a paying guest, taking care of her needs the same way she cared for the other guests.

Kathy threw back the quilt and headed for the bathroom. Well, she'd find a way to repay the dear old lady. Mrs. Flanagan loved roses—red roses, especially. In the window of Madison's shop, she'd spotted some blown-glass rosebuds in vivid crimson. A dozen of those lovely ornaments would help balance the scale a bit. She'd scout around for other rose-themed items, too, and pile a few gifts beneath the tree in the parlor.

Running water for a bath, she considered who else belonged on her Christmas list. Back in Sausalito, she'd always purchased small items for a few of her coworkers—impersonal things like lotion or candles for the women, taffy or fudge for the men. She and Chad had established a silly tradition of exchanging gag gifts. Last year he'd given her slipper-socks with squeakers in the heels, so every time she took a step, a duck quack sounded. She couldn't remember what she'd gotten him.

Sinking into the steaming water, she frowned. Why hadn't she heard from Chad yet? She knew he had to have received her letter by now, unless— Her heart leaped as an idea took form. Unless he had taken time away from the office, too.

Why, of course! Hadn't he indicated he wanted to take some time off? That was probably what had happened. He wasn't at the agency to retrieve his mail. She sagged with relief against the sloped porcelain back of the claw-foot tub. Maybe there was a chance to call him on his cell, tell him to discard the letter, and let him know her decision.

Smiling, she slipped a little deeper into the tub. When she did her Christmas shopping this morning, she'd find a little something for Chad—not a joke gift, but something usable. Something sweet. Something that would help her let him down gently. A good-bye gift. She drew in a deep breath of the scented water and sighed. Problem solved.

After breakfast Kathy tried calling Chad's cell phone, but he didn't answer. Sighing, she made a mental note to try again later and bundled up to head for town.

"Would you like to borrow my trusty sedan?" Mrs. Flanagan asked. "It's a mite chilly for a walk this mornin'."

Kathy shook her head. "No, thank you. I don't drive."

The older woman's thin brows shot high. "You don't drive?"

"I haven't bothered with a license in years." Kathy used a

glib tone, but Mrs. Flanagan didn't smile.

"How do you get to work?"

"I take the ferry to the wharf and the Muni—the bus system," she explained at Mrs. Flanagan's puzzled look, "to the office. I have no need to drive."

Suddenly Mrs. Flanagan's expression turned pensive. "Do you not drive because of what happened to your dear mother?"

Kathy shrugged.

"Ah, my darlin'..." Suddenly Mrs. Flanagan wrapped Kathy in an embrace. "The hurts we carry that we don't need to..." She stepped back and cupped her hands around Kathy's cheeks. "All right, then. I've been prayin' for a healin' of your relationship with God, and if I'm not mistaken, it's taken place. Am I right?"

Kathy let her smile give the answer.

The old woman gently patted Kathy's cheeks. "Then I'll start prayin' for you to let go of your fear about drivin' a car. Not because I think your two legs are incapable of carryin' you where you need to go, but because it just isn't healthy to hold on to a fear." She dropped her hands and turned toward the sink piled with dishes. "Now be off with you. Run your errands. We'll talk later."

Kathy followed Mrs. Flanagan's directions. Her heart felt light. Knowing the woman would be praying gave her a sense of peace that someday she would find the courage to drive again. God would surely see to it. She offered her own prayer. "Let me throw off the fears, Father, and live freely in Your care."

She entered Madison's idyllic shop, happy to be out of the cold air. The scent of cinnamon greeted her nostrils, and everywhere she looked, Christmas abounded. She roved the displays slowly, admiring each item and making careful selections for Lori, Madison, and Deanna, as well as a few people in Sausalito.

Coming to the end of an aisle, she encountered a huge Christmas tree decorated in a theme she could only define as "peace." White doves perched delicately on the tips of branches. A chain of gold pearls hung in graceful swoops, and clear glass balls and gold bows filled in the gaps. At the top, a beautiful angel in a flowing white robe smiled serenely. Kathy wished she could buy the whole tree as a gift to herself.

She'd only used a tabletop tree in her apartment in Sausalito, but when she was growing up, Mom had always decorated a big tree for their living room. She thought of the tree that now stood in the front window of the living room of the house in which she grew up and nearly laughed out loud. She hadn't said anything to Erik because she hadn't wanted to insult him, but his tree was the saddest thing she'd ever seen. Bald green branches holding a spattering of red balls. It needed help.

Suddenly the desire to do something kind for Erik welled up. The peace tree was too frilly for someone like Erik, but surely she could find decorations that would be appropriate for a man's Christmas tree. When she turned into the next aisle, she gasped. A boxed set of blown-glass nativity figures waited, their black eyes peering out of the box as if issuing an invitation to be taken home. A picture of her and Erik standing near the nativity in the park flashed through her mind. She snatched up the box. Farther down the aisle, she found plastic snowflakes covered in silver glitter. She added a dozen of them to her stack. When she located gold foil dog bones, she giggled out loud. Six joined the growing pile in her arms.

A clerk stepped next to her elbow. "Would you like me to take those to the register for you?"

Kathy cheerfully handed them over. "I'll need wrapping paper and ribbon, too. Would you choose something Victorian-looking for me?"

The clerk bustled away, and Kathy continued to peruse the displays, looking specifically for things that said "Erik." To her delight, she found an ornament that resembled a stamped envelope addressed to Santa Claus. She took it from its metal display hook, then examined the entire selection of individual ornaments. He'd said he enjoyed hunting, so she chose a variety of hand-painted blown-glass ornaments—a wonderfully detailed moose, fish, turkey, and deer head complete with antlers. She delighted at a basset hound with doleful eyes; a little house with shutters; a decorated Christmas tree. The last ornament she chose was a pair of gold joined eighth notes to commemorate their time of caroling together.

What was it, she mused with a finger against her lips, about singing together that created a bond with someone? Oddly enough, she'd felt a bond with Erik from the moment he gently dislodged her arm from the mailbox. Her heart fluttered, but she gave herself a little shake. She shouldn't even be thinking about Erik. Not until she had things settled with Chad.

Scurrying to the counter, she paid for her purchases. When she returned to Mrs. Flanagan's, she would try again to call Chad.

Chapter 10

"Oh, hi, babe." Kathy heard Chad yawn, as if she'd awakened him. "You're probably wondering why I haven't called you after you sent that sweet acceptance of my proposal, huh?"

So he *had* gotten the letter! Then why hadn't he contacted her? Kathy settled against the pile of pillows on her bed and cradled the phone against her cheek. "I probably should have called you sooner, but—"

"No, no, that's okay." She puzzled at the quick rebuttal. An odd rustling noise came though the line. "I've kind of put off giving you a call, but. . ." The rustle came again, followed by muffled whispering.

Kathy frowned. "Chad?"

"Just a sec." A tiny *click* told her he'd put his phone on mute. She waited several interminable seconds before another *click* signaled his return. "It's okay, babe. Nothing important."

Kathy didn't believe him, but she had no desire to pursue

the truth. She had something to say, and then she would let him go. "Chad, I—"

"Kath, listen." His urgent tone cut her off. "I know our last conversation was pretty deep. . .talking marriage and all. And it's really sweet you would say yes. But, babe, I don't think it's a good idea. I mean, you're a great gal, and we've had fun, but some things just aren't meant to be, you know?"

Kathy pulled the telephone away from her face, stared at it for two startled seconds, then brought it back to her ear. "Are you dating someone else?"

"Oh, babe, don't take it hard. Sometimes things happen fast. Gina signed on as a new receptionist last Monday, and we just kind of. . .hit it off." In the background, Kathy heard someone running water. Chad's sigh carried through to her ear. "She's moved in with me, Kath. Please don't be hurt."

Hurt was the farthest emotion from Kathy's heart. Relief washed over her. Thank goodness she had come to Mistletoe alone instead of running off to Vegas with him! She said honestly, "I wish you and Gina well, Chad. I'll be praying for you." And she would—for them to realize God had a much better plan for their lives than what they were pursuing now.

She disconnected the call, closed her eyes, and spent some time in prayer. Then she bounced off the bed and began wrapping gifts. For the first time in five years, she was connected with the real reason to celebrate, and she wanted to savor every minute.

Shortly after dawn on Christmas morning, Kathy and Mrs.

Flanagan walked together through a gentle snowfall to attend a short service at Living Word Chapel. Erik was noticeably absent. Lori whispered to her that he'd gone to his parents' home for Christmas. Kathy discovered she missed him. Funny how after five years of daily contact with Chad, she could let him slip away, but only a few days' acquaintance with Erik left her longing to see him.

Yet her heart rejoiced as she raised her voice with the others in "Angels We Have Heard on High." Tears pricked her eyes. *Gloria*, indeed! She'd been given a precious gift—the restoration of her faith.

And God had swung doors open for her all over the place. Mr. Andale had approved her request to work from Mistletoe as long as she attended the biannual board meetings in San Francisco. She and Mrs. Flanagan had agreed on a fair amount of rent for the long-uninhabited carriage house behind the inn. It was really just a small apartment over the garage, but Kathy's needs were simple, and she looked forward to putting her creativity to work in fixing up the little apartment to feel like home.

After opening gifts and eating dinner with Mrs. Flanagan, Kathy visited the homes of each of her friends. Lori's husband, Russell, to whom Erik had entrusted the task of watering his few houseplants and taking in his mail, let Kathy borrow Erik's key so she could hang the decorations she'd purchased on his tree. She hung them with care, placing the gold music notes in a place of prominence. Standing back to admire her handiwork, she released a rueful sigh.

How she'd like to be here when he came home and found her surprise! But tomorrow morning she would return to San Francisco to clear out her office and her apartment. She wouldn't be back in Mistletoe until after the first of the year.

But she would be back! The thought thrilled her. "My new home." She lifted her face toward the ceiling and smiled heavenward. "Thank You, Lord!"

Erik, his arms full of packages, gave the back door a push with his backside to close it. Daisy trotted to her empty dog dishes in the corner of the kitchen and woofed her displeasure.

"Yes, girl, I know. I'll feed you just as soon as—"

He came to a halt in the doorway between the kitchen and living room. His tree! It glittered with color. He dumped the armload of packages onto the sofa and moved to the tree for a closer look.

Apparently Pastor Brown and Lori had decided his tree needed some sprucing up. He touched each ornament in turn, laughing when he found dog biscuits, smiling at the moose. He felt the sting of tears when he found baby Jesus, small and innocent in a manger lined with hay. When he touched the double music note, Kathy's sweet soprano rang in his memory. With a smile, he picked up the phone and dialed Pastor Brown's number.

"Thanks so much for sprucing up my tree," he said when the minister answered.

A low chuckle came through the line. "Sorry, Erik. I can't

take credit for that. A little Christmas elf borrowed your key and went to work."

"An elf?" Erik's heart began to thump with hope.

Another chuckle sounded. "Yep. A redheaded one. I understand those are the best kind."

Erik hung up the telephone slowly. A redheaded elf. So it had been Kathy! "Daisy, c'mon, girl, we're going to go—" He clapped a hand to his forehead. What was he thinking? He couldn't go to the inn and say thank you. She'd only come to Mistletoe for a vacation. By now she'd certainly returned to San Francisco.

He sat in his recliner, his shoulders slumped. Daisy sat on his foot and looked up at him with sad, wide eyes. He rubbed the dog's floppy ears. "I know, girl. I feel the same way."

A week later, Erik walked past the row of shops on his way home from work, and a small sign caught his attention: DATED CHRISTMAS DECOR, 50% OFF. Curious, he cupped his hands beside his eyes and peered through the window. A variety of Christmas items lay in a neat row across a backdrop of red velvet. One in particular captured his attention—a glass bubble holding two penguins standing on a block of ice, their flightless wings touching as if holding hands. The girl penguin wore a painted green scarf tied around her neck. Fluid filled the bubble, and little white dots around the penguins' feet told Erik it was a snow globe. Squinting, he made out the words printed in gold at the base of the ornament: OUR FIRST CHRISTMAS TOGETHER.

—All I Want for Christmas Is. . . You—

Without a second thought, Erik entered the store, plucked the snow globe from the display, paid for it, and carried it home in his pocket. Once home, he gave it a good shake and set it on the fireplace mantel. Then he stood, hands in pockets, and let the image of the two little penguins caught together in a whirl of tiny white pellets conjure memories of standing with Kathy beneath a flurry of snowflakes.

His heart ached with loneliness. He offered the prayer that was now familiar: *Grant her the desires of her heart, Lord.* Then he headed to the kitchen to find something for supper. On the counter beside the sink sat an empty butter tub, clean and waiting to be returned to Mrs. Flanagan. The idea of getting out again rather than staying in his empty house appealed to him.

He peeked in the refrigerator to confirm his initial suspicion. There was nothing in the house to eat. He patted his thigh. "Hey, Daisy, want to take a walk?"

Daisy replied with a low-pitched woof, followed by several bounces.

"Okay, then, get your leash and let's go." Erik would return Mrs. Flanagan's dish, then head to Flossie's for a bowl of chili. Daisy wouldn't mind waiting on the patio in front of the café since Flossie always had a few leftovers ready for a "Daisy visit."

A few minutes later, he reached Mrs. Flanagan's inn. As usual, the place was brightly lit—every light in the huge house was glowing. He rang the bell and waited with his shoulders hunched against the cold. Within seconds a shadowy figure passed the parlor window; then the door opened.

Erik took a step back, his eyebrows lifting. "Kathy?"

341

"Erik!" There she stood, dressed in the rattiest jeans he'd ever seen and a sweatshirt four sizes too large for her frame. With her red hair pulled up into a droopy ponytail, she was too cute for words.

"What are you doing here?" they chorused simultaneously, then they both laughed.

Kathy waved her arm. "Come in!"

"I've got Daisy."

"Bring her, too."

At her invitation, Erik gave Daisy's leash a tug and drew her over the threshold. Kathy closed the door and leaned down to love on the dog. Daisy rewarded her with sloppy swipes of her tongue.

"Hey, girl, did you have a good Christmas?" Kathy cooed.

Erik wished she'd look at him instead. He offered softly, "She liked the dog bone ornaments very much."

Kathy's gaze swung upward, her cheeks filling with a light shade of pink.

"Thank you. I love what you did with my tree."

"How did you know it was me?"

He shrugged, hoping he wouldn't get anyone in trouble. "Pastor Brown let the cat out of the bag."

She pushed to her feet, sliding her hands into the patch pocket on the front of her sweatshirt. "Well, I'm glad you liked it. Decorating can be kind of a personal thing, but I couldn't resist—"

"You chose perfectly. Every ornament was. . .perfect." Suddenly he thrust the empty butter tub at her. "I brought this back in case Mrs. Flanagan wanted to use it again."

She took it and looked at it for a moment, as if she expected something else. "I'm sure she didn't miss it, but thank you." She set it on a parlor table. "She'd thank you herself, but she went next door to take some leftover lasagna to the neighbor. I guess it's her favorite."

Erik nodded. Then they stood staring at each other in awkward silence. Finally, he repeated the question that had gone unanswered. "Kathy, what are you doing here?"

She tipped her head. "I'm surprised you haven't heard—Mrs. Flanagan said news still spreads around town like a wildfire. I'm fixing up the apartment over her garage. I moved here."

For the second time since she opened the door, Erik felt his eyebrows shoot for his hairline. "But—but what about your boyfriend? Your job?"

She peered steadily into his eyes. "I never had a boyfriend. Not in the true sense of the word. As for my job, I've still got it. I'm just working via the Internet instead of in an office in San Francisco." Offering a shy smile, she said, "So. . .once again. . . Mistletoe is home."

He tried to absorb the full meaning of her simple answer, and he discovered the only thing that really mattered was the last word. Home. She'd come home. He smiled, reaching out to give her elbow a quick squeeze. "I'm glad."

"Me, too."

Another silence fell, but it didn't feel awkward. Instead, it was rife with unspoken messages. Suddenly Erik blurted, "I bought something, but I didn't think I'd be able to give it to you. Could you"—he held out Daisy's leash—"keep her for a minute? I'll run home and get it."

"Okay."

The cold stung his cheeks and sent fire to his lungs, but Erik ran the entire three blocks both ways. When he jogged up the porch steps, he found Kathy framed in the door, waiting. His heart thudded as he drew the little penguin snow globe out of his pocket and placed it in her hands.

Warm air caused the globe to fog over, and she wiped it on her sweatshirt before holding it up to the light. With a grin, she shook it, then giggled as she watched the snowflakes whirl.

"Oh, Erik, it's darling!" She beamed up at him for a moment, then turned her attention back to the globe. Suddenly she drew her lower lip between her teeth, and a blush stole across her cheeks.

Erik knew she'd read the message.

Her gaze bounced back up to meet his. Her brown eyes sparkled brightly. "Thank you."

He cleared his throat. "You're welcome." He cupped his hand around hers, where snowflakes fluttered around a pair of penguins. "I have the feeling it won't be our last."

Kathy's smile turned his heart upside down. "I hope not."

And when Erik leaned forward to bestow a kiss on Kathy's rosy lips, Daisy gave a hearty woof of approval.

Kim Vogel Sawyer

Award-winning, bestselling author Kim Vogel Sawyer is a wife, mother, grandmother, speaker, singer of songs, lover of cats and chocolate, and—most importantly—a born-again child of the King. She recently closed her classroom door to live out her childhood dream of being a full-time author, penning stories of the hope we can all possess when we place our lives in God's loving, capable hands.

In addition to writing and speaking, Kim stays active in her church by teaching adult Sunday school, leading the drama team, and participating in voice and bell choirs. In her spare time, she enjoys quilting, calligraphy, and acting in community theatre. A lifelong Kansas resident, she and her husband relish time with their family, which includes three daughters and four grandsons.

To learn more about Kim's writing and speaking ministry, please visit www.KimVogelSawyer.com

A Letter to Our Readers

Dear Readers:

In order that we might better contribute to your reading enjoyment, we would appreciate your taking a few minutes to respond to the following questions. When completed, please return to the following: Fiction Editor, Barbour Publishing, Inc., P.O. Box 719, Uhrichsville, OH 44683.

1. Did you enjoy reading *Montana Mistletoe*?
    ❑ Very much—I would like to see more books like this.
    ❑ Moderately—I would have enjoyed it more if _____
    _____
    _____

2. What influenced your decision to purchase this book?
    (Check those that apply.)
    ❑ Cover   ❑ Back cover copy   ❑ Title   ❑ Price
    ❑ Friends   ❑ Publicity   ❑ Other

3. Which story was your favorite?
    ❑ *Christmas Confusion*   ❑ *Under the Mistletoe*
    ❑ *Return to Mistletoe*   ❑ *All I Want for Christmas Is. . .You*

4. Please check your age range:
    ❑ Under 18   ❑ 18–24   ❑ 25–34
    ❑ 35–45   ❑ 46–55   ❑ Over 55

5. How many hours per week do you read? _____

Name _____

Occupation _____

Address _____

City _____ State _____ Zip _____

E-mail _____

If you enjoyed

Montana

Mistletoe

then read

A Big Apple
CHRISTMAS

*Love Unites Four Couples
During the Christmas Season in New York City*

Moonlight and Mistletoe by Carrie Turansky
Shopping for Love by Gail Sattler
Where the Love Light Gleams by Lynette Sowell
Gifts from the Magi by Vasthi Reyes Acosta

Available wherever books are sold.
Or order from:
Barbour Publishing, Inc.
P.O. Box 721
Uhrichsville, Ohio 44683
www.barbourbooks.com

You may order by mail for $6.97 and add $3.00 to your order for shipping.
Prices subject to change without notice.
If outside the U.S. please call 740-922-7280 for shipping charges.

If you enjoyed

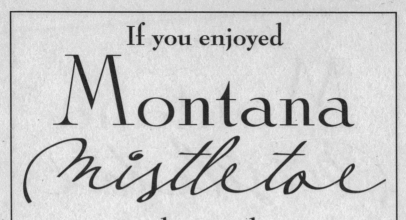

Montana Mistletoe

then read

KANSAS WEDDINGS

by Kim Vogel Sawyer

Three Brides Can Never Say Never to Love Again

Dear John
That Wilder Boy
Promising Angela

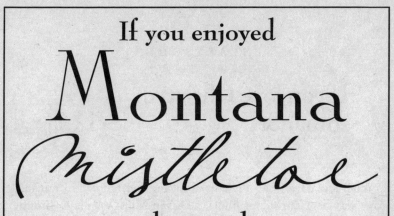

♡

HEARTSONG
PRESENTS

If you love Christian romance...

$11.⁹⁹

You'll love Heartsong Presents' inspiring and faith-filled romances by today's very best Christian authors. . .DiAnn Mills, Wanda E. Brunstetter, and Yvonne Lehman, to mention a few!

When you join Heartsong Presents, you'll enjoy four brand-new, mass market, 176-page books—two contemporary and two historical—that will build you up in your faith when you discover God's role in every relationship you read about!

Imagine. . .four new romances every four weeks—with men and women

Mass Market, 176 Pages

like you who long to meet the one God has chosen as the love of their lives. . .all for the low price of $11.99 postpaid.

To join, simply visit www.heartsongpresents.com or complete the coupon below and mail it to the address provided.

✂-----------------------------

YES! Sign me up for Hearts♥ng!

NEW MEMBERSHIPS WILL BE SHIPPED IMMEDIATELY!
Send no money now. We'll bill you only $11.99 postpaid with your first shipment of four books. Or for faster action, call 1-740-922-7280.

NAME _____

ADDRESS_____

CITY_____ STATE _____ ZIP _____

MAIL TO: HEARTSONG PRESENTS, P.O. Box 721, Uhrichsville, OH 44683
or sign up at WWW.HEARTSONGPRESENTS.COM